DUKE *of* MADNESS

#1 Sisterhood of Secrets

BY
JENNIFER MONROE

Duke of Madness by Jennifer Monroe

Published by WOLF Publishing UG

Text by Jennifer Monroe
Edited by Chris Hall
Cover Art by Victoria Cooper
Paperback ISBN: 978-3-98536-024-6
Hard Cover ISBN: 978-3-98536-025-3
Ebook ISBN: 978-3-98536-023-9

WOLF Publishing - This is us:

Two sisters, two personalities.. But only one big love!

Diving into a world of dreams..

...Romance, heartfelt emotions, lovable and witty characters, some humor, and some mystery! Because we want it all! Historical Romance at its best!

Visit our website to learn all about us, our authors and books!

Sign up to our mailing list to receive first hand information on new releases, freebies and promotions as well as exclusive giveaways and sneak-peeks!

WWW.WOLF-PUBLISHING.COM

Also by Jennifer Monroe

The Sisterhood of Secrets

There is far more for the women at Miss Rutley's Finishing School than an education, for their secretive headmistress will assure her pupils find the happiness they each deserve.

#1 Duke of Madness

#2 Baron of Rake Street

#3 Marquess of Magic

DUKE *of* MADNESS

Prologue

Chatsworth, England, 1825

The carriage shifted and creaked, threatening to send Her Grace, Julia Elmhurst, crashing to the floor in a heap of fabric. Luckily, the quick hands of her lady's maid prevented her from doing so.

"Thank you," Julia said, but Bridget Lowry simply waved off the gratitude, as she was prone to do since first taking over the position of Julia's lady's maid twenty years prior.

"Don't think I saved you out of kindness," Bridget said with a mock sniff. "I'm more worried that His Grace will end my employment if I don't save your life from time to time." This sent them both into bouts of laughter, a sound that helped ease the worry that Julia had felt since receiving a letter from Mrs. Agnes Rutley, known to her students as simply Mrs. Rutley, four days earlier.

Mrs. Rutley was dying and had demanded that Julia come to her bedside. Of course, no one demanded anything of a duchess, certainly not a woman who ran a girls' school, but Mrs. Agnes Rutley was not just anyone. She was a woman Julia admired, a woman for whom she had cared greatly, and thus the reason she had left her estate in

Cambridge the day after receiving that correspondence. If she could have departed that very day, she would have, but even a duchess had limitations when preparations needed to be made.

The carriage slowed, and Julia looked out the window. Her heart caught in her throat at the memory of her last day at Mrs. Rutley's School for Young Women. Housed in a small country estate by the name of Courtly Manor, in the village of Chatsworth just outside of London, the school had not changed much over the years. The once-peeling white paint had been redone, as had the black that framed the windows. The trees were taller, the bushes larger, and more ivy covered the house's facade, but otherwise, it was very much as Julia remembered when she first laid eyes upon it just after her fourteenth birthday.

For a moment, she wished she were young again. Far too much time had passed since she and her fellow students spoke in innocent whispers of their childhood dreams, their futures, and their hope for love.

How often had she and her sisters—that was what she thought of those young ladies who had attended with her all those years ago, they were her sisters in a way—peered out the windows of this house, wondering what was taking place beyond the boundaries of the property or watching to see who had arrived? Many guests had called at the school, and speculation ran rampant when an unknown carriage trundled up the drive as to whom might be hiding within. And on whom they might be calling.

By the end of Julia's final year, eight of the girls—nay, young women—became the best of friends. So many nights were spent whispering secrets well after dark when they were meant to be abed, sharing curiosities and other matters in which women nearing the age of their debut found an interest. Julia remembered hiding away to play games of chance, or climbing trellises to sneak outside when the moon shone at its brightest, or when a challenge was made. Few ignored a challenge.

So lost in thought was she that Julia started when the door opened. The driver dipped his head and moved aside to wait for her to alight. Smiling at Bridget, Julia allowed the man to hand her from the carriage, and for several moments, she felt as if she had gone back in time. She was once again eighteen and eager to set out into the world in search of a husband.

"I'm uncertain how long I shall be," she said to the driver. "I imagine it may be a bit, so I suggest you take your ease. I'll send word when I'm ready to leave."

He gave her a diffident bow. "Yes, Your Grace."

With Bridget at her side, Julia walked not to the portico in front of the entry door but rather to the large oak tree beside the drive, rumored to be nearly three hundred years old. She pressed her hand against the rough bark of its trunk where nine sets of initials had been carved into its flesh—made by eight friends and their headmistress—as a sign of the pledge they had made.

Their oath was simple but heartfelt: If any one of the women in that group was in need of aid, all would answer the call if she was able.

"I never thought our oath a childish endeavor," Julia whispered as she touched each set of initials in turn before coming to a stop at hers. "Even now as a mother, a woman who has traveled far and wide, and a duchess, I never thought it so."

"All promises made from the heart are never foolish, Your Grace," Bridget said. "That's the reason why you're here, and I suspect the others will arrive soon enough."

Julia nodded and turned toward the grand house. In truth, although she wished to see Mrs. Rutley again, she could not help but fear what she would find. A selfish part of her wanted to remember the vibrant woman in her middle years she had known all those years ago, not the frail body likely lying on her deathbed.

Yet, how could she possibly walk away? Mrs. Rutley had loved her as if she were her own daughter. More than once, the headmistress had intervened—subtly, of course—when Julia's father visited with the sole purpose of berating his daughter.

Her father was a baron, but he barked his wishes as if he were a general. Her mother, on the other hand, always kept her head low, and Julia feared that, one day, the woman would collapse from the fear she walked in. Although she did not want to see her father harmed, Julia often wished he would simply disappear. She always had a stab of regret for such a terrible thought, but he controlled every aspect of her life—and that of her mother's—even down to the books she read.

Julia squared her shoulders. It was time to end this dwelling on the past, at least for now. She had come for a reason, and she could no longer delay the inevitable.

"You do understand that I must go alone, do you not?" Julia asked, turning to the woman who was as much a friend as she was a servant.

Bridget bobbed a quick curtsy. "Of course, Your Grace," she replied. "Do you think anyone would mind if I walk through the gardens?"

"I see no reason why not," Julia replied. "Mrs. Rutley has never denied anyone access to most anywhere on her property, and I doubt she has changed enough to deny it now."

As the maid walked away, Julia took a deep breath to calm her pounding heart and walked to the portico. Before she could ring the bell, the door opened to a familiar round face she had not expected.

"Julia!" Mrs. Shepherd exclaimed. The cook wasted no time pulling Julia in for a tight embrace before pushing her away and looking her up and down. "Look how beautiful you are still! Oh! And now I've got flour on your lovely gown!" She began brushing at the front of Julia's dress. "And me calling you Julia rather than Your Grace," she added under her breath. "A right fool, I am."

"Don't distress yourself, Mrs. Shepherd," Julia said with a laugh. "I'm sure Bridget can easily clean flour out of fabric. And I'm still Julia to you." She kissed the cook's cheek. "It truly is so wonderful to see you again. How are you?"

Mrs. Shepherd brushed back a stray strand of hair that had once been dark but now was all silver. "I'm as well as can be expected, I suppose," the cook said, yet the shake of her head belied her words. She clicked her tongue. "Ah now, look at me taking up all your time when you're here to see Mrs. Rutley. Here, let me take your coat and hat."

Julia glanced at the staircase to her left. "Is she... that is..." She clamped shut her mouth. If she did not speak the terrible thoughts that lingered in her mind, perhaps they would not come to pass.

Mrs. Shepherd draped Julia's coat over an arm. "She's fighting as she always has," she replied, her eyes brimming with tears. "She's in her bed. Go see her. She's been waiting for you."

With a nod, Julia walked up the great oak staircase. At the top, she turned right and headed down the long corridor. When she reached the last room on the left, she stopped and stared at the door, giving herself one last moment to gather her courage. Taking a deep breath, she opened the door.

Mrs. Rutley lay in her bed, her head propped upon several pillows. What was left of her once thick, chestnut hair was now sparse and gray. Julia's heart melted. Never had she seen her headmistress so thin and frail. Yet, despite her weakened state, she wore the same radiant smile Julia had always remembered. At least that much had not changed.

"Ah, Your Grace," Mrs. Rutley said, her voice a mere croak, "you came."

Julia hurried to the woman's side. "We have no need for formalities. I'm still Julia. That is how friends address one another, by their Christian name, is it not?" She forced a smile. "I left as soon as your letter arrived. We made a promise, all of us did, and I, for one, keep my word."

Mrs. Rutley closed her eyes. "We did make a promise, and I do hope most of you will return."

"I would think all of us would," Julia said, confused. Her eyes fell to the clenched hand at Mrs. Rutley's side, opposite from where Julia stood. Did she not want Julia to know that she was in pain? "Are you thinking that some may not come? Surely Ruth, above all, will not ignore your summons."

Mrs. Rutley patted an empty space on the edge of the bed, and Julia sat. The small, frail hand took hold of hers. "Sadly, I received word that Ruth died in an accident two years ago," the headmistress whispered. "And Unity and Theodosia moved to the Americas ten years ago, so I doubt they will be able to come. The others..." She lifted her shoulders in what was likely meant to be a shrug. "We shall see."

"Then only six of us remain, including you?" Julia asked. Mrs. Rutley nodded, and Julia gave the thin hand a light squeeze. "Well, I'm here. The others will come, as well, I'm certain."

Her mind returned to the day they had gathered around that great tree. Yes, any who remained in England would heed the call; she could feel it. The bond they shared was so strong that nothing would keep them apart. Except a massive ocean. Or death. Poor Ruth.

"Is there anything I can do for you?" Julia asked. "Can I send Bridget into the village to purchase anything you may need? Or want?"

"No, my dear," Mrs. Rutley said. "I called you here because I must confess a secret to you. A secret that I should not take with me to the grave."

"Concerning me?" Julia asked with surprise. Mrs. Rutley gave a tiny nod. "I must admit that I'm confused. What secret about me could you possibly have?"

Mrs. Rutley closed her steel-gray eyes, and a small smile played at the corners of her lips. "I'll explain, but first you must tell me a story, one about a young woman and the man she came to love. Although I was there to witness its unfolding, I wish to hear you tell it one last time."

Tears welled in Julia's eyes, but she blinked them back. Where should she begin? The day she arrived at the school when she was but fourteen? Or perhaps when she had first heard the rumor about the man she had come to love?

She looked at Mrs. Rutley and smiled. "I remember the day everything took place as if it were yesterday, for it began with Emma in near hysterics and me coming face-to-face with the Duke of Madness."

Chapter One

Chatsworth, England, 1805

Miss Julia Wallace stared out the window of her room at Mrs. Rutley's School for Young Women on a cool September morning. Below her sat the carriage of one Matthew Colburn, 5th Duke of Elmhurst or, as many called him, the Duke of Madness. The reasons behind the moniker were not clear to Julia, but she suspected that it had to do with the rumors surrounding the man's late father, a man who died from madness several years earlier, or so she had heard.

Can someone truly die from madness? she wondered.

Although she had heard many descriptions attributed to the Duke of Madness—hair that fell to his knees, a hideous face, and a tongue so vile that highwaymen would blush in shame, just to name a few—she had yet to lay eyes on him. And she intended to do just that, once her French lesson was completed, of course. Unfortunately, her lesson had gone longer than expected, and the opportunity was lost. As she hurried to the room she shared with Miss Emma Hunter to dress for dinner, she made a mental note to question Mrs. Rutley about the duke. If anyone would know about any man in the area, the headmistress would.

Yet, all thoughts of the duke and her questions concerning him fell to the side when she opened the door to hear a low grumble coming from within. Emma sat upon her bed, ebony hair mussed and face pinched with anger.

"Emma?" Julia asked, hurrying to the girl's side. "What is wrong?"

"I learned a terrible truth today," Emma said in a tight voice, her stark-blue eyes afire. "Oh, Julia, please tell me you did not hide this to protect me as you have done with other matters!"

When Emma had arrived at the school three years earlier, several of the girls set out to tease her. Despite her doll-like features, she was also short in stature, much shorter than most young women her age and rail thin. Julia had done her best to put a stop to the teasing, vowing to see no one, man or woman, ever harm her friend. This was what made her and Emma as close as sisters.

"I've hidden nothing from you," Julia said. "Now, tell me what has upset you so."

Emma sat on the edge of the bed, her hands clenched into fists in her lap. The girl was never one to be quick to anger. Whatever had upset her had to be something terrible, indeed.

"The party Lord Bancroft will be giving next month?" Emma whispered. "I've learned the truth of it, and I'll not have an old man take me away!"

Julia shook her head. "No one will be taking you away," she said. "The party is meant to celebrate the end of summer. The girls from this school have attended in the past as a way to practice what they learned during their time here. You have no reason to be frightened or angry. Plus, if Mrs. Rutley says we must go, we must go. How often have we been allowed not to do as she says?"

"You don't understand!" Emma said. "We will not attend because it's our first party but rather to be shown off to potential suitors."

"Well, of course," Julia said with a light laugh. "Is that not why most parties exist? Or the Season once we are of age, for that matter?"

"Yes, but that is not all," Emma said. "At the end of the night, we will all be taken to the parlor where old unmarried or widowed gentlemen will bid on us for the right to make us their wives! Lord Bancroft receives five percent of the earnings from the auction, Mrs. Rutley receives another five percent, and our parents are given the rest."

Julia brushed back a strand of the girl's dark hair from her face. "Where did you hear such nonsense?"

"Abigail told me," Emma replied. "Oh, I know she can tell the most outlandish tales, but she was weeping when she told me about this. I've never seen her do that before, so she must be telling the truth."

Julia stifled a groan. Abigail Swanson was a cruel girl with bright red hair and a sharp tongue she wielded as savagely as any weapon. Any story she told was likely untrue, but she had an uncanny ability to make every falsehood she told seem real.

"They do not sell young ladies," Julia said. "At least not here. And if we do happen to learn it's true, then we will make our escape into the night." This made Emma smile, and Julia stood. "I'm going to have a word with Abigail. Once you have calmed yourself, we may go for a walk around the gardens if you would like."

"I would," Emma replied. "I'm sorry for upsetting you."

Since their first day together, Emma had been a bundle of worry, and Julia understood why. Mr. and Mrs. Hunter spent the majority of their visits scolding their daughter, berating her for the most trivial of matters.

The sad thing was that Julia's father was no different. His reason for sending her to this school had not been to make her a better woman for her own good. No, what he wanted from his daughter was to attract a far wealthier suitor, who would somehow line his pockets once she married.

Most of her friends had remained home instead of being sent to a school, their mothers proudly teaching their daughters every social mannerism needed to be successful in life. But when one's mother barely speaks above a whisper, and her father belittles her every word, another woman is needed to take her mother's place.

Julia recalled when the decision was made to send her away. The storm outside that day had raged, much like her father's temper. She had winced when the vase shattered against the wall, trembled when he pointed at her mother, and fought back tears when he announced that Julia was going away.

When she had first arrived at the doors of the school, she was frightened, for she had never been away on her own. Yet upon meeting Mrs. Rutley, she knew the decision had been the right one, for the headmistress demonstrated the strength Julia would need to succeed in life.

"You have not upset me in the slightest," Julia assured her friend. "But you must promise me never to pay Abigail any heed again. Can you do that for me?"

"I promise," Emma said, putting her arms around Julia and hugging her tightly.

"Now, I would like you to wash your face. I'll return in a moment."

Leaving the room, Julia marched down the corridor and came to a stop at the fourth door down, which led to the room where Abigail lived. Miss Margaret Tranter, the girl who shared the room with Abigail, was equally fiendish, and the sounds of laughter coming through the open door gave Julia pause.

"When I began to weep," Abigail was saying, "she became so angry!" Her companions laughed all the harder. "That Emma must be the most gullible sprite I've ever met! I feel sorry for the weakling man who will be forced to call her his wife!"

Julia stormed into the room, her hands balled into fists in her skirts to keep herself from slapping the object of her anger. Lydia Gilstrap and Margaret fell silent, but Abigail rose regally from the bed.

"I did not invite you into my room," Abigail snapped.

"And do you believe I care?" Julia asked, pointing a finger at Abigail's face. "I warned you to leave Emma be, but you continue to mistreat her. If you believe I'll not strike you, you are sadly mistaken, for I'll not hesitate to blacken both your eyes!"

The truth was, Julia doubted she would ever strike another person, for violence was not her way, but she might do so if it meant protecting Emma from the likes of this girl!

I'm far too old for this type of trouble!

Abigail placed a hand on her hip. "I was only teasing her," she said. "But the truth is, though there is no auction, she will likely marry an old man, anyway."

"You are an ignorant fool," Julia growled.

"Emma is far too short for a woman, and her children will likely be even shorter." Abigail's smirk deepened. "No decent man wants a pixie for a bride." Her friends burst out laughing at this remark.

Anger flared, and Julia considered making good on her promise to use her fists. Yet, she was a cultured young woman, not a ruffian. Striking Abigail would embarrass Julia more, no matter how much Abigail deserved it.

Julia brought her face close to that of Abigail. "One day, you will marry," she said in an even tone. "He will be a handsome, titled man."

Abigail grinned, but Julia narrowed her eyes and sharpened her voice.

"And each morning, he will awaken, knowing in his heart he married you not for love but for the shipping rights your father owns. Each time you raise a teacup made of fine porcelain, you will realize that is the only precious thing you will ever know. You love no one but yourself and, therefore, will marry a man as callous as you. You will deserve one another, I'm sure."

Abigail's face went a deep crimson. "Leave my room this instant!" she said. "I have no desire to hear your flights of fancy. I may not marry a man who loves me, but life is not the romantic novel you believe it to be. It's practical."

"Leave Emma alone," Julia said, putting as much malevolence in her tone as she could, "or next time it will not be my words that cut deep." Turning on her heel, she marched from the room.

When she reached the bottom of the stairs, she did not find Emma, so she walked toward the office Mrs. Rutley used. The headmistress had to do something about that infuriating girl! Teasing was one thing, but to upset Emma to such a degree was quite uncalled for.

Julia lifted a hand to knock, but the door swung open. Before her stood a gentleman in a deep-blue coat, his long dark hair falling to his shoulders. He was looking to his side as he exited, and Julia did not miss the strong jawline that caused her heart to beat with a new rhythm. He had to be the most fetching... could a man be called fetching? Regardless, she had never seen a man so pleasing to the eye!

This assessment lasted no more than half a breath, for then he muttered a goodbye and took a step forward, right toward Julia. Then everything she had thought about the man changed forever.

She raised her hands to keep the man from colliding into her and gasped when he did just that. He, in turn, grunted and took a possessive hold of her waist. Well, perhaps not possessive exactly, he did not know her, nor she him, enough to be possessive. Regardless, he had a firm hold of her waist, firm enough to evaporate every drop of moisture from her mouth and leave her legs wanting to give out from beneath her. In fact, if he had not had such a hold on her, she would have likely tumbled to the floor!

Yet it was her hands pressed against his chest—a solid mass that seemed made of iron—that made the room spin around her. Her arms went limp, and her hands hurried to grasp hold of something, anything! When they landed on his arms, she nearly fainted. Firm, taut muscles made the dizziness worse. Had the Greeks used this man when they created their famous sculptures?

An alarm of shame rang in Julia's head, and her cheeks heated. What was she doing fixating on a man's physical form? No woman in her right mind considered the body that lay beneath a finely cut coat! A warning tickled the back of her mind, one given to her by Ruth, but for the life of her, she could not remember the consequences for such thoughts.

His curt tone brought her back to reality. "Watch where you are going," he snapped.

Julia withdrew her hands and stumbled when the man released her, but she could only stand there, unable to respond. It was as if her mind had gone blank, and her tongue had been removed from her mouth.

"Your Grace!" Mrs. Rutley said as she hurried to the door and pushed Julia aside. "My apologies! Oh my, your coat. It's now rumpled." In her late forties, Mrs. Rutley came no higher than the man's chest, even with her chestnut hair coiled on top of her head beneath a ruffled mob cap. To Julia's shock, the headmistress smoothed not only the coat he was wearing, but the waistcoat beneath as if she were brushing a mare!

"What in blazes are you doing?" the man asked. "Remove your hands from me this instant, woman. Are you drunk?" He pushed away Mrs. Rutley, who took a step back, unruffled by the harshness of his voice.

Julia licked her lips as he pulled back his hair. Oh my, but how handsome he was! Devilishly so. His eyes were as gray as a winter sky, and his full lips made her feel as if she were drunk on wine. What would it be like to have those lips touch hers?

"What is your name?" he asked.

"Julia," she whispered. "Miss Julia Wallace."

"Well, Miss Wallace, may I advise you to watch where you are going from now on?"

Julia nodded and glanced at Mrs. Rutley, who was motioning to her skirts. Belatedly, Julia dropped into a curtsy and said, "My apologies, Your Grace. I did not—"

The duke raised a hand. "If I wish to be put to sleep, I'll ask you to speak. Until then, remain silent."

Julia's cheeks burned again, this time from annoyance.

"Consider my offer, Mrs. Rutley," the duke said. "I'll call again in five days."

"Yes, Your Grace," the headmistress replied, dropping into a perfect curtsy. "Allow me to see you to the door."

"There is no need," the man said. He turned to look at Julia and added, "I fear I may not make it to the door without a woman throwing herself at me again." Then, to Julia's shock, he winked at her!

When he was gone, Mrs. Rutley smiled at Julia. "Don't mind his words," she said. "He is a man with many burdens."

Julia stared toward the front door. "I understand why he is called the Duke of Handsome." She covered her mouth with a gasp. "I mean madness. The Duke of Madness."

Mrs. Rutley laughed as she guided Julia into the office. "I believe it's you who has been overcome with madness," the headmistress said. "Now, what has brought you to my office?"

His Grace, Matthew Colburn, 5th Duke of Elmhurst, bounced the gold pocket watch in his hand as the headmistress of the school spoke. Mrs. Rutley, a slim woman nearing fifty, still held some beauty with her straight nose and high cheekbones, and he considered the various rumors he had heard about her. According to the gossip hounds, she participated in late-night trysts with a number of barons, which could be true. What he thought was less likely to be true was that she sold some of the girls who attended her school to the highest bidder. That rumor was simply preposterous, in his opinion. Yet, all rumors were based on some sort of truth, so perhaps this particular one came from the possibility that she played matchmaker as well as headmistress and was paid for both.

The truth was, Mrs. Rutley was an intelligent woman who had a certain self-assurance about her that he admired. She held herself as regal as any queen and demanded respect with her mere presence.

The headmistress reminded him of his mother, who had retreated to Scotland soon after the death of his father. As his father's mind deteriorated, his mother had remained strong, although he had found her asleep in her chair from exhaustion on more than one occasion. It had been too long since he had last seen her, and for a moment, he wished she were here.

"Do not worry about me," his mother had once said when he had expressed his concerns. "I'm strong enough to handle this on my own."

He had doubted her strength back then. The burden she had to carry was much too heavy for any one person. Despite his concerns, he found himself replying, "If you insist."

Yes, he could see that Mrs. Rutley shared that same resilience his mother had. Yet, he was not here to regale himself on her better qualities, nor to speculate on the latest rumors of the *ton*. No, he was here to discuss her school, or rather the property on which it sat, which bordered his own.

"Therefore," Mrs. Rutley was saying, "I must say with certainty that I have no desire to sell. I'm sure you were hoping for a different answer, but the school means too much to me to sell it, no matter how much you offer."

Matthew had to bite his tongue. As a duke, he was not accustomed to being denied any requests from those outside his family, and the few experiences he had encountered were not any more appealing than now.

He looked down at the watch while considering his next words. The pocket watch had been a gift from his late father, the 4th Duke of Elmhurst, who had assured Matthew that the timepiece would bring him good luck in matters of business or whenever else he might need it. There were times when the luck of the watch had failed him, but those instances were few and far between. Perhaps he was not focusing enough of his attention on it for it to work its magic. He rubbed his thumb over the smooth back of the housing just in case.

"I'm willing to pay double the current market value," he said, feeling a surge of surety course through him. "Think of the property you will be able to purchase with that money, one that is much larger and will be able to house more pupils. Maybe you can even purchase something in London. Perhaps you can take a holiday abroad or purchase several new dresses?"

The older woman's face remained resolute, and he returned the watch to his inner pocket. "Surely you don't wish to spend the remainder of your days watching over the spoiled children of those hoping to move up in the world and become a part of the *ton*?"

Although the school was deemed a "private school," Matthew had always suspected that the true objective of sending one's daughter there was so parents could be rid of their children to have time to themselves. After all, boys were sent off to boarding schools for that very reason, he was certain.

"My school is not the typical school, Your Grace," Mrs. Rutley said. "The girls who attend are good girls, quite intelligent. What's more, although many come from wealthy but untitled families looking to climb the proverbial societal ladder, as you have judiciously pointed out, several pupils—not all mind you, but some—come from newly titled families. There are also those who have decided it would be best that their daughters are trained by someone qualified to do so—someone such as myself. Their decision to send them away is theirs, and they are not likely to explain their reasoning to the likes of me. And although they practice the usual skills expected of young ladies—music, the arts, and embroidery, for example—they can also hold conversations around philosophy, the sciences, and even history."

"I'm sure they are able to entertain one another with all sorts of fanciful discussions women tend to enjoy," he replied. "I do doubt, however, that they could hold a decent conversation with the likes of most educated men."

Mrs. Rutley offered him a smile that he first thought meant she had accepted defeat. That prepossession disappeared with her next words.

"I would never allow my young ladies to engage in such conversations with gentlemen, Your Grace," she said.

Matthew grinned. Yes, he had won this battle!

"After all," Mrs. Rutley continued, "few men bested by a woman in any way, especially when discussing a topic that requires intelligence and quick thinking, are able to repair the damage caused by the embarrassment of finding themselves in such a situation."

Matthew leaned forward and tapped the table twice with his knuckles with a laugh. "If such a day comes, I'll forfeit my title and work in a millinery!"

When the woman did not join in his laughter, he stopped. Surely, she was not being serious? His Uncle Ezra had warned him that contemporary women were making strange attempts to wiggle their way into the world belonging to men, reading books on topics once forbidden to them, and even going so far as to meet in secret to discuss those topics. Uncle Ezra had assured Matthew in no uncertain terms that if women became knowledgeable in areas in which they had no business, they would become dangerous. Even the Almighty would be unable to intervene and stop them.

"Mrs. Rutley, I've wanted this land for years now. Perhaps we can come to an agreement we both can appreciate. How about you sell me just a portion of your land, a small parcel? Would you be willing to concede at least that?"

The woman blinked but otherwise remained resolute, and his frustration deepened. His pocket watch had failed him, and now he was unsure how to proceed. "This is more difficult than finding a worthy bride," he whispered to himself. Or perhaps not in a low enough whisper if the woman's arched eyebrow was any indication. "You know very well what I mean. You have a houseful of women ready to be married off. Yet even as a duke, I cannot find one single young lady I can trust to be my companion at a party I'm throwing in a fortnight, let alone one I would be willing to marry."

He swore under his breath for admitting this aloud. What was it about this woman that had him laying out his troubles right in front of her?

"Of course, I only speak in jest," he said with a laugh that sounded false even to his ears. "I have plenty of women to choose from, and many more who wish that I would call on them." He rose from his seat, wondering, not for the first time, if he was going mad just as his father had. His blasted tongue continued to cause him grief!

"I have no doubt that the eligible ladies who swarm around you vying for your attention are numerous," Mrs. Rutley said as she, too, stood. "Regardless, I do not wish to sell. Not even a portion of my property is up for sale."

Sighing, Matthew walked to the door and opened it. Turning his head to make one last appeal, his confidence faltered when Mrs. Rutley gave him a smile that dared him to make his request again.

In truth, the land was of little importance to him. His father had tried time and again to purchase the property on which the school sat, and now that he was gone, Matthew continued the attempts because it was what his father wanted.

Yet, there was a second reason for continuing his father's endeavor, one that he had never told another living soul. If he could succeed where his father had failed, such as purchasing the land, he would prove himself different from his father.

He could have laughed at this. Why would he have ever thought this endeavor easy? His father, a man who could have talked a turtle into selling his shell, had been unable to convince Mrs. Rutley to sell.

How could Matthew have done any better? All he wanted to do now was to be gone from this place where his luck had failed him.

He took a step forward, and then everything became a blur.

A creature so beautiful, with hair the color of wheat, stood before him, her blue eyes wide and her delicate hands resting on his chest. Time stood still, and the woman's gaze held his, transfixing him. His hands had a mind of their own as they encircled her waist, and the feeling of holding her made any response stick in his throat. It was as if he had laid claim to her, and now she would reside in his arms forever.

To his shock—and he had to admit, to his pleasure—her hands wandered down to his arms, causing a flame inside him to ignite his entire being. Inhaling sharply in order to find his breath, he instead became lost in her fragrance, a subtle hint of roses mixed with the light scent of soap. For the first time, he considered giving up the vow he had made.

When her hands pulled back as if burned by scalding water, Matthew blinked twice and came to his senses. "Watch where you are going," he muttered and then inwardly scolded himself for the choice of words and the tone he had used.

Mrs. Rutley pushed between them. "Your Grace! My apologies! Oh my, your coat. It's now rumpled."

It was one thing to be touched by the lovely young woman and quite another to be accosted by Mrs. Rutley herself! "What in blazes are you doing? Remove your hands from me this instant, woman. Are you drunk?"

Despite the discomfiture of Mrs. Rutley's familiarity with him, he could not take his eyes off the younger woman. "What is your name?"

"Julia," she replied. "Miss Julia Wallace." Even her voice was a song emitting from her throat!

"Well, Miss Wallace, may I advise you to watch where you are going from now on?"

Her beautiful neck bent just a fraction, and she blushed. "My apologies, Your Grace. I did not—"

He shook his head. As pleasant as Miss Wallace was to look at, he did not have time for a woman he had no business having an interest in. It was just not worth the risk. Besides, when Matthew had mentioned Mrs. Rutley's school to his uncle in passing several years earlier, the man had sneered like a rabid dog. He began a rant on how only unscrupulous women attended such an establishment and were unworthy of their time or attention.

Come to think of it, Uncle Ezra seemed to dismiss any woman he, Matthew, brought up in conversation. Why was that?

Well, he had no time to deliberate his uncle's motives now.

"If I wish to be put to sleep," he said as he pushed both women away, "I'll ask you to speak. Until then, remain silent." He had to get out of here! Being so near this young beauty was sending his mind reeling.

Drat! Why had he taken such a sarcastic tone with her? And a duke did not simply apologize.

"Misunderstandings," he mumbled. There. That was a worthy offering of peace. He turned to the headmistress. "Consider my offer, Mrs. Rutley. I'll call again in five days."

When Mrs. Rutley offered to walk him to the door, he declined, but a mischievous inkling spread through him. "There is no need," he said, allowing the tiniest of smiles to play on his lips. "I fear I may not make it to the door without a woman throwing herself at me again." He winked at Miss Wallace to ease the bite of his words.

Matthew hurried to the front of the house, concerned that Miss Wallace would hear his heart pounding in his chest. Once outside, he drew in a deep breath. Now, *she* would be a wonderful trinket to dangle on his arm at the party! His peers would be so jealous.

But no, it could not happen. He was a duke, and certain expectations had been put into place for him. She was a common woman, likely from a wealthier family if they could afford a private school but common all the same, and would not likely impress his uncle, who had been working tirelessly to find him a suitable bride.

Over the past two months, many eligible young ladies had been paraded before him, but he dismissed each one without much thought. Some were attractive in their way, but most were either quite hideous or needed a great deal of powders and rouges to make them appear attractive. The young woman he had just encountered was unlike those presented to him thus far. Her beauty was natural.

No! He had to push her from his mind! She was not for him.

Yet try as he might, he could not shake the feel of her hands touching him as the carriage carried him back to his home.

Chapter Two

Hardwick Hall was a massive country estate built by Matthew's grandfather, and just one of the dozens of properties he now owned. It had a portico wide enough to hold a hundred men side by side, and a ballroom that could hold a hundred more. No expense had been spared in its construction or the luxuries inside and outside of the home.

Despite its imposing appearance, a certain darkness had loomed over the estate since the death of his father two years earlier. Perhaps it was the silence left behind now that his voice no longer rang through the halls. Or maybe it was when Matthew's mother fled to an estate in Scotland once she was free of her husband's illness. Matthew suspected the sense of foreboding came from the loneliness he felt in his home that caused a certain coldness he could not shake.

At the top of the steps that led to the portico, he stopped and turned to lean against one of the seven white columns. The land he owned stretched for miles, and the estate on which the school sat would make a fine addition. *If* he could convince Mrs. Rutley to sell.

He shook his head. The woman would never sell. His appointment with her had been a waste of time, and time was a luxury he despised wasting.

Yet had it been? The beauty into whom he had stumbled had caused his throat to go dry and his mind to turn to mire. Even those few seconds had made that call worthwhile.

"Miss Julia Wallace," he murmured. "That was her name." The woman had been strikingly beautiful, and Matthew thought—not for the first time—what it would be like to run his hand through her hair. Or to learn how soft the skin on her face was. But such thoughts led to actions, which turned into pledges of commitment and, as he has seen firsthand with his parents, thus turned into destruction.

What a far cry the end had been from the beginning. He recalled as a boy how his father would affectionately take hold of his mother, whispering in her ear and causing her cheeks to redden. How many times had he secretly wished to have a wife to share such joy?

He heaved a sigh, leaving his dreams in the past where they belonged.

A voice behind him made him jump. "Who?"

Matthew turned to face his uncle, Ezra Colburn, younger brother of his father, who stood with a raised eyebrow. From his dark hair to matching boots, the man was draped in nothing but black. Uncle Ezra had not been in Matthew's life much before his father became too ill to see to the needs of the estate. In fact, he could count the number of times on one hand when his uncle had called to the house. But when his father's condition worsened and all appeared lost, Uncle Ezra arrived at Hardwick Hall like some hero out of a story and had remained since.

"Just one of the students at the girls' school," Matthew replied. "A rare beauty. Quite captivating, I must say."

"And one with a father unable to hire a private tutor," his uncle said with a snort of disdain. "Why must you waste your time eying those beneath you? Unless you plan to only bed this woman? In that case, by all means, do so."

His uncle's eyes bore into Matthew to the point that he lowered his gaze. Matthew recalled the first time his uncle had belittled him for a matter he no longer could remember. His father had died the week before, and Matthew had promptly brought up how small his uncle's treatment of him made him feel. Expecting an argument of sorts, he was surprised by his uncle's response.

"My dear nephew, I am here to help you, not to fight. If you cannot trust your own blood, who can you trust?"

Still grieving the death of his father, Matthew had heaved a sigh. He had no one else he could trust, none to whom he could turn. Only his uncle.

"I'm sorry," he had murmured.

Since that time, Uncle Ezra had denigrated Matthew so often, he lost count. Matthew understood it was only to help him grow to become the man his uncle knew he could be. Although there were times he challenged his instruction, Matthew found that agreeing more often kept the peace.

"You really must take care with what you say aloud," his uncle said. "We cannot have you acting as your father did and further ruin the family name. Peter was my brother, and it pains me to speak so poorly of him, even if what I say is true. But you must strive to be perfect in every way to erase—or at least rewrite—the terrible legacy your father left in his wake."

Matthew had to concede that what his uncle said was true. His father had indeed lost his mind in the last few years of his life, and his actions and words had brought great shame to the Colburn name. He was caught having complete conversations with himself or, worse yet, with inanimate objects such as trees. The finest doctors had been called in, yet none could find the source of his madness, and soon, he made few public appearances.

The last straw occurred during a party four years earlier, when his father broke out into a song. That in itself would have been bad enough, but his choice of song was better suited for drunken sailors than for the aristocracy who had been in attendance. The horrified stares of the onlookers were the beginning of his end.

Soon after, his father had gained the moniker *Duke of Madness*, and Matthew feared that one day he, too, would inherit that title just as he had the dukedom.

"I understand, Uncle," Matthew replied. "Though I worry it's too late. I've heard the rumors that I'm like my father, and that the moniker has already been bestowed upon me. I fear the only woman who may take an interest in me may be nothing more than a scullery maid at best."

This was an exaggeration, of course. Although Matthew had heard the rumors, they had not stopped the polite smiles from the numerous ladies willing to overlook his possible malady in hopes to gain the title of duchess.

The larger problem was that he found any sort of conversation with most gentlewomen dreary. None could challenge him in the way Mrs. Rutley claimed the women she trained could. Furthermore, his fear of becoming like his father and siring a child who would follow in their footsteps forced him to push away any possible matches. Why would he wish a woman to suffer as his mother had?

His uncle heaved a sigh. "What you say may be true. Any woman would refuse to see you." Then he grinned. "But not the lady who waits inside as we speak."

Matthew frowned. "What lady? Uncle, what have you done?"

As his uncle was prone to do, he walked into the house without responding. Frustrated, Matthew followed after him. In the foyer, they encountered the butler, Hickson, standing at attention. A short, round man with a ring of hair around an otherwise balding pate, Hickson was a stiff man who knew his place.

"What lady waits for me?" Matthew asked the butler. "You know how much I despise surprises."

"Indeed, Your Grace," Hickson said, yet his eyes shifted toward Uncle Ezra. "She is—"

"Quiet, you bumbling fool!" his uncle said. "Matthew, come with me. You will learn who she is soon enough."

With great reluctance, Matthew followed his uncle through the large French doors that led out to the back garden. She was waiting for him outside? What lady waited out of doors for any man? This had to be a trick of some sort.

His uncle stopped at the doors. "Well, Nephew, tell me, what do you see?"

"I see two ladies," Matthew replied as he peered through the glass panes. Oh, how he despised these games his uncle forced him to play!

"I imagine one is the lady of whom you spoke, and the other is her chaperone."

Uncle Ezra chuckled. "You only see the obvious, but you must look closer if you wish to be a great duke."

Matthew squinted at the women. "I imagine the lady in question is the one who has dark hair. She is rather pretty in a way—"

"Your interest in her should go beyond her looks, Nephew. Her father owns several important parcels of land near the Thames, and the stakes he holds in hotels across London and Oxford are not to be trifled with." He placed a hand on Matthew's shoulder. "The man has also gambled away most of his fortune, so he is desperate. His last true asset is his only daughter."

"How many times have I told you that I'll marry when I find a woman of my choosing?" Matthew asked, though he was determined to never marry if he could help it. His plan was simple: Make excuses and delay all talks of marriage until even his uncle gave up, leaving Matthew blessedly alone. "If her father is in need of financial aid, schedule a meeting to discuss what business we may conduct to get him back on his feet. What I'll not do is discuss marriage, or even courting a young woman with the sole purpose of gaining said business."

His uncle's nostrils flared. "Do you wish me to leave your home? Just say so if you do, for I don't enjoy being made a fool of. You cannot continue to reject my advice as if it comes from that idiot butler of yours."

Matthew shook his head. "Uncle, you must understand—"

"Listen to me very closely," his uncle said with a deep growl, "for I'll never speak it again. In just over two months, you will be a part of the most important meetings you will ever encounter. Your holdings will triple, and no man, save the King himself, will be able to compare himself to your wealth. You are one and twenty and unwed, and I tell you now that you will embarrass this family worse than your father ever could have. At least he married and therefore had an heir, for goodness' sake! You have not even done that!"

The set of meetings of which his uncle spoke was indeed important, for it would determine his rights of shipping from various ports as well as the acquisition of dozens of businesses between Cambridge and London. The stakes were so great that failure could see the Colburn name shamed for generations. Yet not as significant as Matthew being unmarried, a fact his uncle reminded him of daily over the last few months.

The plan Uncle Ezra had was simple. Find a woman, marry her, and quickly produce an heir. Matthew's peers might have time to find a worthy bride, for they did not have a dark cloud of madness hanging over them. Time was running out. All too soon—much sooner, it appeared, for Matthew than it had for his father—Matthew would lose his mind.

Uncle Ezra took a step forward, his stature equal to Matthew's tall frame, but his gaze far harsher. "Now, if you don't wish to speak to that woman, I'll find you another. I know of a lady who will be a guest in my home in just a few weeks. All I ask is that you accompany her on one outing. Will you do at least this one thing for me?"

Guilt tore at Matthew's heart, and he gave a reluctant nod. "Yes, Uncle, of course I will."

"Good. I'll tell the woman outside that you are too busy to see her." He pushed open the door but then stopped. "Why was I forced to mind my brother and now must do the same for his son?"

Another twinge of guilt plagued the back of Matthew's mind as his uncle closed the door behind him. With his father's sudden passing, Matthew had been given little time to grieve as he stepped into the role of duke. Although he had trained since birth for that day, he still found so much of what was expected of him overwhelming. Yet the selection of a bride had been the most burdensome of all.

As he watched his uncle speak to the dark-haired lady, a flash of images played through his mind. Meeting a woman, enjoying outings with her, and eventually marrying. All brought him a sense of joy, but each vision ended the same—becoming as mad as his father and his wife living the tortured life his mother had been forced to endure. A life of watching over her husband as if he were a child. Listening to a spouse at dinner who spoke of animals that could talk and relatives long since dead who he expected to join them for a holiday. And although his mother had remained stoic in her expressions, Matthew had seen the pain in her eyes. A pain he would not wish on anyone.

No, he would marry no woman, the one who stood outside now or any other. He had been able to delay the inevitable thus far, but could he delay it forever? Yes, his luck would continue, he had no doubt.

Smiling, he reached into the inside pocket of his coat, then frowned. The place where he kept his pocket watch was now empty.

He patted his coat, his breeches, anywhere he may have placed his watch. "Where did I put it?" he asked. Had it fallen in the carriage as he returned from the school? No, that was not possible. He recalled turning it in his hands while he spoke to Mrs. Rutley, and he was certain he had returned it to his pocket at the end of that encounter.

Then his eyes widened. "Why, that little thief!" he said in a harsh whisper. What he had believed to be a beautiful young woman using her hands to entice him was nothing more than trickery. While he was distracted, Miss Wallace had stolen the watch from his person and was likely attempting to sell it at this very moment. She was nothing more than a thieving pickpocket!

Fear sank into his chest and caused his legs to stiffen, more for what was lost than for what the girl had done. That watch was the only thing that brought him luck and kept him from becoming like his father.

Soon, anger replaced fear. How dare she take what belonged to him? He would see his property returned to him!

"Hickson!" he shouted as he marched into the foyer.

"Your Grace?"

"See that my horse is saddled," Matthew snapped, his fists clenched at his sides. "It appears our neighbor is housing a thief, and I mean to go retrieve my property."

With a quick bow, Hickson hurried away, and Matthew considered how he would make the girl suffer for the wrong she had caused him.

Julia sat with four of her friends in a circle on her bed. They had insisted she retell the story about her encounter with the Duke of Madness for the third time. When she was done, the room fell silent.

"So, he is handsome as well as mad?" Jenny Clifton asked with a frown as she tugged at the chestnut braid that fell over her shoulder, a terrible habit she had whenever she became confused or frustrated. "I had heard his face is disfigured. Is that not true?"

"It certainly is not," Julia replied. "Though, I would say it's more than simply handsome. Perhaps noble? Yes, that is a better description. He has a noble face. And not mad-like at all."

Beside Jenny sat Diana Kendricks, a girl with the curliest blonde hair Julia had ever seen. "When a man takes hold of a woman's waist in such a way," she said in her typical know-all tone, "he does so as an act of claiming ownership of her."

"No!" Emma gasped.

Diana gave an adamant nod. "Mother told me that, years ago, a man could simply pick up the woman he wished to marry and carry her off, but now societal rules have dictated that they use less aggressive means. But some, like this duke, will apparently lay claim to a woman as a way to honor the old ways."

Louisa Dunston joined in the heated discussion, but Julia sat back to consider what Diana had said. She had never heard of such a ritual, but what reason did she have not to believe it to be so? Diana's mother had proven to be a wealth of knowledge over the years, after all.

For a time, her thoughts drifted to what had occurred several hours earlier. Her imagination burst into being, and in this vision, the duke would not take hold of her waist, but instead, he outright embraced her. Mrs. Rutley would cry out for him to stop, but he would merely laugh as he pulled Julia close against his chest so she could revel in the feel of his strong arms around her. He would then lean in closer, intending to kiss her.

Of course, such actions were unbecoming of a lady, and she would have to put up a pretense of refusing, but he would be far too powerful and would kiss her, anyway. When the kiss came to an end, she would look up at him and whisper, "That was beautiful, Your Grace."

Giggles filled the room and pulled her from her musings, leaving her gasping in horror. Had she said that last aloud? Indeed she had, for Emma was laughing so hard, she tumbled off the side of the bed.

"I was not... that is..."

Footsteps outside the door saved her from having to explain her words; the door opened and two more of her friends stormed into the room, their eyes wide.

"Oh, Julia, come quickly!" Unity Ancell said, gasping as if she had run up the stairs. "The duke has returned, and he is ever so angry! He is in Mrs. Rutley's office shouting so loudly that even the paintings on the walls are shaking!"

Julia shifted to the edge of the bed and stood. "Why is he angry?"

"We don't know," Theodosia Renwick said, "but Ruth is trying to listen at the door."

Diana giggled. "He has returned to claim his possession," she said. "We should all say our goodbyes now."

"That is nonsense," Julia snapped in an attempt to keep civility in the room. "Come, let us go downstairs. Maybe we can learn the truth as to why he is here."

The room emptied as the seven girls made their way down the long corridor, passing other rooms where other girls who attended the school were likely sharing their own bits of gossip. As they descended the staircase, they encountered Ruth, her auburn hair in short curls and a small scar on her cheek.

"I was unable to hear all that he was saying," Ruth said, "but I caught the word 'thief' and something about calling the magistrates?"

"Perhaps he meant the vicar," Diana said. "As a duke, he has the power to forgo the reading of the banns."

Julia looked over the young women who had all become her dearest friends. Although no official title had been given her, she was well aware that the others looked up to her. It was in moments such as this that she knew they needed to act like the ladies they had become and not the young girls who had been sent here years ago. That meant not being caught listening through keyholes. For any reason!

"Enough," she said in a firm tone, and the voices fell silent, "laughing and teasing about such things in private is all well and good, but we are far too old to be discussing them where others can overhear.

We are young ladies, and it's about time we started acting as such. Now, the duke is not here to carry me away. Or to go in search of a vicar." She gave Diana a glare. "We must think before we act. Our actions today will guide our steps tomorrow."

Everyone nodded, and even Ruth sighed in defeat. "I suppose you are right," she said. "But it's rather fun to lose myself in nonsense from time to time."

"We all enjoy those moments," Julia said, "but as I said, there is a time and a place, and this is neither. Now, shall we go for a stroll before we must change for dinner?"

Everyone agreed, and once they had collected their bonnets and shawls, they headed to the front door. As Emma reached for the handle, a familiar voice called out.

"Julia, come here, please." Mrs. Rutley stood just outside her office door.

"Would you like me to accompany you?" Emma whispered.

"No. I'm sure everything is well," Julia replied, although she did not feel so. "Ruth, lead the others around the grounds. I'll join you as soon as I'm finished." She joined the headmistress and immediately recognized something was wrong by the worry on the older woman's face.

"Come with me." Mrs. Rutley rarely spoke so sharply.

Julia nodded and followed the headmistress to her office. Indeed, the Duke of Madness stood with his hands clasped behind his back as he appeared to be perusing the tomes on the bookcase.

"Your Grace," Mrs. Rutley said, "I've brought Miss Wallace as you requested."

Julia's heart thudded in her chest. Was what Diana said true? Was he here to lay claim to her? Why else would he come?

No, that was just plain silly. She realized just how silly when the duke turned toward her, and his face held no expression of lust or happiness for being there.

"Miss Wallace," the duke said in a stern voice, "I advise you to confess to your thievery. If you admit the truth and return what you have stolen from me, I'll never speak of it again."

Julia's head swam in confusion. "Thievery, Your Grace? What thievery?"

He narrowed his eyes at her, but Mrs. Rutley stood between them. "Your Grace, allow me to speak with her, if you don't mind." When he nodded, she turned to Julia. "It appears that His Grace has lost a pocket watch."

"It was stolen, not lost," the duke snapped.

"His watch was stolen," Mrs. Rutley corrected, but a small frown played on her lips. "Did you take it?"

Julia shook her head. "I would never steal. And if I did, why would I need a watch?"

Mrs. Rutley turned back to face the duke and smiled. "You see, Your Grace, Miss Wallace has denied taking your watch. If you will allow me to search your carriage, I would be happy to do so. Perhaps it fell beneath one of the benches."

A deep growl emitted from the duke's throat. "This is ridiculous," he said before moving to tower over Julia. How could a man be so handsome even when he was angry? Yet, his eyes expressed the madness that explained his moniker. "Of course, she would deny it. That is what thieves do."

Despite how frightened she was, Julia did not appreciate the accusation in the slightest. "I swear on my family's name that I did not steal your watch." Forcing the words to come out was akin to pulling an entire spool of thread through the eye of a needle.

"*Argh*!" The duke groaned and turned away to return to his place before the bookshelf, his back to Julia and Mrs. Rutley. "I have no choice but to summon the constable."

Julia choked back a sob. He would not do something so horrible without proof, would he?

"Your Grace," Mrs. Rutley said, "do you not think that is a bit extreme?"

The duke turned on his heel so quickly, Julia looked to see if he had made a hole in the rug beneath his feet. "Extreme?" he demanded. "Mrs. Rutley, you are a respectable woman, but I must reprimand you on your choice of words. That pocket watch has been in my family for several generations, and it has brought me a great deal of luck. Not only am I hosting a party in two weeks, but I also have scheduled some negotiations that are very important to the future of the dukedom.

Without that watch..." He slammed a fist on the desk. "I don't have to explain myself to you, Mrs. Rutley. I must have my pocket watch, and you must train your girls not to be thieves!"

Mrs. Rutley gave a quick dip of her head. Was that a smile? "Your Grace, I would not offend you by detailing Miss Wallace's life to convince you that she is not a thief. But I do find us at a crossroads and am unsure how to proceed." Then her face lit up. "It brings you luck, you say?" she asked in a thoughtful tone with not a whit of a quiver. Julia considered weeping. "I believe I may have a solution to your problem."

"Unless you have my watch, you do not."

"Perhaps I do," Mrs. Rutley replied, unruffled. "You see, Lord Wallace, her father, is a man who enjoys games of chance. He has doubled his fortune through such means."

Julia stared at the headmistress. Why was she lying about her father? He despised games of chance and considered those who wasted their money on such pastimes, fools.

"But Mrs. Rutley—" Julia started to say only to be interrupted.

"Quiet, Miss Wallace," the headmistress snapped. "I will handle this!"

Julia could only gape. Never had Mrs. Rutley spoken so harshly to her before, and her heart trembled. Did the headmistress believe she had indeed stolen from this man?

Mrs. Rutley did not seem to notice Julia's distress. "As I was saying, when Miss Wallace was but fourteen, she sneaked into the room while her father was playing, and he had been losing rather significantly. Now usually, such actions bring about scorn, but her father soon realized that she brought him good luck, for he suddenly began to win."

Had Mrs. Rutley somehow caught the duke's madness? Such maladies were not contagious, were they? Julia considered taking a step back just to be sure, but she was more frightened of Mrs. Rutley at the moment than any malady she might catch from the duke.

The duke rubbed his chin. "How fascinating. I've heard of people possessing such luck, but never a woman. What do you propose?"

"You have made it clear that you are in need of luck, Your Grace, and Julia has that very gift. You mentioned a party you will be hosting.

How you would like a female companion to be there with you? I would recommend that Miss Wallace be your companion for that gathering."

To this, the duke laughed. "Are you mad? She steals from me, and I'm to invite her into my home where I have more items of value?"

"That is not my point at all, Your Grace," Mrs. Rutley rebutted. "You may use her as a decoy to keep your uncle from choosing a wife for you from one of the many women in attendance."

His face turned stony. "How did you know about that?" he asked in a low, menacing voice.

"Rumors abound," Mrs. Rutley replied quicker than lightning. "It's a fair exchange, my lord. Miss Wallace will give you the luck you desire. With your oversight, she will put to good use the skills she has acquired while also keeping at bay any of the other ladies clambering for your attention."

He rubbed his temples. "This is ludicrous..."

"And in return, I'll sit with you at a later date to discuss the sale of a portion of my land to you."

The room spun around Julia. She was first accused of theft, and now they were using her as a bartering tool in a business transaction? How dare they treat her so callously!

"I'm a duke, not a governess. I would not task my gardener with what you ask of me."

Julia closed her eyes. Finally, someone had sense to end this madness.

"Yet, I do find myself in the most unusual dilemma. My lucky pocket watch was stolen, and I am in need of luck." His eyes fell on Julia, and she found her throat suddenly in need of moisture. "Perhaps Miss Wallace will make a decent substitute."

Julia had been compared to many things, but to a lucky pocket watch? Could he be more insulting than to compare her to an inanimate object?

The duke continued, "Do understand that if I entertain this notion of yours, I'll not send for the constable, at least not yet. If all goes well, I'll let the matter drop. Also, this agreement is only to gain land and not as an act of charity toward this girl who lacks basic civility." He paused and frowned. "And I'm to be willing to do all this with nothing more than a promise to sit down at a meeting, to discuss the *possibility* of a sale of a portion of the land? Am I correct in this assumption?"

"Oh no, Your Grace. After these important negotiations you mentioned, we shall sit down, and I *guarantee* you will receive a parcel of my land. Let's say the section of the stream that snakes onto my property up to the hedgerow to the south? We can discuss the finer details at a later point. What say you?"

Julia stared at Mrs. Rutley, pleading with her eyes. If this man thought her a thief now, he would treat her no better than a scullery maid later!

"I'll agree on one condition," the duke said finally. "If my watch is not returned by her"—he pointed at Julia—"within three months from today, the amount of land you sell me doubles. Agreed?"

"You have a bargain," Mrs. Rutley said, putting out her hand. The duke shook it.

Julia's jaw dropped. Her headmistress had just used her as a bartering tool! Suddenly, Abigail's talk of selling students did not sound so foolish.

"I imagine Miss Wallace will need to be advised as to who will be in attendance and any other particulars concerning your party. You'll need to spend a minimal amount of time together so you will both be comfortable with one another," Mrs. Rutley said. "After all, you want her to be prepared. Shall I have her ready for you to collect tomorrow?"

"I'll be here at midday," the duke said as he walked past them. "Don't be late, Miss Wallace. And I would consider righting this terrible wrong by returning my watch well before the three-month deadline."

Once the man was gone, Julia turned to Mrs. Rutley. "How can you allow him to punish me for a crime I did not commit? You know I did not steal anything from that man!"

"You are not being punished," the headmistress said in her usual quiet tone.

"Then why am I being bartered as a good luck charm? I cannot believe you would use me as a pawn in some sort of strange transaction. Do you not believe me when I say I did not steal his pocket watch?"

Mrs. Rutley sighed and placed a hand on Julia's cheek. "Of course, I don't believe that you stole it, my dear, but that does not matter. What does is that the duke believes it to be true. You must make the best of this arrangement and make a day of rain become one of sunshine."

Julia shook her head. "I've been with you for nearly four years, and never have I argued with you. But I must say that I do not wish to do this. The man is mad and has accused me of theft, yet you choose to send me to him, anyway. I would like to know why."

"Right or wrong, it's not for us to say.," Mrs. Rutley said. "He is the duke,. Therefore, we'll do as he requests without question. Now, we have nothing more to discuss on the matter."

Julia sighed and left the room. Never had she witnessed Mrs. Rutley do anything so selfish. Julia did not want to be used! Yet, what say did she have in the matter? None whatsoever. If the duke was truly as mad as he made himself out to be, what other accusation would he make of her?

Chapter Three

All the girls who attended Mrs. Rutley's School for Young Women came from a variety of walks of life. The majority were sent on their untitled family's last farthing, but Julia was not one of them. Not only was her father a baron, but he had insisted on sending her to the school with her very own lady's maid.

Many of the other girls looked upon her with envy at having a trained woman helping her dress rather than relying on one another to see to their many stays and buttons, but Julia ignored their whispers. After all, Bridget had become more than a servant in Julia's eyes; now she was a close friend with whom she confided her deepest secrets, just as she was now.

"The duke believes I'm a thief!" Julia said as she stomped across the room for the tenth time since beginning her telling. "And now as a punishment, I'm to attend a party with him, as well as several outings. I don't know how I feel about being punished in this way." She stopped and turned on her heel. "If Father learns of it, he'll see me married off that same day!" She dropped onto the stool in front of her vanity table, and the wood creaked. "We are friends, are we not?"

At five and twenty, Bridget was seven years Julia's elder and Julia's best friend. A round woman with perpetually rosy cheeks and ash-colored hair, she was never seen without a smile. That same smile had caused more than one man to return in kind, but Bridget never seemed to notice. They had spent many nights speaking of their dreams, and more than once, the woman had provided Julia a shoulder on which to cry.

Bridget picked up the brush and began stroking Julia's hair. "I think that you're a beautiful young lady. And you found the duke handsome, didn't you?"

"Well, yes, that is true."

"'Devilishly so' is how I think you described him," Bridget said, the corners of her lips upturning. "The fact is, you'll be in his company. In his handsome company. Now you tell me, what will there be to anguish over?"

"Besides believing I'm a thief?"

"He doesn't think you're a thief, Miss Julia. Or at least, I doubt he truly does."

Julia turned to face the maid. "I'm confused," she said, frowning. "The man outright accused me, in front of Mrs. Rutley. He even accused her of training us to become thieves. How do you gather that he does not believe I am one?"

Bridget smiled, took Julia's hand, and led her to the bed to sit on the edge. "Men are odd creatures, Miss Julia. They have this strange inability to speak what they truly believe." When Julia's frown deepened, she added, "What I mean is that the duke has taken a fancy to you and is using the missing pocket watch as a means to call on you."

Julia's cheeks burned. "Those are very bold words to say aloud, Bridget."

"That doesn't make them any less true. Don't you see? He was afraid to speak his mind to you—that he finds you beautiful and wants to be near you. He's a duke, not a child, so why else would he act like a child over a silly missing watch? I say it's because he means to get close to you."

Julia considered her friend's words. "One would think that sending a card would be less complicated," she mused.

Bridget laughed. "You'd think so, but we're talking about a duke.

He's likely been spoiled since birth, but I believe that'll change because of you."

"How can I possibly change him?"

"It's as clear as day. Mrs. Rutley told him that you will benefit from practicing your hostess skill, when the truth is, it's he who needs lessons in maturity. If you can make a duke a better man, what else in life must one accomplish?"

Julia smiled. Bridget had always been a wise friend, and she was no less so now. This was not a punishment but rather an opportunity to prove her worth. "Yes, I'll tame the duke and bring him luck." She paused. "Though I'm unsure how to do the latter." She was still confused as to why Mrs. Rutley had chosen to tell lies about her father.

"Do you know what I think?" Bridget asked as she rose from the bed. "I think you'll find your own luck and share that with the duke." She stifled a yawn. "Is there anything else I can do for you, Miss Julia? If not, I think I'll retire for the night."

"No, I need nothing," Julia said, standing and giving Bridget a hug. "Thank you for your wise counsel, once again."

It was common knowledge that a lady's maid was simply another servant. Any hint of friendship between Julia and Bridget would have upset her mother and had her father shaking the pillars of heaven.

Yet too often, Julia found she could not go to her mother for advice. Did the woman care about her daughter? Julia knew she did. The problem was that her mother always seemed a word away from breaking into a sob, and Julia did not want to be responsible for causing such distress. Therefore, when Julia first had questions concerning the opposite sex, she had turned to Bridget rather than her mother for answers. And every other important question thereafter.

"We're friends," Bridget said with a shrug, although her cheeks turned a bright crimson as they always did whenever Julia complimented her. "And I'm honored to be the one you come to when you need advice." She laughed. "I doubt any other lady's maid can say her mistress sees her as a friend as well as a servant."

"Well, that is exactly how I see you," Julia said, kissing her friend's cheek. Bridget's flush spread to her ears.

Once Bridget was gone, Julia looked at the empty bed across the room. Emma had gone earlier to the room belonging to Diana and Ruth and had not yet returned. Although the school had a strict bedtime curfew during the week, Mrs. Rutley was much more lenient on the weekends. As long as the girls were quiet and did not disturb those attempting to sleep, they could visit one another whenever they chose. The only caveat to allowing them to stay up later, if they so choose, was that they were still required to rise at a decent hour in the morning.

Just as Julia was about to slip into bed, Emma entered the room, bubbling with excitement. "There is a man outside of Ruth's window," she whispered. "Come and see for yourself!"

Julia frowned. "A man? What man?"

"I have no idea who he is," Emma said, her slippered toes peeking out beneath her nightgown as she turned around to lead Julia back down the corridor. "But you really must come see!"

When they arrived at Ruth's room, three other girls had their faces pressed to the second window that overlooked the gardens. Ruth stood before the other, which was open.

"What is going on here?" Julia demanded as she went to stand beside Ruth.

Below them stood a young man, perhaps twenty years of age, wearing threadbare trousers and holding a cap in his hands. Julia thought him to be a stable hand or cobbler's assistant at best.

"If ye wan' me to catch ye, ye need to jump," he said.

The girls all tittered.

Undaunted, Ruth placed a hand to her breast and replied, "Prepare yourself, for I'll fall right into your arms. It's my dream to leap into the arms of a man and be carried away!"

The titters turn to downright laughter.

"That is enough, Ruth," Julia snapped. "Who is that man?"

Ruth grinned at her. "I don't know his name, but he is an apprentice to the butcher. When he arrived with a delivery for Mrs. Shepherd, I whispered in his ear that he should come visit me at night, so I could run away with him."

"Have you gone mad?" Julia exclaimed. "Don't forget that you are a trained young woman, but your actions are childish at best! Now, tell that man you will not be leaving and let us all go to bed." It was difficult to ignore the sorrow in Ruth's eyes, but this was for her own good. A butcher's apprentice? And one whose name she did not even know?

Ruth hung her head. "I'm sorry. I simply could not help myself. I was overcome with a fit of mischief."

Julia sighed. Ruth seemed to always suffer from fits of mischief these days. One day, her mischief would get herself, or someone else, hurt!

"Well?" the man shouted. "Are ye comin' or what?"

Ruth stuck her head through the window, but before she could respond, another voice rose from outside.

"I'll come and wallop you across the head with this pan, boy! Now, you'd best run for your life before I beat your head until you're silly!"

Emma's eyes nearly covered her face. "It's Mrs. Shepherd!"

Sure enough, the cook came hurrying out into the patch of light left by the candles from the window, a frying pan lifted above her head. Even Julia could not help but join the others in laughter as the man yelped in fright and ran toward the trees.

Their laughter was cut short, however, when Mrs. Shepherd turned to glare up at them. "I'm coming up there, next, so none of you'd better leave!"

"Oh, my! We are in for it now!" Diana said. "I do hope Mrs. Rutley does not send letters to our parents."

"My father will be irate," Emma whispered. "All of us are doomed."

When Mrs. Shepherd barged into the room still clutching the frying pan, the lamenting came to an abrupt stop. "Now, I'll hazard a guess that this was Ruth's idea?"

"Yes, Mrs. Shepherd," Ruth said as she took a meek step forward from the line of girls. "I came into mischief this morning and invited him to come."

Although her main position was cook, Mrs. Shepherd had also designated herself an unofficial protector of the girls who attended the school. More than once, Julia had heard whispers of a rumor that the woman once murdered a man who had attempted to kidnap one of the students, but that was likely a flight of fancy. Then again, the cook did have a fiery temper, so imagining her thwacking someone across the back of the head—either a man overstepping his place or a student misbehaving—was not a stretch.

"You must stop this mischief from taking hold of you, girl," Mrs. Shepherd snapped. "And the rest of you shouldn't encourage her. Remember, you're no longer the children you were when you arrived at this school. I'd suggest you all think on the shame you'd bring your parents if they knew, or even worse, what you're doing to your own reputations."

"Will you be informing Mrs. Rutley?" Emma asked, her voice squeaking.

The cook sighed. "I should, you know, but I won't. If I catch any of you doing something this... this featherheaded again, so help me, I'll kill you faster than I did that man years ago." She punctuated this with a firm nod before turning and leaving the room.

The girls stared after her, but Julia did not miss the twinkle in the woman's eyes. It had likely been she who started the rumor as a way to frighten the girls into doing as she said.

"I told you it was true," Ruth said. "See, she even admitted it!"

Diana sniffed. "I still don't believe it."

Soon all the girls were arguing over whether Mrs. Shepherd had indeed committed murder. Julia, however, yawned and headed back to her room. The last thing she wanted to do was remain awake until first light, arguing over a subject that likely was untrue. Even one as exciting as Mrs. Shepherd murdering someone.

Saturday mornings were typically reserved for traveling into the village for various needs, although on this Saturday, Julia chose to remain in her room. Bridget helped her don a yellow dress with intricate white flowers stitched into the bodice and along the bottom hem. A matching yellow ribbon had been added to her bonnet, and she had pulled on white gloves to finish the ensemble. All this to be ready to meet the duke.

A collection of butterflies flittered in her stomach as Julia considered the time she would be spending with that duke. Would he spend that time berating her for the pocket watch she supposedly stole and demand that she return an item she did not have? Or would he choose to engage in pleasantries, instead? She hoped for the latter but feared the former was more likely.

"You really shouldn't be so distraught," Bridget said as she dabbed a bit of perfume on Julia's neck. "I know ladies prefer a lighter complexion, but you appear sickly. Trust me, you have nothing to fear."

Julia sighed and stood. "It's just that I find this whole arrangement so odd, I'm struggling to understand what is supposed to come of it."

Bridget shook her head. "Maybe you're right," she said with a sigh, much to Julia's surprise. "I'll inform Mrs. Rutley that you'd rather have Mr. Horace Pernhope call on you again, instead."

"You would not dare!" Julia said with a gasp.

Mr. Pernhope, although a nice young man, had sent a letter the very day they met and every day thereafter, professing his love for her. It was not until Mrs. Rutley sent a letter to his father that the correspondence stopped. If she had not, the man likely would have used every scrap of parchment he could find by now!

"Oh, I'm only teasing," Bridget said with a laugh. "But you really must allow yourself to enjoy the outing. Remember, it's you who'll be training him, contrary to what Mrs. Rutley told him. And I'll be there with you, so there's no need to worry. I'll make sure everything goes well enough."

It had taken much insistence on Julia's part to convince her father that she did not need both a lady's maid and a chaperone; Bridget would do well enough in both positions. Plus, in a school filled with girls, she had any number of possible chaperones. The idea of having an old spinster following her around, as her father had wanted, made her skin prickle. Perhaps a bit of luck had come her way when her father had agreed.

She nearly laughed. It seemed even the idea of being around a man destined to madness had already had an effect on her. Luck, indeed! It had been her ability to present her side clearly and concisely that had gotten her what she wanted, not luck.

Julia prayed her friend was right as they made their way to the foyer. Mrs. Rutley was waiting for them just outside the parlor, her dress a lovely green muslin.

"His Grace is inside waiting," she said in lieu of a greeting.

"Already?" Julia gasped. "He is not due to arrive for another thirty minutes!"

"Be that as it may, he is here now." Mrs. Rutley looked her up and down and smiled. "You look beautiful. Now, I'll see that tea is sent up in a bit. His Grace refused my offer, but I suspect he may change his mind." Her eyes twinkled.

"Mrs. Rutley," Julia said, lowering her voice, "what do you plan to tell my parents concerning the duke and me?"

"At this time, nothing," the headmistress replied firmly. She placed a hand on Julia's arm. "You have no need to worry. If they happen to learn of this arrangement, I'll placate them. After all, you have a chaperone and are of age to have suitors." She glanced toward the door. "However, if we stand out here and continue prattling on, it will be His Grace with whom we will have to contend."

Julia gave her a small nod and entered the parlor, Bridget following behind her. The duke was peering out a window, his hands clasped behind his back. Just as the day before, his hair fell in waves around his shoulders rather than kept short as most gentlemen preferred these days.

"Don't stare," Bridget whispered. "It's rude."

Julia nodded and averted her eyes, turning to stare at the plush cream-colored couch and matching chairs. Several paintings hung from white walls, gold trim framing them. Purple drapes were held back by gold cords with purple tassels.

"It's also rude to whisper," the duke said. "Especially in the presence of a duke. Though, after your act of thievery, it should come as no surprise that you whisper with others rather than use common courtesy and greet a guest."

Indignation filled Julia. "I'm no thief," she said. "Stealing is an immoral act, and I assure you, I would never do anything that would harm you or anyone else in any way."

He walked over to stand before her, and Julia's heart began to thud against her chest. His harsh words sent a shiver of fear down her spine, but that was not why her heart pounded so terribly. There was something about this man that she could not place, but even as he glared down at her, she somehow felt safe in his presence. Just another item to add to the growing list of all that was strange about this situation.

"The truth will emerge soon enough," he said. "Now, let us sit and conjure some sort of topic to discuss, or our hour together will seem like two."

Julia took Bridget by the hand and led her to the couch, but the duke remained standing, staring at her as she sat.

"Not even a curtsy?" he said. "A thief and an untrained chit. Why does this not surprise me?"

An untrained chit? Julia thought. How dare he be so callous in his description of her! Yet her embarrassment was far stronger than her anger, for she had indeed forgotten her courtesies. "Forgive me, Your Grace," she muttered as she stood and dropped into a perfect curtsy. When she rose, the duke wore a strange grin.

"There is hope for you after all, Miss Wallace," he said with an air of surprise. Did he truly believe she did not know how to make a perfect curtsy?

Once she returned to her seat, he sat in one of the chairs across from her. "Mrs. Rutley informed me that the students here have studied the sciences and philosophy. I had heard that some of the girls' schools advertise they offer such instruction, but I must admit that I did not believe it."

Julia was uncertain if there was an underlining question, or if it was simply a statement that did not need a response, but she chose to address it, nonetheless. "Indeed, we have studied a variety of subjects. I particularly enjoy learning about history and philosophy. I find the sciences less appealing."

"My uncle says that educating a woman will cause the world to erupt in fire," the duke said.

Julia could not stop a tiny snort at the absurdity of that statement. Yet when the man frowned, she swallowed it back down.

"And what is your opinion on the matter?" Julia asked.

"I believe he is correct in his estimation. Women should learn how to run a household and deal with servants, how to devise a menu, and the best ways to decorate a home. Any other instruction is simply a waste of time."

Did all men share the same opinion? Her father had said very much the same, as did her uncle and other men she had known in her life. What the duke proposed was nothing new, which made the conversation quite boring. As he continued to speak, Julia found her mind wandering. Is this what she would be forced to endure in the coming months? Was it possible to die from boredom?

"Miss Julia," Bridget hissed, "His Grace asked you a question."

Julia started, and her eyes widened. "Forgive me, Your Grace. Would you ask your question again?"

The duke stared at her, a stoic expression on his face. Would he now refuse to speak? He was acting more a child than a grown man as time went on!

Finally, he sighed and said, "Since you are supposed to be this great student of philosophy, I propose a simple scenario. If you had a servant steal from you, would you see that he or she was brought before the magistrates and thus punished for the crime, or would you show compassion?" He leaned back in his chair, that mischievous grin she had seen before playing at his lips.

So, he chose to continue with the topic of his accusation, did he? Well, Julia refused to admit defeat. If it was a duel of the minds he desired, she would accept.

"And what is this item that the servant is accused of stealing?" she asked.

"Does it matter?" the duke asked.

"Of course it does."

"There are many items one might steal, but in this instance, let us say it's a pocket watch." A twinkle of mischief danced in his eyes.

Julia tapped her lips as if in thought. She was far more prepared to play this game than he realized! "And it's certain that the servant stole it?"

"Nothing in this life is certain, Miss Wallace, but for the sake of this example, then yes, it's certain."

Julia considered for a moment and then replied, "I would ask the servant why he stole the pocket watch. Was it for greed? Or did he wish to sell it to feed his family? Not all employers pay a fair wage, after all." She could not help but smile when the duke's grin fell.

"I pay more than a fair wage," he countered.

"Yet, you never mentioned that you were the employer, Your Grace," Julia said. "I devise my answers around the information I'm given, and I refuse to make assumptions or statements without proof. Although, it appears some do."

The gasp Bridget gave told Julia she had overstepped herself with that last statement, but he did not make simple conversation easy. "My apologies, Your Grace. I did not mean—"

The duke raised a hand, and Julia closed her mouth. "We shall say that the servant stole the watch out of simple greed," he said. "Is that not the reason all thieves steal? Now, based on the information you have, what is your response, Miss Wallace?"

Julia could only stare at the duke. Perhaps Bridget had been correct; this man desperately needed her help. She drew in a deep breath and slowly released it before responding.

"I would show compassion," she replied. "You see, I believe everyone is capable of learning and changing, and even a servant can learn that thievery is not the best way to travel through life. If a true change occurs, the lesson was learned, and no one needs to suffer."

The duke moved his hair behind an ear to reveal more of his handsome face. Julia considered having Bridget pour water over her as the man bit at his lip in thought. Oh, but he was handsome!

"So, you would show compassion to a man from such a low station? Why?"

"That is easy, Your Grace," she said, smiling. "Oftentimes, those with little deserve much. If we treat only our peers, meaning those with wealth or of our same station, with respect, what does that say about us?"

Chapter Four

Matthew had arrived at Mrs. Rutley's school with one simple purpose in mind—to get Miss Julia Wallace to confess to stealing his pocket watch. It did not take a Bow Street Runner to see that the manipulative woman had used her hands the day before to pickpocket him and relieve him of that which belonged to him. With careful words to challenge her on an intellectual level, he had devised the scenario as a means to bring the woman to a full confession.

Instead, he found her much more challenging, and more astute, than he had expected. Her final statement about showing mercy to those beneath his station had given him pause. He had been trained to see servants as nothing more than furniture that did his bidding, and the idea of using compassion with furniture seemed strange. Now, however, he had been forced to consider that these were human beings worthy of mercy.

Of course, he would never admit this to Miss Wallace outright, for her pride would swell to the point she would be unmanageable.

Even as he thought this, he could not help but soak in her finely sculpted features. With hair as bright as the morning sun and the faintest of pink in her cheeks, he found her more beautiful today than she was yesterday. Then, he caught a hint of the fragrance of fresh flowers that sent his head spinning.

He pushed aside the desire that rose in him. He was not here to indulge in the woman's beauty. What he wanted—no what he needed —was a confession from her. And the return of his watch.

Yet, a strand of doubt crept into his mind. Had she indeed stolen the watch? What if he had in fact lost it in the carriage as Mrs. Rutley suggested? If so, perhaps his driver had taken it, although Matthew had asked the man, and he had proclaimed his innocence. What Miss Wallace did not know was that he had already shown compassion, for he chose not to dismiss the driver, despite his suspicions the man could have been the culprit. Even without proof, Matthew had every right to dismiss a man he did not trust.

"If I've offended you, Your Grace," Miss Wallace said, breaking him from his thoughts, "I apologize. It was not my intention."

It was not the apology he was searching for, but it was a beginning. "I'm curious about this luck Mrs. Rutley says you possess. Were you aware of this rare ability before your father recognized it?"

She shook her head but said nothing.

"I'm surprised that he allowed you to observe as he played his games of chance. Few men would allow any woman near a gaming table, let alone his daughter. But if he believes you bring him good luck, I can see the wisdom in such a decision.

"Perhaps I should also take advantage of this luck you supposedly carry now that what does bring me luck is gone. In less than two weeks, I'll be hosting a party, and I must have luck on my side. You see, a man will be in attendance, a man I don't particularly like, and I must be able to convince him to invest in a business venture."

"And this pocket watch, did it bring you luck in matters of business?"

"Of course it did," Matthew replied. Did women not understand the value of charms that bring luck? "Some men keep a particular coin in their pocket, but I've found the watch to be as equally blessed. It has been in my family for several generations and is more valuable than the gold from which it's made. My great-grandfather was carrying it with him when a carriage nearly ran him down. He was convinced that without it he would have been crushed to death. My father had a similar experience. He was on a ship bound for Spain when a storm struck. If it had not been for that pocket watch, the ship may have been thrown against a wall of rocks along the coast. My luck has not included saving my life, thank heavens, but I've carried that watch with me to every business meeting I've attended. Nearly every time, I've gotten exactly what I wanted. Now, I'll need you to attend my party to give me the luck that was taken from me, so this man and I may come to an agreement."

The door opened and Mrs. Rutley entered, carrying a silver tray. After setting it on the table, she poured them each a cup of tea and left the room without speaking a single word. When she was gone, the room became eerily quiet.

Matthew shifted in his seat. He did not like silence. "I trust you have attended parties in the past?"

"I have, Your Grace," Miss Wallace said. Had she snickered? No, of course not. Surely, she had more training than that! "I promise that I'll conduct myself perfectly. You have no need for concern."

He frowned. "I'm not concerned for your conduct but rather the luck you can bring."

It was not until red blossomed on her cheeks that he realized he had spoken the words aloud. Cursing himself inwardly, he took a sip of his tea to give him a moment to think. What else would the girl need to know? He had scheduled a number of outings with Mrs. Rutley earlier, which would allow him the opportunity to ask his questions.

"There will be in attendance one Lord Talbot. I find him a bit annoying, but he's necessary if I'm to be successful in purchasing the hotel in Brighton I want. Your duty will be simple—don't speak unless spoken to and remain close." He reached for his cup, and a new thought came to mind. "There will also be other distinguished guests in attendance, including my uncle. His expectations are high, so do make certain that you remain as 'perfect' as you have claimed you are capable of being."

"Yes, Your Grace," Miss Wallace replied. "I understand."

Matthew went to speak but caught the corners of her lips rising. It was a lovely smile, one that made her eyes sparkle, and he found himself admiring them. But had she not used that same tactic before to steal from him? The thought made him look away. He really would need to be on his guard. If he was not careful, he might lose everything he owned!

When his thoughts returned to the party, he said, "I presume you understand that we will be at the party as acquaintances and nothing more. If anyone makes inquiry as to how you managed to become one of my guests, simply state that I've extended my charity to your school by allowing you to attend."

"Of course, Your Grace," Miss Wallace replied. "I certainly had not planned to tell anyone the truth."

He stared at her for a moment. Was that sarcasm or was she simply stating a fact? Most women were far less cryptic. Why was it so difficult to read the meaning behind this woman's words?

"Nonetheless, women are prone to flights of fancy and tend to see romance blossoming where there is none. I simply don't want you believing that this arrangement will go beyond friendship—if it even goes that far. All I wish is to utilize your luck and then receive the land that is promised me."

Miss Wallace nodded, but a flash of sadness appeared in her eyes. For some unknown reason, this caused a twinge of guilt in Matthew. "What I mean to say, is that many women would see such an invitation as something more than it truly is."

"I'm not many women," Miss Wallace said. "In fact, I find that I'm quite different from most. Although your invitation is... solicitous, you can rest assured that I see it as nothing more than a means to an end."

Matthew could not stop himself from snorting. "I know how women can be, Miss Wallace. They do what they can to distract most men to weaken them, all so they can trap them into agreeing to a marriage they don't want."

"Then you truly have nothing to fear, Your Grace, for you are unlike most men, or so I assume." A tiny smile played on her lips as she said this.

Matthew found her boldness both alluring and shocking, but how should he respond? If he argued, he placed himself in league with the common man. Yet, an agreement would only encourage her to use her mind, which was outright dangerous.

Rather than forcing a decision, he stood and buttoned his coat. "I have pressing matters I must attend to," he said, though the truth was that he was not as prepared for an intellectual battle today as he had believed. After all, without his watch, he would lack the luck he needed to prevail. "I spoke with Mrs. Rutley and arranged to call tomorrow at one. We shall be gone for two hours, so please be prepared."

Miss Wallace dropped into a deep curtsy, and her eyes gleamed as she said, "Yes, Your Grace. I look forward to receiving more instruction from you."

Was she mocking him? He searched her face for any evidence of mockery but could find none. What he did see was such beauty, he should have been blinded.

You fool! he berated himself. *She is using the same charms to fool you as she did yesterday. Don't fall for them again or you may likely lose something more than your watch!*

"Good day to you," he said with the slightest nod of his head before hurrying out of the room.

Mrs. Rutley stood beside the door, dipping into a curtsy as he approached. "If I may be so bold to ask, how have you and Miss Wallace gotten along, Your Grace?"

The truth was that, if he thought about it, it was one of her students who had taught him, but what man in his right mind made such an admittance? "She is stubborn, Mrs. Rutley, and believes herself to be more intelligent than she is. But I'm a duke, and she'll soon realize her place."

The headmistress smiled. "I have no doubt that you will succeed, Your Grace," she said as she opened the door for him. Although she smiled again, this time there was something behind it, something he could not identify.

The door closed behind him, and he let out a heavy sigh. "Not only am I losing my mind," he whispered, "but this house is full of women who are madder than I am. The headmistress, the pupils... are they all insane?"

A sudden shout made him turn to see an aproned woman barreling from the side of the house, a large frying pan raised above her head as she chased after a young boy.

"If you come into my kitchen and try to steal another pie from me, Reginald Burns," the woman shouted, "I'll beat some sense into you!"

Indeed, it seemed that madness was everywhere.

As Matthew stepped through the front door of Hardwick Hall, Hickson attempted to whisper at him.

"My hearing is just fine, Hickson," he snapped. "Speak clearly, man."

"Your uncle is upset, Your Grace," the butler said, his voice trembling. "He asked me where you had gone and was clearly unhappy with my response."

Footsteps echoing down the corridor made Matthew turn to find his uncle approaching. Dressed once again in all black, Matthew suspected the man owned no clothing of any other color.

"Tell me you did not return to that school!" Uncle Ezra bellowed. When Matthew did not respond immediately, he added a sharp, "Matthew?"

"I did," Matthew replied, removing his overcoat and hat, then handing them to Hickson. "I made a pact with Mrs. Rutley. We shall receive a parcel of the land on which the school sits." He paused. Why had he said "we"? Was he not the duke and the rightful owner of this estate?

The thought disappeared when his uncle shot the butler a glare. "Do you plan to give your opinion on this matter?" he demanded.

Hickson's eyes widened. "No, my lord."

"Then leave us, you nosy old fool!"

"Must you speak to him so harshly, Uncle?" Matthew sighed. "He has been employed in this house longer than I've been alive. Does he not deserve even the tiniest amount of compassion?"

His uncle snorted, and for a moment, Matthew wondered if the man would slap him. "I refuse to respond to such foolish words. Now, let us have a drink while you explain about this agreement you have made with *that woman*."

They went to the parlor, and Matthew went to the sideboard. "The land is important," he said as he poured them each a brandy. "Father wanted it, as do I." He went to hand his uncle one of the glasses but paused at the narrowed eyes trained on him. Anger bubbled, and he matched the glare. He *would* finish the purchase his father started, and no one, not even his uncle, would stop him!

"There is more important business to concern you, and none includes dealing with women." He snatched the glass from Matthew's hand, sending the brandy sloshing over the rim. His uncle did not seem to notice. "That land is worthless, and you waste your time attempting to gain even a blade of grass that grows upon it."

"Father did not think so."

"Your father also thought the house was built upon a cache of hidden treasure," his uncle snapped. Then he gave Matthew a sideways glance. "I pray you are not having the same delusions."

"Of course I'm not," Matthew replied, his face hot with shame. "It's a simple trade, and in three months, I'll add to the land upon which this house sits."

His uncle sighed and walked over to the unlit fireplace. "I suppose you may as well explain the sort of bargain you made with that woman. As if I don't have enough to handle watching over you."

The last was mumbled, but Matthew heard the words, nonetheless. "You forget yourself, Uncle."

His uncle's eyebrows rose in surprise. "That came out much harsher than I intended. I'm afraid my days have been quite frustrating as of late."

Matthew frowned. "What is it about Mrs. Rutley that you find so disagreeable, Uncle?"

"She is a female," his uncle replied. "Need I say more? Now, what is this bargain you made, which I've asked you about three times now?"

"One of her students, a Miss Julia Wallace... Mrs. Rutley and I've come to an agreement. I provide an opportunity for Miss Wallace to polish the skills she's learned as hostess at one of my dinners. This will add credence to her school's reputation. In exchange, I'll purchase the land I want."

His uncle downed the entire measure of brandy in one gulp. "Is this the same woman you mentioned yesterday?"

Matthew nodded.

"I assume she will be a guest at your party?" Before Matthew could respond, his uncle sighed. "And why would she not be? You are merely a duke and every eligible lady will be in attendance. Perhaps you should invite Mrs. Rutley, as well, so she may teach you to do embroidery. Or will poetry become your newfound pastime?" A scowl erupted on his face as he raised the empty glass above his head and hurled it into the fireplace before rounding on Matthew. "You are a fool for chasing after this woman. Do you want to ruin our family's name further? Had your father not done enough?"

Tired—and he had to admit a bit confused after his encounter with Miss Wallace—Matthew stood and glared at the man he had always looked up to. "What I seek to gain from Miss Wallace is my business and none of yours. I may be a fool, but I see her as a means to get something I want. If you think I'll suddenly become soft and begin reciting love poems, then you don't know me at all!"

"I've underestimated you, nephew," his uncle said, chuckling. "It seems you do have a backbone after all. Perhaps you may finally become the duke you need to be."

"I'm much stronger than you give me credit for," Matthew said, although he did not feel as such. He felt alone and... what? Indecisive? Yes, that was the best word to describe his current feelings. Well, he would never admit that aloud, especially to his uncle. The man thought little of him as it was.

"Then come with me to the office," his uncle said as he moved past Matthew.

Curious, Matthew followed him to the next room where a massive oak desk sat in front of a large window.

"Your signature is required," Uncle Ezra said as he handed Matthew a piece of parchment.

Matthew perused the document. "Lady Dyer seeks to gain an audience?"

His uncle placed a quill in Matthew's hand. "You must decide what is important. Do we extend charity that gives aid to this suspected unscrupulous woman, or do we allow her to fall into the dregs of society? The choice is yours, but I believe if we were to answer her call, we could benefit from her current situation."

"And what is her current situation?"

"She is a widow without an heir to control her husband's estate, who has been shunned by the *ton*. Should we not show some semblance of mercy toward her?"

Matthew frowned. "Mercy? To a widow? Uncle, I admit that I'm confused. You preach that we should care nothing for the troubles of others. That my priority is to our own affairs, and all else is unworthy of even the slightest acknowledgement?" He reached into his pocket to grasp his pocket watch before remembering that it was gone; a fact he had purposefully not told his uncle.

"I had thought that a woman suffering would be the exception," Uncle Ezra replied. "Have you not often told me that watching your mother suffer bothered you?" He heaved a heavy sigh. "Very well, I'll write and inform Lady Dyer that her concern is not ours."

Matthew held up a hand as his uncle reached for the letter. "Wait," he said with a glance at the man who had been there for him since his father had first taken ill. He and his uncle may not always agree, but he did not want to see a woman hurt—widowed or not.

An image of his mother weeping on the portico came to mind, making his stomach clench. Perhaps something good would come out of a meeting with Lady Dyer, although he was unsure what.

Not bothering to read over the response his uncle had written, Matthew leaned over and signed his name before returning the pen to its holder.

"Good," his uncle said, clapping him on the back. "Now, enjoy your day. I've other business I must see to."

Matthew gritted his teeth. "I find myself increasingly needing to remind you that I'm not a servant and you are not the duke. It would serve you well to remember that."

His uncle laughed. "You're being far too sensitive, Matthew. It appears to me that it's you who has forgotten our roles as of late. Am I not the instructor and you the student?" Matthew went to speak, but his uncle continued, "I have no desire to usurp you. Instead, I hope to guide and mentor you in the absence of my brother. But if you no longer require my assistance, then simply say so. I'll happily return home first thing tomorrow morning." He offered a sympathetic smile. "But remember, I'll always be here to serve you and our family name. No matter what you think of me."

Oh, how the man could heave guilt on him like a heavy blanket! Matthew could not deny that his uncle had been a key part of his upbringing, but the man also could be quite overbearing at times. Perhaps Matthew had taken his anger a bit too far. One thing was certain, he could not allow their disagreement to lead them to a falling away.

"You are right, Uncle. You are only looking out for me, and it is appreciated."

When Matthew reached the foyer, he stopped and closed his eyes, listening to his surroundings. All was quiet except the occasional shuffling of feet of a servant moving down one of the corridors. He sighed and walked into the drawing room. Great paintings depicting famous wars hung from the walls, and exquisite vases sat on highly polished tables. He was surrounded by items of great value, yet rather than give him a sense of achievement, a sense of being, they seemed to mock him.

His breathing quickened, and he ran to the door of the library. There, too, was an expanse of wealth, just as there was in the great ballroom and the sitting room. All the luxury, all the comforts seemed to taunt him, for he had no one with whom he could enjoy them. And as the walls of the corridor drew in closer, Matthew fought to drag air into his lungs as a sudden realization came to him.

For the first time in his life, he understood how truly alone he was.

Chapter Five

The gardens of Courtly Manor could rival many of the greater estates in the area with its flowerbeds and cobbled paths. The back corner ended at a copse of trees, and Mrs. Rutley had insisted on having several benches placed in various spots to allow the pupils a quiet place for contemplation. She understood how trying living with a number of other girls could be, or so she said.

Julia strolled down a particular path that led to a fence at the back of the official gardens. Her thoughts were on the duke, who had left two hours earlier. For such a handsome man, he was rather odd. Who would cling to the idea that everyday trinkets held some sort of magical powers to give a person luck? And to think that a duke believed such rubbish perplexed her further.

When they had spoken of the imaginary servant—she was not daft enough to believe he was speaking in hypotheticals but rather about her—the duke had smiled during the discussion. He needed to smile more often, for doing so only increased his handsomeness.

She could not help but laugh, for she was certain she had outwitted him. His eyes had expressed his surprise at this, as had his frown. Few men could endure a woman's true intellect, but he seemed especially incapable of suffering it. That lack of acceptance likely stemmed from having an uncle who saw women as nothing more than a means to gain an heir. Now, that was one man she did not look forward to meeting.

At the back of the gardens, she stopped at the low wooden fence that marked the boundary for the pupils at the school. Mrs. Rutley had been adamant that none of the girls were to go beyond that fence without her explicit permission. And with an appropriate chaperone. That, of course, did not stop Ruth from sneaking away at least three times in the past year, much to Julia's chagrin. It was not that she, Julia, was responsible for the younger girl, but as the eldest of their group, she acted the role for all the girls' sake.

She looked out over the wide expanse of field. Just beyond the horizon lay the great house belonging to the duke. Was he there at this very moment? Perhaps he was entertaining a female guest. She doubted rather highly that he was, for he clearly had no interest in romantic entanglements. No, he was more likely entertaining a gentleman offering a potential for investment or other form of business arrangement. What was it about men and their incessant need to do business? Was finding ways to gain more riches all men found important in life?

This made Julia sigh. Were all men like her father, who believed that women were nothing more than a means to grow men's coffers? Or to give their husband an heir to carry on the family name?

Yet the duke had seemed different, somehow. The fact he made an attempt to have a philosophical discussion with her said as much. Oh, he certainly believed in growing his coffers, or he would not have been so certain luck could help him. And he had also tried to trick her into confessing to a crime she did not commit, which had failed to deliver the results he likely had expected. Even so, she found herself wanting to learn more about him, to see if her suspicions were true.

"Julia."

She turned to see Mrs. Rutley approaching.

"Forgive me for not speaking to you sooner," the headmistress said as she joined Julia at the fence. "How went your time with the duke?"

Julia gripped the top rung of the fence. "It was baffling. He proposed a scenario in which a servant stole from him—a pocket watch, of course—and asked me about the appropriate punishment for such a wrongdoing."

"And how did you respond?"

"I told him that the person who had been wronged should question the servant as to why he or she stole the watch. From there, depending on the response, he should show compassion. I'm unsure if it was the answer he expected, but it was my honest response."

"That was a wise answer," Mrs. Rutley said. "I believe that by the end of this arrangement, the duke will be a better man because of you."

Julia flushed. "I hardly think a woman can truly change a man, Mrs. Rutley, for few want to change."

"Well, I believe she can." Mrs. Rutley turned to face her. "Julia, I see how the girls look to you for guidance and follow your instruction. His Grace will be no different. After all, he does lack proper counsel." She lowered her voice, a tiny smile playing on her lips. "But if you repeat that, I'll deny saying it with my dying breath."

Julia laughed, yet she was also confused. Her mother, as well as the tutors at the school, had insisted that women should always hearken to men. What Mrs. Rutley implied was that she should see that the duke listened to her.

Then there was the issue of being used as a form of payment. "Mrs. Rutley, why did you use me as a bartering tool in the sale of your land? I know you did not do it with ill intentions, but I feel as though I'm merely a bargaining chip. Or a mule."

"Do you truly feel that way?" Mrs. Rutley asked in that sympathetic tone she used when she wanted her pupils to put great consideration into a response. "Or is your curiosity getting the best of you?"

Julia sighed. This woman knew her far too well. "I suppose it's more my curiosity."

"Then I say remain curious but do so with caution. Take my instruction now just as you do with any other lesson I've taught you. There is no need to question it, not for the time being."

For so long, the headmistress had been more a mother to Julia than her own mother, and she trusted her explicitly. "Yes, Mrs. Rutley," Julia replied, embracing the woman. "I'll not ask again."

"See that you don't," Mrs. Rutley said, though her voice had a hint of teasing in it. "Now, I'll leave you to your thoughts."

When Mrs. Rutley was gone, Julia returned her attention to the field that separated her from the duke's home. She did trust Mrs. Rutley. The woman never did anything to hurt one of her students. In fact, she did all she could to help them in every way possible.

How strange, Julia thought. She looked forward to seeing the duke again. Then her thoughts turned to his party. How many would be in attendance? Would there be music and dancing? Of course, there would be. What gathering without dancing would be considered a party?

Sighing, she imagined the duke asking for a dance. He would take her hand, lead her to the line, and smile down at her as if she were the only important person in the room. They would perform the steps so well that the other guests would watch with admiration.

"What are you doing?" Emma asked, startling Julia from her thoughts. "You are thinking of the duke, are you not?"

Ignoring the teasing tone in her friend's voice, Julia dropped her hands to her side. She had raised one in the air as if acting out her thoughts. "Of course not," she replied, but her cheeks were so heated that she had to be as red as the nearby roses. "I was... that is... oh, drat! I cannot lie. I was thinking of him."

Emma giggled. "You are not in love with the man already, are you?"

"Love?" Julia said. "Don't be silly. I hardly know him. Every couple must take certain steps to reach such a conclusion, and we are only at the first." Realizing what she had just said, she quickly attempted to change the subject. "How was your excursion into town?"

"It went well enough," Emma replied with a shrug. "I purchased a new pair of gloves. Oh, and Mother wrote to say that she has a surprise for me, but she refused to say what it is. She is coming to visit next month and will reveal it then."

What sort of surprise could her parents possibly have for Emma? Her parents visited twice a year for all of two hours, and the entire time was spent berating their daughter. To them, her curtsies were never good enough. Her posture was always too slack, her voice, too loud or too low. In fact, Julia had never heard Emma mention a single instance when her parents were happy with her. They did not see a young woman with feelings. Instead, like many parents of the lower class, she was a path to higher society.

Julia frowned. She could not bring to mind a single student at the school whose parents encouraged her. Every parent who bothered to take the time to visit said nearly the same thing. Their daughter needed further improvement to be ready to receive possible suitors during the coming Season. None seem to notice the advances she had made. All they expected was perfection in exchange for the tuition they paid.

Many of the girls looked upon the London Season with great anticipation, but Julia was not one of them. Her father, much like Emma's parents, was in a rush to see her married and be free of her. And sadly, like most women, she had no say in who her husband would be.

"How wonderful for you," Julia said, returning her thoughts to Emma. "Perhaps they have purchased you a new dress or some other gift?" Highly unlikely, that, but she would not have her friend spend the next month worrying.

"I hope so," Emma replied. "If it's an offer of a new dress, I hope they allow me to visit one of the dressmakers in London. Madame Badeaux is not so terrible, but she will never be as good as those in London."

Julia giggled. Madame Badeaux was the village's only dressmaker, and although she was competent, what Emma said was true. And despite her French surname, Julia had always believed her accent was contrived. That was an unfair assessment, as Julia had never been able to master French, but she could not help but be suspicious of the woman.

"Do you think our parents love one another?" Emma asked. "My father seems to have only harsh words for my mother."

"In their way, I suppose they do," Julia said, sighing. "But it's nothing like the romantic stories I've read." She put her arm through Emma's and began the trek back to the house. "In those stories, they fall madly in love and live a wonderful and perfect life."

"That is what I want," Emma said in a dreamy voice. "I hope the man they choose for me feels the same. If not, I'll have a miserable life, indeed."

Julia could only nod, for she shared the same fear—to be married off to a man who would scoff at the notion of love. And for some reason she could not explain, she wondered what the duke thought of that notion.

On Tuesday afternoon, the duke had called again. Under the watchful eye of Mrs. Rutley, Julia had poured the tea and offered various topics of conversation as she awaited the approval of her guest. Yet, with each topic she suggested, he responded with simple answers that lacked any interest. She had to admit that she was finding their time together equally drab, but what more could she do?

Then, an idea occurred to her. Had his silence been a test in the hope she would break decorum and verbalize her frustration with him? Or could it be he thought himself so great and her so low that she deserved no recognition for her abilities?

Regardless, if the duke did not put forth the effort to converse, she could do nothing more to improve the situation. In truth, if he was unhappy with her, perhaps it would provide a way out of his service. That thought brought Julia a small sense of relief.

That is until Mrs. Rutley made a suggestion that had Julia's eyes widen in shock. Now she found herself sitting in a carriage beside Bridget, with the duke across from them, as they made their way to a picnic.

The duke looked out the window, giving Julia a moment to admire his striking profile. Rather than lying around his shoulders as it had been in the past, his hair was now pulled back and tied with a ribbon at the nape of his neck, allowing her to fully see a jawline that could rival that of any ancient statue.

Her breath returned to normal, however, when her eyes fell to his hand. Was that a spoon he held? Why would he be rubbing a thumb over a spoon of all things?

"Do you have something you wish to say, Miss Wallace?" the duke snapped. Julia shook her head. "Then why are you staring at me?"

Julia glanced at his hand again. "Are you... are you holding a spoon?"

The duke gave a single nod. "I tasked my butler to find me an object that would bring me luck, one that would replace my stolen watch until it's returned to me." He leaned forward. "Who knows? Perhaps when I search my carriage later this afternoon, it will suddenly appear, as if it were returned to me."

Julia had to bite her lip to keep back a retort. How dare he accuse her again of taking his watch. And here she had been admiring his jawline! Perhaps his madness was contagious, for what other explanation could there be as to why her thoughts had taken on the sudden flight of fancy about this man?

All became silent between them. This arrangement was nothing but a dreadful mistake. Maybe simply confessing to the crime would allow her to retain what little sanity she possessed. The only problem was, she did not have the watch to return to him.

"I noticed several students wandering the grounds upon my arrival." The suddenness of his voice made her start. "Do you actually study, or is all your time spent in leisure?"

Julia frowned. Was he insinuating that they were a lazy lot? "We study most of the day, but we are also encouraged to take time out of doors when the weather allows for exercise and fresh air. Being forced to remain indoors for long periods of time is unhealthy, at least according to the headmistress. Did you not think my previous display of skills spoke to the training we receive?"

"I must admit that you exceeded my expectations, Miss Wallace," he replied. "The question is, can you do it again?"

Julia's cheeks burned as the carriage slowed and then came to a stop. She was right in her estimation! He had been testing her!

The door opened, and a footman set the step on the ground.

The duke alighted from the vehicle and then offered a hand to Julia. She took it, albeit reluctantly, and allowed him to help her alight. What she preferred to do was tell the driver to turn the carriage around and return to the school.

"I'll see to this," he said, taking the basket from the surprised footman. He then offered the arm that had no blanket draped over it to Julia. "Miss Wallace."

They walked down a short path, Bridget following behind, that opened up to a lovely spot that looked out over a great expanse of land.

"Is this all yours?" Julia asked in awe.

"It is," he replied as he stopped at the top of the low hill. "There is a small river up ahead," he said. "A brook or stream would be a better description, I suppose. I often go there when I need to escape."

From what a duke could possibly escape Julia was uncertain, but she kept the question to herself. Her only duty was to appease the man so Mrs. Rutley and he could complete their transaction. And to teach him to be a better man.

Indeed, just over the embankment flowed a stream four feet across. It did not appear deep, although the center was deep enough that she was unable to see the bed beneath. The banks, however, were shallow and provided the pleasant trickling sounds one would expect from water flowing over rocks.

"It's lovely," she whispered as she glanced around them. Then she stumbled, and with a shriek, she pitched forward. If not for the duke reaching for her, she would have tumbled down the hill and likely landed in the water below. Whether from embarrassment or the strong hands that held her, she was unsure, but her head felt full of cotton wool.

"Are you hurt?" he asked as he looked her over. "Your ankle? You have not sprained it, have you?"

She could not help but smile at his concern, but this only made his frown deepen. Then she realized she was gawking at him like some sort of hussy! Squaring her shoulders, she replied, "I'm well, Your Grace, thank you."

He gave her a nod, placed the basket on the ground beneath the shade of a tree, and flicked out the blanket. Bridget winked at Julia, and Julia returned it with a small, yet uncertain smile.

"Here we are," the duke said once the blanket was in place. "Allow me." He offered his hand, and she took it. That had been a mistake, for not only was her head filled with cotton wool, but his touch also made her legs want to buckle beneath her. This would not do. How would she manage any bit of good if she was unable to think or stand?

To make matters worse, once she was seated, he did not immediately release her gloved hand. For the span of a heartbeat that felt as long as a day, they stared into one another's eyes. She was jolted back to reality when he released her, and Julia had the strange sensation of missing his firm grip.

The duke looked into the basket, and a small smile played on his lips. "It appears that Mrs. Rutley saw fit to include a bottle of wine in our basket," he said. "I find her selection good, for it will pair nicely with the scenery." He produced the bottle and two glasses. "My apologies, Miss Lowry. It seems Mrs. Rutley did not include a third glass."

Bridget's cheeks turned pink. "I'm here only as a chaperone, Your Grace. I don't need any wine but thank you."

He pulled at the cork, but it did not move. Chuckling, he said, "I must admit that whenever I attempt to remove the cork in one of these blasted bottles, it breaks. I suppose I should have allowed that footman see to it after all. He likely has much more experience than I."

He seems nervous, Julia wondered with surprise. Not wanting to see him suffer, she said, "I'm sure you will have no trouble this time, Your Grace. Besides, I'm here to bring you luck, am I not?"

He grinned at her. "That is true," he said. "What a wonderful opportunity to see if you do indeed possess luck. Maybe you will prove more worthy than my spoon."

Julia was uncertain if that was meant as a compliment or an insult.

When the cork came out without so much as a crack, his smile widened. "Well, it appears you do bring me luck!"

As he poured the wine, Julia found herself curious as to his fascination with charms and their abilities to bring good luck. "If I may ask," she said, choosing her words carefully, "when did you begin believing in luck?"

For a moment, she thought he would not respond, but he handed her the wine glass and said, "My father believed in it. He thought it to be the single most important factor in one's life. Whether it was business or in everyday occurrences, he believed that luck played a part in it. It's what separates successful men from those who encounter failure." He cast his gaze down and added in a soft voice, "And I fear being the latter." His cheeks went crimson. Apparently, he had not meant to speak that aloud.

"Well, I for one don't think you are a failure," she said, hoping to encourage him. She had no idea if he was or not, but it seemed the right thing to say.

"You say that because I'm a duke."

"I say it because the cork did not break," she said, smiling.

He laughed, but unlike the few times he had laughed in the past, this had a pureness to it that created dimples in his cheeks that had not been there otherwise. "You are as witty as you are intelligent, Miss Wallace. Tell me, what other surprises do you hide?"

Julia glanced down at her wine glass. She had barely sipped any, yet her body felt flushed. Then again, she did not drink wine often, so perhaps this was the effect it had. "I often think of myself as adventurous," she said. "Within reason, of course."

"Within reason?" he asked. "How so?"

Her mind scrambled to find a story that would not bring her embarrassment, but then she smiled and replied, "Such as agreeing to a picnic with a duke who believes I stole his pocket watch."

With another laugh, the duke leaned back on his elbows and looked up at the sky. "I'm beginning to believe that you may not have stolen it," he said.

She stared at him in disbelief. What had brought on this sudden change? What she had to determine was whether his statement was genuine or one of his tricks to fool her again.

"The problem is," he continued, "I have no idea where it went. My driver assures me he did not steal it, nor did he find it while cleaning the carriage. And he has no reason to lie." He shook his head and sat back up. "It does not matter, for you, Miss Wallace, are with me now."

Her heart pounded so hard that she was sure he could hear it. This was a different man from the one who shouted at her the last time he was at Courtly Manor, and she found she enjoyed this man's company far more than the other.

Yet, his next statement made her rethink this opinion.

"You will bring me luck until I'm able to find another trinket to replace the pocket watch."

She pursed her lips. So, he saw her as nothing more than a simple trinket, did he? She had not expected the man to profess his love for her, but to be compared to a spoon, or whatever object he deemed lucky, was humiliating! "This luck I'm to bring you," she said, doing all she could to keep her voice even, "how do you plan to use it?"

He sighed. "The party I'm hosting, the one you will attend, as I said before, concerns a business matter for which I'll need a great deal of luck. There will also be women there who will do all they can to catch my eye and fathers who will offer me the moon if I only accept their daughter's hand in marriage. Yet, I have no interest in marrying for convenience."

This admittance surprised her. He was not like other men, after all; he was like her! "Are you saying you wish to marry for love?" she asked. "How wonderful! That is what I hope, as well."

The duke frowned. "Love? Love is for fools. I simply have no desire to marry at all. Let us just say it would not serve my wife well to be married to the likes of me, and, I daresay, what would happen to our children." He waved a hand. "Let us change the conversation to other things."

Julia sat in stunned silence. Not only was she disappointed, she found his admission crushing. Yet, the latter made no sense. Why would she care that he did not believe in love? Then there was the mention of children. What did he mean by his words? And why did his saying so give her a sense of shame and make her feel vulnerable?

"Forgive me," she said, handing Bridget the glass. "I would like to stand beside the brook if I may."

He hurried to stand, but he made no offer to escort her. "I'll prepare the bread and cheese, then," he said instead.

Why did Mrs. Rutley feel the need to put me in this situation? Julia wondered as she approached the brook. How could a man dismiss any notion of love, consider it as nothing more than a foolish endeavor, yet still believe a pocket watch could change one's fate?

And why did her heart hurt so terribly learning this?

Chapter Six

Uncertainty warred inside Matthew. He leaned against a birch tree and watched Miss Wallace as she stared down into the brook. He clearly had offended her, which made him feel a complete fool, but the voice of his uncle kept him from going to her to apologize.

"You are a duke, and she is merely a woman!" the voice chastised. "A duke should never apologize to anyone."

Why had he allowed the fact that he no longer believed she stole his pocket watch to slip from his lips? Worse still, when had he come to that realization? No, that last he knew immediately; he had seen it in her eyes. He had seen the honesty in them, as well as her beauty, her intelligence, and that humor he so relished.

He sighed. His future held nothing but madness, which would only hurt the young woman. Glancing toward the lady's maid, he saw that she was absorbed in some sewing or needlework. Perhaps he could have a moment with Miss Wallace without the long ears of her chaperone. Not that he planned to be inappropriate, but rather as a means to say what needed to be said without an audience. It was bad enough he had to embarrass himself in front of Miss Wallace.

Sighing again, he walked down the short embankment and joined her beside the brook. Neither spoke as they watched the water trickling over the smooth stones in the brook's bed.

"If I caused an offense, Miss Wallace, I apologize. My intention was not to hurt you. I enjoy hearing you speak."

"I appreciate your apology, Your Grace," Miss Wallace said in a small voice, "but there is no need."

If there was no need as she said, why did guilt tug at his heart? He had spoken the truth about his views on marriage. Revealing his reasons why he felt as he did was going too far. He had already made himself look the half-wit as it was.

"You mentioned adventure," Miss Wallace said, breaking him from his thoughts. "What sort of adventures have you experienced as of late?"

Matthew considered the question as a sparrow flew past them. "Since my father died two years ago, I've done nothing but focus on my responsibilities. I do attend parties and other such gatherings, but more out of obligation than for enjoyment. Come to think of it, even before my father's death, it had been some time since I went on any adventures. And you? What sort of exploits have you participated in?"

She turned to look at him. "I attend my classes and on Saturdays go into the village. Some of the younger girls get themselves into mischief, but I typically choose not to do so." Her blush heightened her beauty. "But I must admit that I've joined them on occasion."

This made him smile. "I'll not ask you to reveal these mischievous acts for fear they may shock me." This made her laugh, a light, airy sound that made his skin pebble. "Truth be told, I've done nothing that can remotely be considered adventurous for a very long time." He frowned. "Come to think of it, my last memory of adventure happened when I was ten, and I leaped across this very brook."

Miss Wallace twisted her lips as if in thought. "It does appear quite challenging," she said. "And were you successful in your attempt? Or did you return home drenched to the skin?"

He laughed. "I made it across without a drop of water touching me. Of course, I thought it as wide as the River Thames at the time, but as I grew older, I realized that was not the case."

A light breeze caught the wisps of hair within her bonnet, and Matthew wondered if there was any woman more beautiful than she.

"What about friends, Your Grace? Do you have any you would consider close?"

"I have associates," he replied honestly, "though I suppose I would say they are more acquaintances. My uncle has me concentrating my time on my role as duke, but I imagine there will be time for making friends later, once my legacy is established. And you? I would guess you have many friends at the school."

"A few of us have grown quite close, close enough to feel that we are more sisters than friends."

"And back home?" he asked. "I assume you have many close acquaintances there waiting for your return."

She shook her head. "The day I return home I'll begin the arduous process of welcoming possible suitors, so my father may choose a husband for me. Whether he believes this is his right as a baron or as a father makes little difference. There will be no time for diversion. Those days will be behind me."

Matthew had not realized her father was a baron, nor had he considered that she came from nobility. Perhaps that was poor insight on his part, but how was he to know, given that few of the aristocracy sent away their daughters for training?

The image of another man calling on her and later asking for her hand did not sit well with Matthew, yet he could not have explained why if he were asked. "Perhaps you can delay it," he said, although he knew she could not. Few women in Miss Wallace's position were given the choice when it came to marriage. She would be told whom to marry and when, and he hoped whoever did was kind to her.

"I suppose if you were to marry me, I would no longer have to worry about suitors," she said with a laugh before whipping her head around to look at him, her eyes nearly covering her face. "Forgive me! I was only jesting. I did not mean—"

Matthew laughed. "I understand your point better than you know. My uncle urges me daily to marry soon so as not to bring shame upon the family. You see? That is why I need you near me, to bring me luck so the ladies he parades in front of me are kept at bay."

She raised her chin. "Are you saying I'm some sort of vicious dog who will scare away any prospects? Do you find me that repulsive?"

"Don't be silly," he said, laughing again. "You are quite beautiful—" He pursed his lips. Uncle Ezra was right! He would drive the dukedom into bankruptcy with the way he spoke without thinking.

Her blush deepened. "It appears we have a few things in common, Your Grace," she said. "We both are to be married at the behest of others. Your uncle sounds very much like my father in that he believes he knows what is best for my life." She sighed. "I suppose he does, but I would like the chance to decide for myself." She turned to him and grinned. "But we both are in need of some sort of thrilling adventure in our lives. It has been far too long. For either of us."

He raised an eyebrow. "And what sort of thrilling adventure do you propose we take?"

Miss Wallace motioned toward the brook. "I say we jump across the River Thames."

He waited for her to laugh or to say she was teasing, but neither came.

"We cannot do that," he said, confused. "I'm a duke, and you are a young lady. We are not children to frolic through the woods and leap over rivers."

"You are correct, there are many reasons we should not, but I believe it would be entertaining. Plus, who will know? I certainly will not tell anyone. Will you?"

Matthew glanced at the brook. If his uncle learned that he had been acting like a child, he would treat him like a child. He enjoyed the company of Miss Wallace, but this silliness had to come to an end, and it appeared it would be he who would have to end it.

"I say we return to our food and wine," he said.

She inched toward the bank of the brook. "I'm unsure if I can make it alone," she said in a tight voice as if he had not spoken. "I pray no harm comes to me if I fail." She placed a foot forward, and her arms began to flail at her side.

He took two steps forward. "I insist we return to our picnic," he said. "This immaturity is unbecoming, and if we are caught, our good names will be ruined."

"Then let us be quick about it," Miss Wallace said, catching hold of his arm with a tight grip. "Let us jump by the count of three. One... two... three!"

With no choice but to follow her, he jumped, and when his feet touched the opposite bank, a sense of excitement coursed through him.

"Now," she said, laughing, "was that so terrible? No one witnessed our acting like children. No one other than those of the *ton* watching us, that is."

Matthew glanced around them and then laughed. "Why did I look?" he asked. His sides were aching with his mirth. "You were right, it was fun. I had forgotten how much enjoyment this brook can bring."

"It's not the brook, Your Grace," Miss Wallace said. "It's simply facing our fears. Come on, now, let us do it again!"

Before he could even consider arguing, they were leaping again and then once more. His laughter died down as he looked at her flushed face. Her eyes glimmered with life, and her look of delight created a bond of sorts between them that he had not expected.

"I have no friends," he whispered. "But I would be honored to call you one. With your permission, of course."

Her smile was brighter than the sun as she replied, "The honor would be mine. Friends have much in common, and I believe we share much more than we realize."

"Then so be it," Matthew said. "I decree that we are now friends, and as such, I must insist that you call me Matthew, at least when we are alone." He glanced up at the place where Miss Bridget was seated. So focused was she on her sewing that she may as well have been staring at them. "Or relatively alone. And if you find it acceptable, I'll address you as Julia."

"I would like that." Her response was breathy and sent his heart racing. As he looked into eyes so like the ocean, he considered kissing her but stopped himself. They were merely friends, and friends did not share in kisses. Yet the temptation remained all the same.

Taking one final leap over the brook, they sat on the bank. And although he did not kiss her, he also did not release his hold on her hand.

Friendship. That was what Julia and Matthew had agreed to, though she felt—no, she wished—it was more. Not because he was handsome, or that he was a duke, it was far more than that. For the first time in her life, she had been herself in the company of a man, and her behavior had not been met with scorn. Not that she found herself in such a situation often in her young life, but enough that few would have agreed to enjoy a leap over a brook as a means of enjoyment.

She was uncertain what had compelled her to jump over the brook. It went against every bit of training she had received, yet that simple act had drawn her and Matthew closer. Plus, it left a very pleasant, warm feeling in her heart.

"Your cheeks are still red," Bridget said with a wink. "No doubt caused by the bright sun today. We certainly can't attribute it to the duke, now can we?"

Julia looked up at the portico. "I should prepare myself for the questions Mrs. Rutley is bound to ask," she said. "Do I mention that the duke and I spent the afternoon leaping over a brook?"

Bridget laid a hand on Julia's arm. "I think she'd enjoy hearing about it. How could she possibly become angry? Wasn't she the one who arranged it all?"

Julia glanced at the carriage that had been sitting in the drive upon their return to the school. "It appears she has a guest. Now would not be the best time to tell her."

They entered the house, and Julia was immediately set upon by three of her closest friends, all likely wanting to hear every detail about her outing.

"I'm so glad you are here," Emma said in a hurried whisper. "Your parents have arrived, and they don't appear happy."

"It's true," Theodosia said. "Your father has been shouting at Mrs. Rutley nearly ten minutes now."

Alarmed, Julia wondered why her parents would visit. And why was her father so upset?

Diana reached out and took hold of Julia's hand. "If he tries to beat you, scream, and I'll come to your aid."

"My father does not beat me," Julia assured her friend, though her stomach began to knot with worry. What she said was true; her father had never laid a hand on her, but his words hurt far worse than his hands ever could have. "I'll go see what the problem is."

She made her way down the corridor toward Mrs. Rutley's office. The girls had not lied, for her father's voice erupted from the room like flames from a fire, causing that familiar sense of fear to rise within her.

"I did not send my daughter to you to be paraded around by a man not of my choosing!" her father was saying. Or rather it was what he was shouting. He turned, purple-faced and breathless, to face Julia as she entered the room. "And you! How can you disappoint me once again, child? What must I do to see that you obey my wishes? Have you manipulated your headmistress as a means to rebel against me? If you were a son, I would banish you from my life for your actions!"

This was not the first time Julia had been called rebellious for simply making a decision without first gaining her father's permission. He had said this was one of the reasons—this supposed insurrection—for sending her to the school.

"My lord, if you would allow me to finish explaining the reason why I—" The headmistress's words were cut off as Julia's father held up a hand.

"I have had enough of women in my life explaining their actions," he barked. "Remain silent and I'll speak to you in a moment."

The fact Mrs. Rutley did not cower in the face of her father's ire as most did was a trait Julia admired in the headmistress. If only she could be half as strong!

Julia glanced at her mother who, as was typical, said nothing. She had been cowed for as long as Julia could remember, just as her father wished her to be. Then Julia looked at Mrs. Rutley who, to Julia's surprise, winked at her!

"Well, child?" her father said. "What have you to say for yourself?" He did not wait for her to respond but instead said, "You have embarrassed me for the last time. Go collect your things. It's about time I brought you home and took matters into my own hands." He then turned back to Mrs. Rutley. "And be assured I'll notify the other parents what you are doing at your school."

Leave? Julia thought. She did not want to leave the place where she felt more at home than anywhere else. Her friends were here, and so was Matthew. She paused. When had the thought of not seeing him again become so terrible?

"Father, I—" she began, but Mrs. Rutley spoke over her.

"Lord Wallace, if you will allow me to explain, I believe you will find my reasoning sound."

Her father snorted. "Sound, you say? Mrs. Rutley, your actions show me that you are far from sound." He paused for a moment, glaring at the headmistress. "Well, out with it, woman! What excuse could you possibly make that will make me change my mind?"

Julia said a silent prayer, hoping that Mrs. Rutley could find the words to appease her father. Knowing him, however, the task would be nearly impossible. She would be better off spending her final moments saying farewell to her friends.

"His Grace came to me with a most important request," Mrs. Rutley said. "When a man of his immense wealth calls, especially a duke, I must listen."

"You are willing to listen to the rants of a madman, you mean," her father snapped. "Duke or not, it's quite obvious he is not in his right mind."

"He is rich, my lord," Mrs. Rutley replied. "And his lack of knowledge in the wool trade may be the very opportunity in which someone with your expertise may be able to help. While also filling your own coffers, of course."

His scowl faltered, and he stroked his chin. "Perhaps you make a good point. The man is wealthy, and I do have a firm understanding in that arena, which he may find beneficial. Go on."

"He is hosting a party and is in need of a companion. His cousin, a wonderful woman who is experienced in such gatherings, has sadly fallen ill and is unable to attend. He came to me to help find someone willing to take her place."

Julia could only stare at the headmistress. Had she always been able to lie with such ease?

"Is that so?" Julia's father asked.. "Are you saying that he wanted a girl to parade at his party and you offered my daughter?"

"Not at all," Mrs. Rutley replied. "He requested a young lady, not a girl. One who was not spoken for, and with not only an impeccable reputation but also comes from a family with good standing. One who would be the envy of his peers."

The corners of her father's lips twitched. "Is that so?" he asked, thoughtful. "A family of good standing, you say? A woman who would be the envy of his peers?"

"Indeed," Mrs. Rutley said. "Julia was the first to come to mind. After all, few have your standing, my lord, even when measured against those of higher title. When I mentioned the Wallace name, His Grace recognized it immediately and inquired about your wool trade. He seemed quite interested in your business relations, but I could not speak on your behalf. I'm merely a woman, after all."

"That was wise," her father said as he lowered himself into the empty chair beside Julia's mother. "And what arrangement did you make?"

"Julia is to be there as his companion. Bridget will be joining her, of course. I would never consider sending one of my students without benefit of a chaperone. In exchange, he is giving her the opportunity to put into practice all that she has learned here in an authentic setting. Few of my pupils are given such an opportunity, my lord. I did promise His Grace that I would not mention this arrangement, but he did ask that I speak to you about the possibility of him doing business with you at a later time. I, of course, refused, but he urged me to at least mention it to you." She dropped her gaze, and Julia stared in amazement. Her headmistress would have done well on stage!

What surprised Julia more, however, was her father's reaction to what Mrs. Rutley had said. Gone was his ire, replaced by a thoughtful expression. And a rare smile.

"Did I not tell you, Penelope? Word of my wool trade has reached the wealthiest among us! Very well, if this duke wishes to conduct business with me, I'll allow him to do so despite his... malady." He rubbed his chin in thought. "Though, I should wait before contacting him. I certainly don't wish to appear too eager."

The room fell quiet until her father finally said, "Julia will remain here to complete her training. This arrangement with that duke will continue, but I'll not contact him until spring. That should be sufficient time for him to approach me rather than going through you." He waved a finger first at Mrs. Rutley and then at Julia. "Not a word of my plans to this man, either of you. I'm in control of this situation, and I wish to retain the power that control gives me. I'll not have a woman ruin everything with her inability to hold her tongue. Do I make myself clear?" He frowned. "Does the man have any romantic notions toward you, child?"

"No, Father," Julia replied. "Not in the slightest. He is a practical man, quite businesslike, and seems eager to complete this agreement as soon as possible."

"Good. He may be a duke, and a connection to him will be valuable to my business, but there is the chance he will become as mad as his father was. If that happens and you are somehow entangled with him, everything for which I've worked will be lost."

Julia stared at her father in surprise. "You know of him?"

"Of course I do, you silly girl," he said with a chuckle that made her feel like a child once more. "The antics of his father are well-known all over England. I'm sure his son will inherit many of his afflictions. What woman in her right mind would wish to have his children? They, too, will be as cursed as this man is, and I'll not have my daughter living under such duress."

Curses and luck? Did no one believe in sensibility any longer?

"Well, it makes no difference if he has a romantic interest in you," her father said. "Lord Howe has already asked for your hand in marriage, and I accepted on your behalf."

"Lord Howe?" Julia asked, stunned by this new piece of information. "But he is nearly forty—"

"Silence," her father snapped. He then turned to her mother. "I warned you that your rebellion as a youth would return with our daughter, and now you see I was right."

"I'm sorry," her mother whispered, not raising her head even an inch.

Julia wished to comfort her mother, but the last time she did so in the presence of her father, his admonishment had left her weeping in fear.

"You, child, will finish your training, and when you return home, we shall begin the preparations for your wedding. Hopefully you will make a good impression, for he has requested to court you before you marry to see that you meet his approval." He glanced at her mother, a sneer on his lips. "I don't blame the man. If I had known then what I know now, I would have demanded the same. Instead, I now must endure the likes of a weak woman who does nothing more than mope." He turned to Mrs. Rutley. "Now, as to the rest of her training."

As her father and the headmistress discussed what would take place during the remainder of her time at Courtly Manor, Julia felt as if the world was collapsing around her. She had met Lord Howe, an earl who thought himself a duke, at least once on one of her visits home, and she found him to be a shrewd businessman who was rumored to have a mistress in every town and village. When he looked at her, her stomach twisted into a knot and bile rose in her throat.

It was not until her parents stood that she woke from her thoughts.

"Next time," her father was saying, "I expect you to write to your mother and me before making a fool of yourself. And mind your posture. You sit like an old woman. Like your mother."

Julia straightened her back. "Yes, Father," she whispered as she stood.

Her parents swept out of the office. There were no hugs nor any words of encouragement before the door closed behind them. As a single tear rolled down Julia's cheek, Mrs. Rutley pulled her into her arms.

"Don't worry," the headmistress whispered. "All will work out as it should. Trust me."

All Julia could do was pray the woman was right, for at the moment, she saw nothing but heartache in her future.

Chapter Seven

Ezra Colburn stood outside the country estate of one Lady Dyer, a young widow at the age of three and twenty. Her husband, the late Baron Averill Dyer, had been an old man when he married his young bride, and when he died not three months after, no one was at all surprised, least of all Ezra.

Yet, the old codger left this world before paying his debt to Ezra, and Ezra was growing weary of not getting what was due to him. A year was plenty of time to mourn in his opinion, if the lady did mourn, and it was more than enough time to realize that the man's holdings were nearly depleted. That meant nothing was left for Ezra to claim.

Crestview House was a modest place with no upper level and only four bedchambers. The small gardens that surrounded the home had long been overgrown with weeds and the place reeked of despair. This, of course, only made Ezra smile all the more.

Lady Dyer had not written the letter presented to his nephew. That had been penned by Ezra himself as the first step of many he had planned. Now, he would need the woman to aid him in the next stage of his quest. Fah! How he despised relying on a woman to get to what he needed!

Walking to the door, he knocked twice. A liveried man answered. "My lord," he said with a bow of his head.

Ezra ignored the man as he pushed past him. In the small foyer, he took in his surroundings. Gone were the intricate vases that had been there last, as was the lavish tapestry that had hung above a side table. He suspected it would not be long before the house itself was sold, for no heir had been found to take over the baron's title or to inherit what little the baron had left upon his death.

"Lady Dyer awaits you in the parlor, my lord," the butler said. "If you will follow me."

"I'm well aware of its location," Ezra snapped.

He went to the first door on the left and entered, having been there on various occasions to discuss business with Lord Dyer. Ezra had even been present for the wedding when Lady Dyer and the baron spoke their vows. He had also attended their first party—and their last. He was well-acquainted with the Dyers. And their house.

The baroness stood at the window, a beautiful woman with auburn hair that fell in curls around her innocent face. Despite her loveliness, Ezra had no desire to hold her in his arms, but rather to place her in the arms of his nephew. There, he could take better control of her assets as well as those of Matthew.

Lady Dyer's father had been a wealthy man years ago, but between supporting many mistresses and losing at the gaming tables, he had nearly gone bankrupt. He had auctioned off his daughter to pay off all his debts and purchase a small parcel of land near Oxford, where he could hide himself away from the temptations that had gotten him into trouble in the first place.

"Lady Dyer," Ezra said. The woman was so deep in thought that she clutched at her chest and gasped. "Forgive me for startling you."

"Not at all, Lord Ezra," she replied, dropping into a curtsy before him. "I'm pleased to see you and curious as to the urgency of the letter you sent. Does it concern the party His Grace will be hosting soon?"

When his nephew had returned, raving about his outing with Miss Wallace, Ezra began to worry. The boy had not admitted it, nor was he likely to, but his expression had spoken volumes about his admiration for the young woman. If Matthew continued to call on her, he might consider courtship, and that would not do well at all. Not only did Ezra disapprove of that doxy, but his growing business interests would also grind to a halt. Such a woman becoming the Duchess of Elmhurst would ruin everything Ezra had worked so hard for, and he would not allow that to happen.

He was no fool. Agnes Rutley was a shrewd woman, defiant and opinionated, and her pupils would likely leave the school possessing those same traits.

"Not at all," Ezra replied to her question. "I'm here because of my concern for your wellbeing."

Her green eyes widened as she took his hand in hers. "You have no reason to be concerned about me," she said. "I'm doing well."

Although setting his plans into motion was of the utmost importance, Ezra knew he must tread carefully. The last thing he needed was to arouse any suspicion. "I've heard things," he said, "concerning your estate. That you are having to sell off your most precious items to have enough on which to live. Please tell me this is only a rumor."

The fact was that Ezra had come to learn Lord Huxley, a baron well-liked by many of the *ton,* had gone unaccompanied to the house of Lady Dyer. It was only when he threatened to tell everyone the man was having an affair with the baroness that Lord Huxley admitted his true motive, which was to buy various items from the house.

Lady Dyer dropped her gaze and gave a sad nod. "Lord Huxley agreed not to speak a word to anyone, but it appears I was wrong to trust him."

"Few men can be trusted," Ezra said, guiding the woman to the couch. "That is why I'm here, to see if there is any way that I can be of service."

She smiled at him. "Since Averill's death, you have been the only person who has inquired about my wellbeing. I thank you for that."

It was true that Ezra had inquired but not as an offer of friendship. His real motive was not to collect the debts that Averill owed but rather to purchase his estate before it went into bankruptcy. If Lady Dyer were to wed Matthew, Ezra would be able to purchase the estate for a fraction of its value. The property held no mines or copses of trees for timber, but he could either sell it later for a tidy profit or add it to the already great expanse of properties he owned.

"What will you do?" Ezra asked, allowing commiseration to drip from his words. Or he hoped it was commiseration. He had no idea what it felt like to have sympathy for another person and therefore was never quite sure he had hit the mark. He had seen it often enough to at least simulate it, however. "Once all your valuables are gone, you will have nothing left to sell but the house itself. I'm sure it will provide money for the short term, but what about the future?"

"I'm uncertain," Lady Dyer replied. "I spend every day trying to devise a plan to save my home. I could marry again, but I have nothing a man would want. You are too kind to say it aloud, but you see the state this house is in. Then there are the rumors that I'm barren, but that is a lie." She removed a handkerchief from the sleeve of her dress and dabbed at her eyes.

Ezra patted her hand. Although he would never admit it to anyone, it had been he who had started those rumors in an attempt to keep away any eligible bachelor or wealthy widower. His sole purpose here tonight was not only to gain her estate, but as a first step to acquiring something far more valuable.

When his brother died, Ezra had seen an opportunity to gain control of the dukedom, allowing himself to run the estate as he saw fit. Manipulating the boy had been easy. All he, Ezra, had to do was teach his nephew to rely on him for everything until he lacked the confidence to even lift a fork, without looking to his uncle for reassurance he was doing it correctly. And Lady Dyer would play an important role in continuing what he had already begun.

Now, more than ever, was the perfect time to strike.

"Frances..." This was the first time he had used her Christian name, and her look of shock was pleasing. "There are so many cruel men out there, but honorable men do still exist. I know of one who has spoken very highly of you, which is the true reason I'm here."

The baroness blinked. "Are you saying you know someone who is interested in possibly courting me?" Her eyes went wide, and she pulled her hand away. "You don't mean yourself, do you?" Her cheeks turned pink. "I did not mean—"

He laughed. "I'm far too old and clumsy for a lady of your elegance," he said. "No, I speak of my nephew, Matthew. I must be honest, for I was the one who invited you to his party because he was too shy to do so himself. I tried to reason with him, that you would be more than happy to accept his invitation, but he has some silly notion that you will reject him."

"I would do no such thing," she said aghast. "From what I've heard, he is a good man. It would be an honor if he were to personally invite me to his party."

"I could not agree with you more," Ezra said, taking her hand in his again. "But that does not change the fact that he was reluctant to ask you. Now, a most unfortunate situation has arisen, one in which I need your help."

"Of course," she said. "But what could I possibly do?"

Suppressing a grin, he said, "In desperation, he has invited a most inappropriate young woman to be his companion for the evening. Oh, she is not immoral in any way of which I'm aware, but she has a quick tongue and tends to embarrass herself and those in her company with her outbursts."

The baroness frowned. "I don't understand. Do you wish me to speak to the woman?"

"I would not insult you by asking you to stoop to such levels," he said, pleased to draw yet another smile from her. "I would simply like you to attend the party as planned, but when I introduce you to my nephew, do what you can to keep him occupied. If you are monopolizing his time, he will have no time for the other woman. At the same time, you may show your interest in him." He narrowed his eyes at her. "Surely you would be interested in a duke, would you not?"

"Well yes, of course," she said, although her brow knitted. "It's just that I don't see why—"

"You must not worry about anything," Ezra said. "If you do this, I can arrange something far better, something that will not only save your home but also will solidify your future."

"How so?"

Her eyes held such wide-eyed innocence, Ezra nearly laughed. Now was the time to execute the most important stage of his plan, for if the baroness agreed to his terms, he would leave today well on his way to greatness.

"Marriage," he said. "Continue helping me in setting my nephew on the correct path, to help him reach his potential, and I promise he will marry you."

"Marriage? I don't know about that. Now that I'm widowed, I would like to have the choice in whom I marry. I don't even know this man, and marriage is the least of my concerns at this moment."

Any sensible lady in her position would have jumped at the chance to become a duchess, yet her reaction sent a surge of anger through him. He rose with a frown and buttoned his coat. "Then we have nothing more to discuss," he said crisply. "I have no other way to help you. If you need a solicitor to navigate the sale of your property, please let me know, and I'll direct you to someone who may be of help."

When she began to tremble, he added, "Don't forget that your departed owes me a great sum of money. I'll have little choice but to collect once the property is confiscated and then resold. Good day to you."

"Wait," she called after him. He stopped and smiled, his back to her. "All you are asking of me is to keep him away from this woman at the party? Then I'm to convince him in the weeks that follow that I have an interest in him? And this will save my home?"

He could hear the struggle in her voice, which made his smile widen. Yet, he dropped it as he turned and sighed heavily. "I wish you to help him become the duke he should be, and by doing so, you will also become a duchess, never having to worry about money again. Not only will you save this home for which you seem quite fond, but you will have another twenty over which you will have control. The *ton* will no longer hold you in contempt but will instead admire you. If I had the means, I would simply give it to you, but alas, I do not. Perhaps your father can be of help?"

She dropped her gaze in shame. He knew already that her father could not afford the price of a new suit, let alone the funds needed to bring the house back to its former glory. "I don't know," she said. "I cannot help but feel as if it's trickery."

"Goodbye, Frances," he whispered, but before he could even turn back around, she hurried after him and grasped hold of his arm.

"I'll do this," she said. "I make no commitment to marriage, so whatever plans you have, I refuse to hurt him in any way."

"Hurt him?" Ezra asked, doing his best to hide his sense of triumph. It had been easy to manipulate her thus far and would be the same once she and Matthew were wed. To think she would have a say in that matter showed how naïve she was. "My dear, I would never make such a request. By the end of all this, he will be thanking you."

Chapter Eight

Mrs. Barbara Gouldsmith was instructing Julia and several of the other girls in the art of dining decorum, and Julia was struggling to keep her excitement under control. All she could think about was readying herself for the party, which would take place this evening.

Since the picnic with Matthew, he had called on her twice more. Getting to know one another was how Mrs. Rutley put it. And Julia had learned a few things about Matthew that surprised her. For one, his uncle was as overbearing as her father, so much so that they joked that perhaps the two men were brothers. She had also been surprised how much he could make her laugh. My, but how her heart was warming toward him!

Of course, his belief in superstitions was still an oddity, especially with how much he relied on them to guide his life, but she did not care that he held such beliefs. She found him much more fascinating than she had thought previously, and he was the only male with whom she could converse as a friend.

"Miss Hunter," Mrs. Gouldsmith snapped at Emma, breaking Julia from her thoughts, "you enter a room like a scared child. All you will manage to do is embarrass yourself and your family."

Julia's heart went out to Emma, who stood just outside the door and appeared on the verge of tears.

"She enters like a child because she is one!" Abigail whispered to the girls who were always in her presence, causing them to giggle.

Clenching her fists beneath the table, Julia threw them a stern glare that immediately quelled their laughter.

"I'm sorry, Mrs. Gouldsmith," Emma said. "I cannot help myself. I get very nervous when I enter a crowded room."

The tutor sighed. "You have been at this school for nearly four years and still you struggle with basic skills. Do you not wish to catch the eye of a potential suitor? Or perhaps you would prefer to dedicate your life to a convent instead."

This time, Abigail and her followers burst out in outright laughter.

Julia pushed back her chair and stood. "I don't believe ridiculing her will help her to improve," she snapped at Mrs. Gouldsmith before she could stop herself. "We must use compassion to help one another improve." She glared at Abigail again as she said the last.

"What you say is true, Miss Wallace," Mrs. Gouldsmith said in a tight voice, "but only as it pertains to those of feeble minds. A lady wishing to attract a husband needs a firm hand. Now, Miss Hunter, try again. And if you fail, you will remain here tomorrow to practice until you get it right while the other girls go into town."

Julia went to her friend's side, ignoring the tutor's look of surprise. "Don't be afraid," she whispered to Emma. "Pretend no one else is in the room except the handsome gentleman you wish will notice you."

Emma smiled.

"It's for him and no one else that you enter the room perfectly. Now, imagine it and try again."

"Miss Wallace!" Mrs. Gouldsmith said. "I demand that you return to your seat immediately."

Julia did as the tutor requested but not before winking at Emma.

Emma stepped out into the corridor once more and disappeared around the corner.

"We are waiting, Miss Hunter," the tutor said. "Our time is nearly over, and the other ladies would like to get on with their day."

For a moment, Julia worried Emma had run off, but then she

appeared in the doorway, her head held high and her eyes fierce. She took two steps into the room, grasped hold of her skirts, and dropped into a curtsy so low, so perfect, that her nose nearly touched the floor. Theodosia, who was acting as her chaperone, then escorted her to the chair across from Julia. In a series of quick motions, Emma was seated, her posture perfect throughout.

Miss Gouldsmith placed a hand to breast. "Ladies, it appears that Miss Hunter has set an example for you all. Do strive to match her perfection. You are now dismissed."

Abigail led her group of followers from the room, but Julia, Theodosia, and Jenny hurried to congratulate Emma, who was beaming with pride.

"Oh, thank you, Julia," Emma said, hugging her. "I could not have done it without your advice."

"You most certainly could have," Julia said. "I've told you time and again that those girls are simply jealous of you because they will never match your beauty. That is the reason they choose to tease you. Now they are afraid, for they can see you for who you truly are." She glanced up at the clock and gasped. "I must search out Bridget! I have only three hours to prepare for the party tonight!"

"She is already waiting for you," Emma said, wearing a grin. "As are the other girls."

"Other girls?" Julia asked. "What other girls?"

Jenny heaved a dramatic sigh. "You are attending a party with a duke. Did you believe we would allow you to dress without our help?"

Before Julia could respond, Emma grasped one of her hands and Theodosia the other and whisked her away upstairs. After being nearly shoved into her bedroom—to a chorus of giggles—Julia laughed when she saw Bridget standing between Diana and Ruth.

"Unity is lying down," Diana said. "Her head is aching, but she sends her best wishes to you for tonight."

Julia looked at her friends. "All of you wish to help me dress?" she asked in surprise.

Everyone nodded, and before she could argue, Ruth began undoing the stays of her day dress. Emma hurried to the wardrobe and removed the green gown Julia had chosen to wear.

"Yes, this will be perfect," Emma said. "The duke will have no choice but to look at you the entire night and ignore all the other ladies there."

"I was not invited to have him ogle me," Julia said.

"We don't have time to speak about what you believe will happen," Emma snapped, causing the others to laugh. "Now, let us get this dress off you so we can begin our work."

Julia had never felt more loved, despite feeling pulled in multiple directions. All her friends meant well, after all.

When her layers were in place and her gown was cinched, they took a step back and allowed her to look at herself in the mirror.

"It looks wonderful!" Julia exclaimed.

"We are nowhere near finished," Diana said. "Now, we must make you more beautiful than you already are." She shoved Julia onto the stool in front of the vanity. Emma and Diana saw to the cosmetics while Bridget styled her hair.

Jenny opened a box and removed an emerald necklace. "This was a gift from my mother," she said. "It's exactly what you need for an evening such as this."

"What if I catch it on something or lose it? No, I have several necklaces that will do just fine," Julia said. "I cannot wear something so valuable, so precious!"

"All the more reason you should wear it," Jenny said. "To make the duke realize how precious you are."

The emerald hung from a green ribbon, allowing the pendant to hang against the hollow of her throat. Did they not understand that she and the duke were only friends? That they had shared in no conversation nor even hinted of anything more?

Yet, what if tonight presented an opportunity to move beyond friendship? What if the duke was so overcome by her beauty that he had no choice than to admit he cared for her? Would she accept if he offered her his undying love?

No, that was not how it worked. Did they not have to court first before such an admittance was made? If he did ask to court her, how would she respond?

Then she smiled as she considered her reply. "You may be handsome, Your Grace, and your arms may be strong, but I'm not easily wooed by you."

Giggles erupted around her, and she realized she had voiced those words aloud! Why could she not guard her tongue?

"And yet they are 'merely friends'," Ruth said as she passed the curling iron to Bridget. "Why must she lie to us?"

"I'm not lying!" Julia insisted. She turned to Emma. "You believe me, do you not? Tell them that Matthew and I are only friends and nothing more, please!"

"You see?" Emma sighed as she slipped a white glove over Julia's hand. "She even addresses him by his Christian name. You are my friend, but I'll not lie for you. It's clear you adore the duke, despite your insistence to deny it."

Julia pursed her lips as Bridget wrapped a strand of hair around the curling iron. What if they were correct? Could a woman be enamored with a man and not realize it?

"Now, it's important to gauge the temperature of the iron before applying it," Bridget was saying as if the girls had not used a curling iron before. "Slightly warm, and it fails to create a decent curl. Too hot, and one will be forced to wear a hat for at least a month!"

As her friends talked amongst each other, Julia had never felt so grateful to be surrounded by those who loved her. And as she looked at each one, she knew they were more than just friends. They were sisters, just as she had told Matthew.

Bridget set the iron on its holder, and Julia stood.

"Oh, Julia," Emma gasped, "you look radiant!"

Julia looked at herself in the mirror. Gone was the girl she had been, replaced by a woman she did not recognize. Two long curls hung on either side of her face, and the remaining curls had been pinned into a bun on the back of her head. The cosmetics were just enough to give her some coloring but not too much to be inappropriate. And the gown! The rich green color matched the emerald exactly.

"I believe you're ready," Bridget said with a wide smile. "No lady will be able to compete with you tonight."

Julia turned to her friends. "Thank you all so much," she said. "You have made this night already wonderful. I'm sure the duke will appreciate your hard work."

Diana added a dab of perfume behind each of Julia's ears, on her wrists, and beneath the emerald in the hollow of her throat. "There, now you smell like a garden," she said, grinning.

When they reached the foyer, Mrs. Rutley stood waiting. Her hand on a hip, she gave Julia a critical look. Did she disapprove of the dress? Julia had thought it modest enough for a duke's party—not too low in the neckline but also not with a collar that went up to her chin. Was the necklace too much? Perhaps the perfume was too overwhelming, though Julia enjoyed its fragrance.

All her worries fell away, however, when Mrs. Rutley kissed both of Julia's cheeks. "You are a true beauty," she said. "This night will be magical if you allow it to be. Now, Mrs. Garvey will be your chaperone tonight. Bridget will not do, not for a party as important as this."

Mrs. Hester Garvey was a woman Mrs. Rutley commonly used as a chaperone. A widow in her mid-thirties, she was a trusted friend to the headmistress.

"Are you ready, Miss Wallace?" Mrs. Garvey asked.

Julia nodded. "I'm more than ready."

A chorus of farewells and cries of good luck followed her as she headed to the waiting carriage. Mrs. Rutley was right; the night would be magical as long as it was what she wanted it to be.

Chapter Nine

Matthew stood in the middle of the immense ballroom that in less than an hour would be filled with guests, including the few friends he had, business associates, friends of his uncle, and those who received invitations due to their title.

Lord Talbot fit in more than one of the aforementioned categories, and they would discuss the possibility of Matthew purchasing a hotel near Brighton. The man had been reluctant in the past and would need to be convinced that selling was in his best interest. That would require Matthew to carry a strong charm, to be sure.

Matthew patted the place where he usually kept his pocket watch before remembering that it was no longer there. Where had it gone? He had left behind the spoon for fear of what people would think if he were caught with it. Carrying a pocket watch on one's person was one thing, but a spoon was quite another. Now, however, he considered returning to his room to fetch it just in case he needed it.

No, he would be patient and wait to see if Julia would provide the luck he needed. If not, this night was for naught.

His eyes darted to a portrait of his father, a man who had been tall like Matthew, but that was where the resemblance ended. Where his father had kept his light hair cut short, Matthew preferred to keep his darker hair long. His father had brown eyes, but Matthew had inherited the gray eyes of his mother. Would he retain his mother's sanity or received his father's...? No, he would not dally on that now, not before such an important event.

"Tonight, I'll complete this agreement," Matthew told the portrait. "I'll not make a fool of myself or shame our family name. Or I hope not to. A young lady, Miss Julia Wallace, is to attend, so I have the luck I'll need to see the bargain struck."

He smiled as an image of that woman appeared in his mind. She was no doubt beautiful, but her outlook on life—and more so, how she saw others—intrigued him. For a moment, he imagined courting her and then making an offer of marriage. They would share the most wonderful life together.

Until he went mad like his father.

"Matthew what are you thinking?" he whispered under his breath. "Would you allow Julia to live with that pain?" What of a child they would have together? Would he allow a son to suffer as he had? How he longed to share these fears with someone, but how could he? He scolded himself for being selfish and daring to dream of what could be.

He recalled the many nights he was awakened by his mother's sobs. Or by his father marching through the corridors, shouting that thieves had invaded the house when there were none.

What tore at Matthew's heart most was when his father no longer recognized his mother, before death claimed him. Rather than allowing her to care for him as a wife would, he ranted and raved at her, sending her away at every turn. This became such a common occurrence that when he eventually died, she retreated to an estate in Scotland to hide from the embarrassment of what she had been forced to endure.

"You left me with title and wealth," Matthew said to the painting, "and the idea that I could have a future with a woman of my choosing. Yet, that cannot be, can it? I'll never leave Julia in despair, to endure what Mother was forced to endure, no matter how much I believe I care for her."

Uttering the words aloud had made his heart skip a beat. Although he and Julia had grown close, what gave him the idea that he cared for her? He enjoyed the friendship they shared, to be sure, yet he would never allow his feelings for her to develop into something more.

"I'll purchase the land from Mrs. Rutley and use Miss Wallace for her luck, but I'll not be like you and hurt her by marrying her." He turned away, ire pumping through his veins, to find his uncle walking down the corridor. He walked in long strides, a smile on his face.

"Promise me you will not be speaking to that painting when our guests arrive, Nephew," he said. "We must quell any and all rumors tonight, not begin new ones."

"I'll not embarrass us," Matthew replied. "My goal for this evening is to see the agreement with Talbot closed."

This made his uncle snort. "I've warned you that he is a most stubborn businessman. Don't think your pocket watch will bring you the luck you need this time."

Matthew straightened his shoulders. "I'm in possession of something far greater," he replied. "Have no doubt I will succeed."

Although he spoke the words, he added a prayer that what he said would come to pass. Surely, if Julia's father doubled his fortune because of her, Matthew could complete a simple business agreement.

"See that you do," his uncle said. "Now, you have guests arriving. I would suggest you see to them."

With a nod, Matthew followed his uncle to the bottom of the grand staircase in the foyer where an elderly couple already waited.

"Ah, Lord and Lady Montgomery," Matthew said, placing his best smile on his lips.

The older gentleman bowed, and the lady did her best to curtsy, although her curved back did not allow much in the way of movement. "Your Grace," Lord Montgomery said, "it's an honor to be in your home after so many years." He then turned to Matthew's uncle. "And Lord Ezra, we must talk business later."

"Perhaps," his uncle replied, "if we have time."

Hickson returned with another couple, and for the next hour, Matthew greeted each guest, pretending to accept their praise and honor for receiving an invitation. Yet all the while, he looked over their heads and awaited the arrival of one particular guest.

As the foyer became near to overflowing, she appeared before him, causing his breath to catch in his throat. Julia wore a rich green gown, and in the hollow of her throat lay a matching emerald pendant. Her lovely wheat-colored hair was pulled up into a perfect chignon, exposing her lithe neck. Her cheeks and lips had a hint of red to them, and the blue of her eyes reminded him of a summer sky.

Yet, it was her smile that captivated him. He truly understood about which the poets of years past had written. Julia had been created by the heavens, for she was without a single blemish.

Matthew's heart thumped in his chest as she stepped forward, with whom he assumed was her chaperone, and offered a perfect curtsy.

"Your Grace," she said.

Making every attempt to regain his breath, he gave her a bow, ignoring the whispers of the *ton,* wondering what woman could cause a duke to bow so deeply.

"Miss Wallace, I'm honored to have you here," he said.

A hand on his shoulder made him start. "Do you not believe your guests have waited long enough?" his uncle whispered.

Matthew nodded and turned to the group that now filled the foyer. "Let the party begin!"

The first notes of the orchestra filtered into the corridor as he led his guests, ordered by station, to the ballroom. Many headed straight to the drinks table, and soon the room was alight with laughter and talk. Matthew searched the crowd for Julia, a difficult task when everyone vied for his attention. For a moment, panic seized him. Where was she?

With a sigh of relief, he found her standing across the room, her chaperone at her side.

"I must say, Your Grace," Lord Talbot said in that simpering voice that Matthew found grating, "the wine you selected for this evening is absolutely marvelous. Does it come from your vineyards?" Baron Talbot was a tall, wiry man with lines across his forehead and down his cheeks meant for someone much older.

"It does," Matthew replied. His stomach knotted. Why should he be nervous about discussing business with this man? It was not as if he were just out of swaddling!

It was a relief when they spent several minutes speaking about trivial matters, allowing Matthew time to gather his thoughts.

"Although I must admit the idea of going in together to purchase this Brighton hotel has intrigued me," Lord Talbot was saying. "I've given it a great deal of thought and have decided that I no longer wish to be a part of it." He lifted his wine glass and smiled, making the creases around his mouth deepen. "Now, if you wish for an investor in your vineyards, that would interest me."

Matthew could only stare at the man. He knew he should be arguing that the opportunity in Brighton was well worth the risk, but the words would not come. He would fail, just as his uncle had predicted, and shame coursed through his veins. Had the luck Julia was to provide already failed him?

No, he had to do what he could to save this accord. "Now, Talbot, as Brighton expands, those who claim their stakes early will profit the most. The risk will pay off far more than you realize."

"I don't know," the baron mumbled, frowning into his glass.

Just then, Julia walked past, and Matthew placed a hand on her arm to catch her attention. "Miss Wallace, may I introduce a dear friend of mine? Lord Talbot, Miss Julia Wallace."

Julia smiled and dropped into a curtsy. "It's a pleasure to meet you, my lord," she said.

Lord Talbot took a rather large drink of his wine before replying, "The pleasure is mine. And how are you and His Grace acquainted?"

She laughed. "Oh, we are merely friends, my lord."

"Wallace..." Lord Talbot said quietly. "Is your father Edmund Wallace?"

"No, my lord," Julia replied. "My father's name is Henry."

The baron went red to his ears as he downed another full glass of wine in one gulp. "Oh, yes, that was who I meant," he said in a rather loud voice. "Yes, I remember you now. I always knew his daughter would become a fine lady one day. And to think that the two of you are friends. How wonderful! I would very much enjoy asking after your father, but perhaps we can discuss him later. At the moment, His Grace and I are discussing a hotel venture we are planning."

Matthew suspected that Lord Talbot had never heard of Julia's father. But why would he feel the sudden urge to pretend he did? He had a reputation for knowing everyone but perhaps wanted to spare himself the embarrassment that he, in fact, did not.

Julia tipped her head and smiled. "I'll await your company," she said before withdrawing to another part of the room, her chaperone trailing behind her.

Matthew could not believe his luck! No, he could believe it. Julia had proven she could bring someone luck. Now he knew he had to keep the young woman close at hand!

Was it possible for any woman to feel as honored as Julia did as she walked away from Matthew and Lord Talbot? To be introduced by a duke to another man of title left her with an exhilarating feeling, to be sure, but it was far more than that. It was also the way Matthew had looked at her this evening.

The moment his hand touched her arm, a tingle rushed down her spine. Mrs. Rutley had been correct in her prediction. The evening was already proving to be magical, and this was merely the first hour!

When she and Mrs. Garvey arrived at the drinks table, the older woman said, "You may have a small sip of wine but don't drink too much. Drunkenness in a young lady is not very becoming."

"I promise to only take small sips," Julia said, giving her chaperone a small smile.

The footman handed them each a glass of red wine, and they walked over to a line of chairs. Julia watched the other guests, admiring the elegant gowns of the women and the fine suits of the men.

Then her gaze fell on Matthew, and she could not stop a small sigh from escaping her lips. How handsome he was among the other men, standing above them in height and spirit. He was unique, not only because he was a duke, but because he possessed a kind heart so few titled men seemed to have.

When she had nearly fallen at the stream, it was not only the act of protecting her from the fall but what had followed.

"Are you hurt?" he had asked. The words were simple but conveyed much more. They confirmed what she had suspected. Somewhere deep inside him was a kind man.

"I'll not inform Mrs. Rutley how His Grace accosted you," Mrs. Garvey said as she swiped invisible lint from her blue dress. "He may be a duke who believes he is above reproach, but grabbing your arm was barbaric, and he had no right to do so." She patted at her dark hair as if to put back into place hair that had not fallen loose.

Julia simply smiled. "Mrs. Garvey, may I ask about some of the older traditions?"

Mrs. Garvey laughed. "I'm not quite that old, but you may ask."

"I heard that in the past, men would choose their brides by simply taking hold of them. I'm uncertain whether to believe this, but I'm curious whether matters of courtship have always been the same."

"My late husband, Felton, was a romantic," Mrs. Garvey said. "He would read me poetry, bring me carefully selected flowers, and dare any man to look upon me, for he cherished me so."

"How wonderful," Julia said.

Mrs. Garvey sighed. "No, that was how I thought he should be, not how he truly was. The truth is, we courted for two months before he met with my father to ask for my hand. He never mentioned marriage to me before then. Don't think that men are like those in stories, for such heroes are rare indeed. As you enter your first season, you will learn soon enough that all men are the same. They believe women are meant to warm their beds, bear them children, and see to the home. Otherwise, they are to remain silent and do as they are told."

Julia nodded, but she did not agree. Matthew was a far better man than any she had encountered. Not that she had much experience with men, but she was sure he would not treat her so offhandedly.

Searching for the man in question, however, her confidence in that belief began to wane, for another woman stood at his side. Never had Julia seen a woman so lovely, with her thick auburn curls and a green gown made of finer fabric than Julia could have ever considered. The woman's smile radiated around the room. Did she have an interest in Matthew? Or was he simply playing the attentive host?

Julia shook her head. When had she become a jealous ninny? Yet, her jealousy only worsened when the woman laughed and placed a hand on Matthew's arm in a far too familiar way.

When she went to take another drink of her wine, she was surprised to find it gone. "I would like to return my glass," Julia said, standing. "Oh no, I see no need for you to accompany me, Mrs. Garvey. I'm not going far."

Mrs. Garvey appeared ready to argue but then smiled and replied, "I'll be here waiting."

Julia walked up to the refreshment table and exchanged her empty glass for a full one. When she turned back around, she nearly collided with a man she had seen earlier. There was a sinister air about him that sent a shiver down Julia's spine.

"Miss Wallace?"

"Yes?"

He gave her a bow. "It's a pleasure to meet you. I'm Lord Ezra Colburn, uncle to His Grace."

So, this was the overbearing uncle of whom Matthew spoke.

"The pleasure is mine, my lord," she said. "Matthew has spoken highly of you."

"As he does you," Lord Ezra replied. "His spirits have improved considerably since being in your company. I hope they continue to do so, for his sake."

Julia had to school her features from showing her surprise. "You do?"

"Of course," Lord Ezra replied. "Matthew has been unusually hard on himself as of late, though everything I try seems to fail. With your newfound friendship and his interest in Lady Dyer, I believe he will become a far better man."

Julia's heart quickened. "I'm afraid I'm not acquainted with Lady Dyer."

Her worst fears were realized when Lord Ezra motioned to the lovely woman who stood beside Matthew. "She is the woman in the green gown. I have never seen Matthew so happy. Have you?"

Julia had to admit that Matthew did appear extremely content. "I have not, my lord," she managed to say.

"If you will excuse me, Miss Wallace, I must speak to someone concerning business. If you require anything, please feel free to ask."

"Thank you, my lord," Julia said, her heart aching as he walked away.

As she took another sip of her wine, she thought about what Matthew's uncle had said. Matthew never mentioned Lady Dyer to her. Yet, why would he? She, Julia, was merely a lucky trinket to him. Lady Dyer was clearly the woman to whom he had an attraction.

Her despondency only deepened as couples lined up for the first dance of the evening. Heaving a heavy sigh, Julia thought of the words Mrs. Rutley had told her about this night being magical. Indeed it was, but it was not she who would benefit from the magic it offered. That favor belonged to Lady Dyer.

Chapter Ten

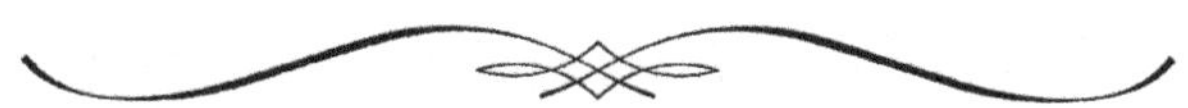

As Lady Dyer continued to speak, Matthew was finding attentiveness difficult. The lady herself was not the cause of his frustration but rather that he would have preferred his time spent with Julia. Instead, she stood alone in front of the punch bowl. He could have had even the slightest of moments alone with her if the baroness was not monopolizing his company. Each time he glanced in Julia's direction, her gaze was cast down. Was she somehow sad? If so, he wished to know why.

"I must say, Your Grace," Lady Dyer was saying, "when I received my invitation to tonight's soiree, I was elated."

Matthew gave her another polite smile, one that matched the several dozen he had given her thus far. He had laughed at her attempts at humor and smiled at her stories, all to please her. When his uncle had introduced them, he had requested that the baroness tell Matthew about a marquess with whom she was acquainted. Rather than the easy tale he had expected, it turned into a long-winded story that threatened to take the entirety of the night in its telling.

Matthew had a story he wished to share, but it was for Julia's ears only. He wished to express how important the luck she carried was to him, how it had brought Lord Talbot to his side, and convinced the man to invest with Matthew. Now, that was a story worth telling.

Finally, Lady Dyer paused in her storytelling, and Matthew chose that moment to make his escape. "If you will excuse me, I must speak with..." He glanced back toward the drinks table, but Julia was gone.

The music changed, and several couples took to the middle of the floor.

Uncle Ezra placed a hand on Matthew's shoulder when the music paused. "It would be wise to ask the lady to dance," he whispered. "Everyone is looking at you to begin."

Stifling a sigh, Matthew offered a hand to Lady Dyer. "May I have this dance?"

"It would be an honor, Your Grace," the baroness replied.

They took their places, and soon the groups began to move, fingertips brushing those of their partners. The two lines stepped forward, coming together in the middle, and the ladies twirled before stepping out once more. Back and forth the couples moved, but all Matthew could do was pray for the set to end. Why should he be forced to dance at all?

Because you are the duke, and the host of this party, he chastised himself silently. If he could have found Julia, this dance would have been much more enjoyable. Lady Dyer was pleasant enough company, of course, but he had to speak to Julia. She needed to know how important her attendance had been to him.

When the set finally ended, he returned Lady Dyer back to her place, offered quick apologies, and hurried in search of Julia. Yet, she was nowhere to be seen. Several men called his name, but he gave them no more than a polite nod as he hurried past them.

He entered the foyer and was surprised to see Hickson placing Julia's wrap on her shoulders. They were meaning to leave!

"Julia!" he called before chastising himself for not watching his tongue. "Miss Wallace, are you leaving already?"

"I am," she replied. "My head is aching, and I would like to return home to take a powder. I do hope you enjoy your evening."

Something was terribly wrong, but he could not place what it was. Although everything inside him begged to tell her how he wished to have her stay, that he promised to be more attentive, instead he said, "I have the most wonderful news. Do you remember the business proposition I wished to make with Lord Talbot?" She nodded. "We have come to an agreement." He lowered his voice, hoping her chaperone would not overhear. "You brought me the luck I needed. Thank you."

"Of course, Your Grace," she replied. "Thank you again for inviting me, but I really must be going."

"Please stay," he said. He wished to tell her how much he wanted her at his side, but his uncle approached, Lady Dyer close behind.

"We meet again, Miss Wallace," his uncle said. "Lady Dyer, I would like to introduce Miss Julia Wallace. She is an acquaintance of Matthew's and a pupil at the young ladies' school held at Courtly Manor. She has been receiving lessons in comportment, but every young lady should be given the opportunity to benefit from practical experience. Perhaps you'll be willing to add some of your wonderful knowledge in this area. After all, few can match your poise and etiquette."

"It's a pleasure to make your acquaintance, my lady," Julia said. "But I really must be going."

Matthew's temper flared as he turned to his uncle. Could the man have been more degrading in his words? "Uncle, Miss Wallace is a young lady, and any arrangement I have with her is not meant to be shared with others as a source of idle gossip." He turned his back to his uncle in order to speak to Julia, but she gave Matthew a painful look and hurried away. Lady Dyer's eyes widened, and she took a step back. But her shock was not as strong as that of Matthew himself. Never had he crossed his uncle except in private, but he felt it necessary given the circumstances.

"If you prefer, I'll become a mute in your presence," his uncle snapped before storming away.

Matthew closed his eyes but opened them again when he felt a hand upon his arm.

"It may not be my place, Your Grace," Lady Dyer said in her soft sultry voice, "but I believe I may know why your uncle is upset. Is there somewhere we may speak in private? I feel it's important no one overhears us."

A new set had begun in the ballroom, and Matthew nodded, leading the woman away. "Hickson," he called to the butler, "is the parlor lit?"

"It is, Your Grace."

"Good." He threw open the doors to the parlor, and once Lady Dyer was inside, he closed them again. "Forgive me, but we must hurry. If we are caught alone, we will only provide fuel for the wagging tongues of the *ton*, whether you are a widow or not."

"Which is the very reason I requested we meet in private, Your Grace. However, as a widow and an outcast, the tongues would be spewing other tales than misconduct, I assure you." She lowered her gaze. "I'm well aware of how much I disgust them."

"I would disagree," Matthew said, shaking his head. "You are friendly, intelligent, and have a gift for conversation. You should not speak so poorly of yourself."

She looked up at him and smiled. "I appreciate you saying so, Your Grace. But what I must say has nothing to do with what others think of me. A man was here earlier, a guest of your uncle's, though I don't know his name. He made a mockery of you in front of your uncle, for he made insinuations about Miss Wallace being a pupil of the girls' school. He had already consumed a great deal of alcohol before arriving, or so I understand, so your uncle instructed him to leave. Then he—your uncle, that is—requested that I engage in conversation with you. I must admit it was far more delightful than I had expected." She gave him a bright smile. "The reason I mention that incident is because I believe it's why your uncle made that cruel comment about Miss Wallace."

Matthew rubbed his temple. Again, his uncle was looking out for Matthew's best interests in his bristly way. Yet how did he repay the man? By shouting at him.

"If you are angry, Your Grace, you may shout at me. I'm strong enough to endure it, for my husband shouted at me as a way to release his anxiety."

How could anyone have such disregard for a widow? Or how could a husband treat his wife with such disdain? "I'm not angry with you,"

Matthew said, "and therefore have no reason to shout at you. What you did for me this evening was well intended, so I thank you."

"It was my honor, Your Grace," she said, dropping into a deep curtsy. "I have few friends, but I do enjoy helping others when I can." She turned toward the door and then stopped. "Forgive me, Your Grace. I did not mean to assume we are friends. It's just that I found our time together this evening a pleasant experience, and I felt as if we have known one another for years. I've also been so alone and..." She sighed. "Forgive me. I tend to ramble like a fool sometimes."

She cracked open the door, but Matthew called after her. He understood quite well how she felt. "What you say is true. We are friends."

"Thank you, Your Grace. I've not had anyone treat me with such kindness in a very long time." She slipped out of the room.

Matthew paced the room for several minutes. Julia had been mocked and ignored. The fact that she chose to leave early on such a special night was terrible. This was all that Matthew disliked about his life, that someone with a heart as wonderful as hers should be forced to endure such treatment. He would make it up to her somehow, but first he needed to search out his uncle and apologize for losing his temper.

For a duke, he had so much yet to learn.

Julia stood at the window gazing up at the stars and listening to the steady breathing of a sleeping Emma. She had endured a cacophony of emotions during her life, but what she felt now confused her. It was as if she and Matthew had developed a strong bond only to have it severed like a strand of thread. Worse still, she felt more alone now than ever before, and the reality of her father wishing her to marry Lord Howe only made matters worse.

Had she hoped Matthew would somehow save her from such a plight? In truth, she had secretly wished he would become so enamored with her that he would have no choice than to ask to court her.

And if they were courting, Lord Howe would no longer be a problem. That is, to anyone except her father.

The rustle of blankets behind her made Julia turn to find Emma rubbing her eyes.

"Julia? What are you still doing up?"

"Thinking," Julia replied. She had no desire to reveal to her friend what had occurred at the party. For now, it was not yet real.

Emma padded over to Julia. "What is wrong?" she asked. "Why are you home so early? What happened?"

Emma would not allow her a wink of sleep! Julia sighed. "When I first arrived at the party, it was so lovely—"

The door creaked, and Diana entered the room. "Oh, good, you are awake," she said. "I want to know everything!"

Emma gave Diana a sad look. "She was just about to tell me but be forewarned. It did not end well."

"Please, go on," Diana said.

"Yes, well, as I was saying, it began exactly as I would have expected. No, better. I've never seen such lovely gowns in my entire life."

She moved on to one particular green gown and the events that surrounded Lady Dyer and Matthew. By the time she concluded her retelling, Jenny and Ruth had joined their small group.

"I've never been so embarrassed in my life than when Matthew's uncle stated that I needed further training. And Lady Dyer, she is so beautiful, far more than I. She has the loveliest red hair and carries herself so well. And although she also wore green, her gown was far better than mine. I understand why His Grace was enamored with her and decided to spend the evening in her company rather than mine. What can I possibly offer him when he has someone far more cultivated to catch his attention?"

"Oh, rubbish," Ruth snapped so loudly, everyone turned to glare at her. "My guess is that she is nothing more than a hussy laying a trap for her next husband." Where Julia chose her words carefully, Ruth spoke aloud the exact words that came to her mind, without thought for how they would be received. Her words or actions, oftentimes both, got her thrown into the cooking pot on far too many occasions.

Emma and Jenny gasped, but Julia shook her head. "I don't believe so. She is far too graceful and elegant to need traps."

Ruth glowered, her hands on her hips. "Did you not say the duke searched you out to ask you to remain, but this woman appeared and interrupted you?"

"Well, yes, but—"

"Then this woman sees you as a threat to her plans to entrap the duke," Ruth continued. "She realized that the duke had eyes for you, which upset her enough to do what she could to come between you." She pointed a finger at Julia. "And don't think that I say this only as a means to make you feel better. I say it because it's the simple truth. That hussy is jealous of you."

A sense of hope washed over Julia. Was what Ruth said true? Perhaps Lady Dyer was indeed jealous of her. Yet, a new question arose. "Your assessment of the situation does make me feel better, but what of Matthew? What if he is distracted by her?"

This time it was Jenny who added her opinion. "If he was so distracted by this woman, as you say, why did he request that you remain?" She clasped her hands in front of her. "When I returned home last winter, I accompanied my parents to a party given by a friend of my father. His son, who is quite handsome, asked me to remain when I mentioned I wished to leave."

"What happened?" Diana asked.

"I did remain. And later I made excuses to leave the ballroom, met with the man in a dark corner, and gave him a kiss."

"No!" Emma said with a gasp. "Jenny, how could you do such a thing?"

Jenny shrugged. "It's quite simple, really," she said, a proud expression on her features. "If a woman desires a kiss, she should have it. After all, men may kiss any woman they please without repercussion. I say we should be able to break societal rules as long as no one witnesses it."

As the girls debated this statement, Julia returned to her vigil at the window to contemplate Matthew. He had asked her to stay. Why would he do so if he had an interest in Lady Dyer? The answer was, he would not.

Feeling much better, she returned her attention to the group. "Thank you for your advice," she said. "I've come to realize that I have much more to offer than I believed. Matthew does care about me. How much remains to be seen. Yet he did ask that I stay at the party, so at least I have that."

Julia gave each of her friends a hug and wished them a goodnight. One by one, they left the room. Just as she was pulling back the covers of her bed, the door opened once more, and Mrs. Rutley entered.

"I spoke with Mrs. Garvey," the headmistress said. "She mentioned that your head was aching, but I have a suspicion that something else hurts instead."

All Julia could do was stare at the woman. How could she possibly know such a thing?

As if confirming she could hear the thoughts of her pupils, Mrs. Rutley added, "I know all too well what it's like be hurt, so be truthful with me."

Julia nodded. "I don't wish to retell the story, but let us just say that I was disappointed, and perhaps a bit jealous. Oh, very well, quite jealous when I was unable to speak to Matthew more than I did. But after discussing it with my friends, I believe I may have acted in haste. After all, a host must not spend his entire night in the company of one particular woman."

Mrs. Rutley chuckled. "At least you remember one lesson I taught you," she said, although her voice lacked the slightest tone of reprimand. She pulled a letter from her dressing gown. "This arrived a short time ago."

"Thank you," Julia said. She ran a finger under the seal and unfolded the parchment.

Dear Julia,

The party tonight was a success, though I fear as I write this it will never end. Circumstances beyond my control kept me away from you, but it will not happen again. If Mrs. Rutley agrees, I shall call tomorrow at one to speak with you further on this matter.

Until then,

Matthew

Julia sighed and clutched the letter to her breast. All her worries had been for naught, and she could not help but smile at Mrs. Rutley.

"Now," the headmistress said, "I believe you need to sleep. One o'clock will come early tomorrow." She winked.

Soon, Julia was in bed still clutching the letter. Even as she drifted off to sleep, her thoughts were on Matthew and the time they would spend together.

Chapter Eleven

The last of the leaves clung to the tree limbs in the gardens of Courtly Manor as Julia and Matthew strolled down the stone path, Bridget walking a discreet distance behind them. Matthew had arrived at the promised hour, but neither he nor Julia had spoken more than a few words of greeting in the quarter hour they had been together.

The path split where a large elm tree grew, the two new paths bounding away on either side. A small outbuilding sat alongside the wall to Julia's right, used to house the necessary tools needed by the gardener. Thankfully, the man was not there today, allowing Julia and Matthew the relative privacy they needed.

When Julia glanced at Matthew, she could not help but sense his worry. "Your party was lovely," she said. "The finest I've ever attended, though I must admit I have only attended a few."

Matthew merely nodded but said nothing.

"And your business negotiation? I'm so glad it was successful."

This made Matthew smile. "It was the luck you brought with you," he said. "You did not lie, nor did Mrs. Rutley. You do possess a great deal of luck."

A twinge of guilt pierced Julia's heart. She did not approve of lying but had learned from a young age that there were times when skirting or distorting the truth was necessary. What she wished to do was tell Matthew the truth, that she possessed not an inkling of luck, but if she were to do so, Mrs. Rutley would be terribly displeased. And Matthew distressed.

"I would like to discuss Lady Dyer," Matthew said.

Julia's legs wobbled beneath her. This was the topic she wanted to discuss above all, but now that it had been broached, she wanted to return it to the unspoken.

"She was a guest of my uncle," Matthew said. "She is a widow, and our estate does business with hers."

Our estate? Julia wondered. This was not the first time he had referred to what he owned as a shared possession, but she kept her thoughts to herself.

"I admit that her company is pleasant enough, but she spoke so much I thought my ears would fall off."

Julia laughed at this. "I'm pleased they did not," she said.

"As am I," Matthew said. Then he sighed. "I scolded my uncle for his choice of words, but you had already left. I learned that although they may have seemed unusually cruel, he had a reason for using them. Earlier in the evening, a particular guest arrived well into his cups. He spoke disrespectfully about me to my uncle, so my uncle was forced to eject him from the party. You see, Uncle Ezra wants nothing more than our family's name raised to its former glory. But I assure you, he meant no harm by what he said. He only wants what is best for everyone he encounters, and by recommending Lady Dyer as a possible mentor, he was merely expressing the fact that he sees potential in you."

Julia considered this for a moment. Perhaps she had been hasty—and immature—in wanting to leave the party early. What would she do when someone mistreated her at a party she hosted? Would she simply run upstairs and throw herself onto her bed, leaving her guests without a hostess? The idea was ludicrous. She was nearing her debut into society, and it was about time she started acting the part.

"But overall," Matthew said, "I wish to say that I'm sorry."

"There is nothing to forgive," Julia said, smiling. "I understand better now. Thank you for explaining it to me."

Matthew grinned and whispered, "I cannot express how beautiful, how intriguing you are. And you possess such a pure heart. If I had you, I would need nothing else in this world." His eyes widened and filled with alarm. "Oh... I... forgive me! It's as I said before, I tend to have bouts of madness and speak before thinking." His entire face and ears were so red, he appeared to have spent several days in the sun.

Julia could have spent those days with him as dry as her mouth had become. Yet, she managed to form words, despite the fact breathing was difficult. She placed a hand on his arm. "You are not mad. I cannot count the number of times I've spoken without thought. I'm honored you believe I'm beautiful, for I think you quite handsome. I cannot think of a single gentleman who compares to you."

Mrs. Shepherd could have heaped a shovel full of hot coals on Julia's cheeks, and they would not have been hotter. What had compelled her to speak so candidly?

And why did her head reel, and her heart feel as light as a feather?

Matthew gave a despondent sigh. "I appreciate your kind words, but they could not be further from the truth. You must understand, my father *did* go mad. The first indication of his madness was him speaking to himself, carrying on conversations when no one else was in his presence. It only worsened over time. Rather than speaking to no one, he began speaking to inanimate objects—chairs, statues, even trees.

"By the end of his life, he recognized no one, but my mother grieved for her husband long before he was dead. When I assumed the title, I found myself unable to erase the shame he had caused. If anything, I only make things worse. The probability of me repairing our family name is low, for I'm likely to follow in his footsteps." He sighed, his head hanging low. "I'm sorry. I did not mean to bring up such matters."

What could she possibly say that would ease his pain? She knew no one who was afflicted as his father had been and thus had no words of wisdom to share. Yet, she could share the fears that overwhelmed her. They may not be as complicated or as terrible as his, but it was all she had to offer.

Searching his eyes, she said, "I'm sorry your parents suffered so terribly. Although I may not understand the fear of saving your family name, or what it's like to endure what you have been forced to endure, I do have fears of my own." She sighed. "Though, now that I consider them, they are minuscule compared to yours."

He smiled. "Fears are just that—fears. Please, tell me. I would like to know."

Julia sighed. "When we returned from our picnic, my parents were waiting. They arrived unannounced to tell me that my father had found me a suitor." She forced herself to ignore Matthew's flinch at this. "I care nothing for this man, I assure you. I feel he looks at me as if he is assessing a mare he wishes to purchase. My fear is that one day he will come and whisk me away to marry him, for if he does, I will never be truly happy. My mother endured very much the same, although she would never admit it to me. Her life has been nothing more than walking in the shadow of my father and being forced to endure him belittling her. That is my fear, that I shall live my mother's life."

Matthew took her hand in his. "I'm sorry you are frightened," he said. "What will you do? I imagine your father will never allow you to have a say in the matter."

"He would choose my wedding gown if he could," she said with a light snort. "All I can do is make the most of my time here at the school, enjoy the friendships I've developed with the other girls and with you. I must endure until the day my father comes to collect me and present me to a man I do not love. However, if I spend my days dwelling on my future, it will suffocate me."

What a fool she was! Here Matthew was concerned that he would go mad like his father, and she compared that to the possibility of doing what most young ladies must do and marry a man she did not love. She gave a weak laugh. "I may have only made matters worse," she said. "If I made your concerns seem as frivolous as mine, I apologize."

Was all now lost? Would he go away, hoping never to see her again? After all, no one wished to hear that madness was a frivolous problem. Yes, she was indeed a fool!

Matthew had never been a confident speaker, but with Julia, it was different. She had taken hold of him unlike anything else in his life. He had no doubt that his recent success with Lord Talbot resulted from her, and he had to make certain that luck was not wasted on another man, one who cared nothing for her. Whoever this other gentleman was, it made no difference, for he would never be good enough to appreciate all Julia had to offer.

When he had shared his fears with her, he had been surprised at the relief it brought him. And he had not lied when he said that her fears were not less than his, for he now felt a camaraderie with her he had never before had with anyone else.

They were friends, and he cared for her deeply, more so than any other person in his one and twenty years. He could never love her, of course, for he could never put her in the terrible position his mother had been forced to endure. But he would do what he could to see she did not suffer too much, for he had something his father never had. The insight into the possibility he could lose his mind. At least he could send Julia away once the madness began and see she was protected from the inevitable.

As he gazed into her lovely blue eyes, he brushed away a tear from her cheek. "How could I have ever believed you were a thief? And your troubles are not frivolous, for they are yours, just as mine may seem frivolous to someone who has suffered worse than me. I had foolishly believed you were a form of luck or a means to acquire property, but now I've come to realize that you are far more. You bring me the peace I so desire, and the friendship we share is important to me.

"Now I have a new fear. That one day what we share will be lost, and all for the wants of others. Your father wishes you to marry another, and my uncle insists I find a bride..."

He paused. Perhaps he had the solution to solve both their problems! If he were to court her, it would give his uncle one less thing to pester him about. In turn, it would save Julia from having to marry another, at least until the right man came along.

Worry washed over him. What if this courtship ended in marriage?

What then? Loving her, which was a likely outcome, would do nothing but hurt her in the end. He searched her face. No, he had to help her. No matter the cost, he would push forward and do whatever he could to protect her. There was no other way.

"Yes, that just may be the answer!"

"What?"

He grinned down at her. "I would like to court you."

To his surprise, and pleasure, she leaped into his embrace. "Yes, of course! I would like nothing more."

A breeze caused a strand of her hair to blow across her face as the world around them became quiet. With her head against his chest, his confidence grew. It was as if his worries had disappeared. He was at peace and no longer alone, and he would never let her go.

If he had been given the choice, he would have remained there, holding her forever, but as strong as his feelings were, he took a quick step backwards. "We cannot risk being caught," he said. He glanced at the lady's maid, who made every effort not to look in their direction. At least, they would have an accomplice there.

"You are right," Julia said, glancing toward the house. "Thankfully, I see no one peering out the windows. Should I write Father and tell him the news?"

For a moment, he considered her question. There were proper ways to go about such things. Any gentleman worthy of a lady would speak to her father in person, to ask for her hand in the right way.

Then worry cramped his stomach. How would he broach the subject with his uncle?

Yet, it was more than that. He had just made a commitment he already feared he could not keep. Oh, what had he done? Would it not be best to end it and hurt her now rather than later?

No, the decision had been made, and he would see it through to the end. That did not mean they should not be cautious, at least for the time being, for a host of reasons, but for the good of overbearing family members included.

"No," Matthew replied, "there is no need at the moment. We have no idea how he will respond, and there is no reason to rush anything. Plus, he may disapprove if I don't ask before you inform him."

"Yes, that makes sense. We have so many steps to take beforehand. For now, I say we simply enjoy one another's company."

"I would like that," he said. He offered his arm. "I have meetings tomorrow and the day after, but I'll send you and Mrs. Rutley an invitation to dinner soon."

"That would be wonderful," Julia said as they came to a stop beneath the shade of an overhanging bough, in front of an outbuilding they had passed earlier.

Although it was tempting to take her into his arms and kiss her lips, he withheld the urge. Gentlemen simply did not behave that way. Plus, her lady's maid had already ignored their brief embrace. Ignoring an outright kiss was asking too much.

"I sense that you and your lady's maid are close," he said, glancing over his shoulder.

Julia nodded. "Father insisted I have a lady's maid when I came to the school, and I'm glad he did. She has been with me nearly four years, and I hope to keep her with me once I'm married. A woman needs a confidante, someone with whom she may share her secrets." Then a grin spread across her beautiful features. "Though a gentleman should come first in such matters. If he is the right gentleman, that is."

Her smile, her very being shone brighter than the sun above, allowing Matthew to be himself for the first time since childhood. Or if he ever had been. "My mother has a lady's maid who has been with her nearly thirty years. You would think they were sisters the way they speak to one another when they are alone."

"What is your mother like?"

Matthew pursed his lips. "At one point, she was very much like you. Whenever she entered a room, all attention was drawn to her. But as Father's illness worsened, her smile faded. Now, she lives alone with only a handful of servants. I've seen her only once since my father died, and that was two years ago. We have corresponded in writing over the years, but I do miss her."

The realization of this truth disturbed him. Sometimes he was unsure whether he had abandoned her or if she had him, but he was certain she was far better suited for Scotland than a place where she was forced to remember what his father had put her through.

"I would like to meet her," Julia said. "If you believe I'm presentable enough, that is."

Matthew chuckled. "You are more than presentable, Julia. You are the embodiment of what every lady should strive to be." Her blush sent a warming sensation through his heart. Telling her such things came easily, for they were the truth.

"And you are what every gentleman should strive to be," she said. "Intelligent, well-spoken, and although lacking in the area of philosophy, well-studied."

He laughed. "Is that so? Do you honestly believe you can outwit me?"

"Of course I do," she replied. Then she bit at her lower lip. "But don't worry, Your Grace. I'll never reveal that to a single soul and thus save you from any embarrassment."

Keeping a stern stare, Matthew replied, "I believe that is a wise decision, for I would otherwise be forced to reveal to everyone how you stole my pocket watch."

She gave him an indignant glare. "Surely, you would not shame me by making such an outrageous accusation!"

Matthew shook his head. "I could never hurt you, Julia."

When she took his hand in hers, he smiled. "You are a duke, a strong leader, and a man with a heart so pure I could never fathom you hurting anyone."

Desire rose in him, and before he could stop himself, he decided to grasp the nettle and lowered his head to kiss her.

"Mrs. Rutley is coming!" hissed the lady's maid.

With his heart pounding in his chest, Matthew took a step back, stumbling on a small rock. If it had not been for the outbuilding, he would have ended up on the ground and unable to explain how he got there.

Mrs. Rutley came into view and stopped to drop into a curtsy. "Your Grace, we are honored to have you here with us again."

"Mrs. Rutley," he said, bowing to hide his embarrassment. Was that a mischievous grin she wore? No, of course not. She could not have seen his attempt to kiss Julia. "I was just telling Miss Wallace that I must leave, but I'll be sending the two of you an invitation to dinner later in the week."

"Then we shall humbly await that invitation, Your Grace," the headmistress said.

Matthew glanced at Julia, wishing he could tell her that he did not truly want to leave. They had pushed their luck all too far as it was. Yet, the sparkle in her eye and her tiny nod told him she understood all he was thinking.

Bidding them a goodbye, he made his way to the front of the house and his waiting carriage as thoughts of the afternoon played in his head. He had sworn to keep her safe, more so away from this man her father wished to court her. If it were up to him, he would choose to court her forever. That way, he would never have to marry.

Once the thought came to mind, however, he could not stop but wonder what life would be like married to Miss Julia Wallace.

Chapter Twelve

Three days after Julia and Matthew had strolled through the gardens, Julia had told no one about their courtship, save Bridget, though she very much wanted to do so. Yet, it would do no good to have rumors erupt before Matthew was ready to make the announcement. When that would be Julia was uncertain, but she had to trust he would know when the right time came.

She glanced around the small room where a dozen girls sat with needle and thread, working on their embroidery. Mrs. Rutley walked behind each pupil, observing with a careful eye and stopping from time to time to make a suggestion or dole out a compliment. The girls were encouraged to talk to one another, as long as the conversation was deemed fruitful, a lesson Ruth was currently struggling to grasp.

"A lady does not converse with other ladies about the types of liquor her father keeps on hand," Mrs. Rutley said. "Do you not have a particular book to discuss? Or perhaps practice your French by discussing your favorite flower or a gown you noticed the last time you visited a dressmaker. After all, you are falling behind in your French studies."

"I'm sorry, Mrs. Rutley," Ruth said and then continued speaking to Louisa. Not in French and not about gowns. "Did you hear...?"

Julia smiled. She had to give Ruth credit. Mrs. Rutley did not say she could not gossip.

She looked down at the handkerchief with the initials "MB" in blue thread embroidered on it. Now to complete the edges, also in blue, so she could present it to Matthew as a gift. Yet, it was more than a gift. It was a piece of her heart. She may not believe in charms of luck, but Matthew did, and a handkerchief would be a far better replacement for a spoon in a gentleman's pocket.

"I spotted him on Saturday," Emma whispered beside Julia.

"Whom?"

"The baron, Andrew St. John," Emma said as if Julia should have known. "When we were in the village, he was exiting the Red Fox. You will never believe! He looked directly at me... and winked!"

"He did not!" Julia said, appalled at such forward behavior. "And you? How did you respond?"

"How could I respond?" Emma replied. "Do I admit outright that I found his boldness appealing?"

Julia dropped her needlework into her lap. Emma had spoken of the baron before, but never had she made any reference to an attraction to the man. Now it would be up to Julia to explain how wrong he was for her. After all, he had a less than sterling reputation, far less sterling than most.

"Gentleman simply don't act thus," Julia said in a harsh whisper. "Have you not heard the rumors about him? There is a reason he is referred to as the Baron of Rake Street. He is a rogue, Emma, so don't grin like a child receiving a gift when he does something so forward. After all your training, you should be repulsed by such behavior."

Three other girls had turned toward Julia before she realized she had raised her voice. Luckily, Mrs. Rutley was on the other side of the room talking to Unity, or she would have demanded to know their topic of discussion.

"I cannot help that I find him handsome," Emma said with a pout. She placed her embroidery hoop on her lap and looked up, a dreamy expression on her face. "To think that a man who spends his time playing games of chance and lives a life of adventure would wink at someone like me."

Julia clicked her tongue. "Such flights of fancy must be dismissed," she snapped. The onlookers nodded their agreement. "There is nothing wrong with finding him handsome, but you cannot entertain romantic notions with a man such as he, you simply cannot!"

Emma sighed and returned to her needlework. "Yes, you are right. I have no idea what has come over me, but since that day, I've thought of little else."

Returning to her handkerchief, Julia had to admit that she understood all too well how Emma felt. Her own thoughts had been scattered since Matthew mentioned courting, and although she knew the process would be slow, she had already begun considering their eventual wedding. How many guests would attend? Would he allow her to invite Emma? She saw no reason why she could not invite any number of her friends from the school.

Yet, the most important thing was the matter of her feelings for Matthew. Julia was uncertain what love was, or when it introduced itself to a lady, but whatever emotion she felt for him was strong. Being in his arms, or even in his presence, made her feel alive. Their conversations warmed her heart, and she looked forward to dining with him in the coming week.

As her fingers deftly worked the needle, her thoughts returned to their time in the garden once more. The commitment they had made to one another had been wonderful, but the way he had looked at her as they stood beside the outbuilding said he had wanted to kiss her. She would never admit it to anyone, even Bridget, but since that day, she had a strange desire to learn what it felt like to be kissed.

"Although he did not kiss me, it will happen, and it will be wonderful."

A chorus of giggles made Julia gasp in horror. "I was reciting poetry," she snapped at the others, wishing for a hole in which she could hide. "It's—"

"Ah, yes, a translation of a poem by Monsieur Fabian," Mrs. Rutley said, and the room fell quiet. "I'm impressed by your ability to make such a complicated translation, Julia." The headmistress winked at her, and she sighed with relief. This was not the first time Mrs. Rutley had saved her from embarrassment. She would have to thank the woman later.

A timid knock at the door had Mrs. Rutley meet a maid, who whispered something to the headmistress.

"Emma," Mrs. Rutley said.

"My parents have come!" Emma said with a smile. When Julia raised an eyebrow, Emma added, "Well, who else would call on me?"

"Lord St. John," Diana said in a whisper that carried, making the other girls laugh.

The door opened wider to reveal Mr. and Mrs. Hunter, Emma's parents, and an older gentleman who appeared to be her grandfather.

Julia returned her attention to her work only to find she had missed a stitch. She really had to keep her mind from wandering. With a sigh, she pulled out the stitches to the place she had made the error and resumed her work.

Fifteen minutes later, Mrs. Rutley returned, a look of worry on her face. "We will break early," she said. "Mrs. Gouldsmith will expect you in one hour, so don't be late."

A collective sigh of relief resounded around the room, and the girls quickly went about gathering their sewing.

Jenny joined Julia, her things piled on top of her sewing basket. "What do you think has happened?" she asked. "Mrs. Rutley did not look at all pleased."

"I have no doubt that Emma's father is here to berate Mrs. Rutley," Julia replied. "He seems to find it a favorite pastime. She is a strong woman, but a woman can only endure so much from a man such as him."

"You are both fools," Abigail Swanson said as if she had been a part of their conversation. "Mrs. Rutley pries into other people's business. It's about time someone told her off for it."

Julia clenched her jaw. "Mrs. Rutley is not a busybody. She cares about her students. Why would you say something so horrible?"

Abigail sniffed. "Father told me that she is well-known for prying into the affairs of others. It's why she never remarried. No potential suitors could bear her meddlesome ways. Therefore, she was forced to find other means to live, by opening this school."

"If your father believes Mrs. Rutley is such an unworthy tutor," Jenny said, "then why did he trust her enough to allow you to study here?"

Abigail's smile dropped, and her face reddened. "Emma is exactly like Mrs. Rutley," she spat. "They want nothing more than to be accepted by the upper class, yet they will always fail. As to my being here, that is my concern, not yours." She lifted her nose into the air and marched out of the room, pushing Theodosia out of her way in the process.

"Why is she so cruel?" Jenny asked. "We have been nothing but nice to her, and she never has a kind word to say to anyone."

"My guess is that her parents are unkind to her," Julia said. "Those who lash out in anger tend to be the most wounded."

Jenny frowned. "But there are many here who have parents who are unkind, and they don't treat others so horribly."

Julia smiled. "That may be true, but no two people respond in the same way. Just ignore her. Think of it as practice for when we must endure unpleasant people once we are married. You know there will be at least one woman who is as disagreeable as Abigail, if not more."

"Yes, that is a wonderful way to look at it," Jenny said.

They made their way to the gardens where the others were enjoying the unusually warm day. Julia listened as her friends spoke of what their futures would hold, and although she tried to listen, she could not help but think of what the future held for her and Matthew.

And what could possibly have caused Mrs. Rutley to look so distressed.

That evening after dinner, Julia returned to her room rather than join the others in either the library or the parlor as they were apt to do. The purpose of the school was to find the best in women, and unscheduled gatherings were encouraged to give the pupils opportunities to practice what they had been learning. Although she enjoyed spending time with her friends, she preferred to have some time to be alone with her thoughts. The last thing she needed was to reveal her secret to the entire school.

She had expected to receive today the invitation to dinner, but it had not come. Well, there still was time, so she would not concern herself. That did not stop a tickle of disappointment to gather in the back of her mind. As a duke, Matthew was decidedly busy, and Julia would simply have to remain patient, although that was proving to be difficult. Every time she allowed her dreams of marriage to take over her thoughts, a stab of worry would send them scattering.

The light creak of the door made her sit up. "Oh, Emma," she said, clutching her chest, "you startled me. I'm so glad you have returned. How was your outing? And what surprise did your father... Emma? What is wrong?"

"Nothing," her friend replied as she went straight to her wardrobe.

"Nothing?" Julia repeated, swinging her legs over the edge of her bed. "Don't try to hide those tears. You are like a sister to me. Now, out with it. There is nothing you cannot tell me."

"No, there are some things I cannot say," Emma said in a choked sob. "Please, I cannot discuss it."

Julia pursed her lips. Whatever this problem was, there was no doubt Emma's father was behind it. "I don't care what your father says. You are a beautiful young lady. And intelligent. Don't allow his words to hurt you so deeply."

Emma made no reply as she rummaged through the wardrobe. When she turned, she held a carpetbag in her hand. "It's time for me to say goodbye," she whispered. "Just know that I love you and will miss you terribly when I'm gone."

Panic coursed through Julia. "Your father wishes you to leave tonight? Surely, he would not have you travel after dark. The sun sets very soon." She forced Emma to look at her. "What are you not telling me?"

Emma dropped her gaze. "Please, if you are my friend, let me sneak away tonight. Don't try to stop me."

Julia frowned. "Sneak away? If your father is not taking you..." If the realization that came over her would have been a sudden gust of wind, she would likely have gone crashing to the floor. "You cannot run away from your problems, Emma."

"I have no choice. I'll write to you soon, but please, don't tell Mrs. Rutley, not until I've been able to get far enough away not to be found." She closed the carpetbag and kissed Julia on the cheek.

Julia stared at the now closed door. What should she do? On one hand, she could not betray Emma's trust by telling Mrs. Rutley that she had run away, but allowing Emma to travel alone was far too dangerous.

The door flew open, and Diana hurried into the room, Unity at her heels. "Oh, Julia, Emma is planning to run away!"

"I know," Julia replied with a heavy sigh. "And although I don't want to, we must inform Mrs. Rutley."

"We most definitely must," Diana said. Unity nodded her agreement.

Julia moved past the two girls and hurried down the corridor, Diana and Unity whispering behind her. A door opened, and Theodosia joined them. Then another. By the time they arrived at Mrs. Rutley's office, they were seven in number.

Knocking once and not waiting for a reply, Julia entered the room to find Mrs. Shepherd and Mrs. Rutley speaking.

"What is the meaning of this?" Mrs. Rutley asked.

"We are sorry to interrupt, but it's Emma," Julia said. "Something has upset her, so she is running away!"

Mrs. Rutley rose from her chair behind the desk. "Where is she now? Has she left already?"

"I don't believe so, but I don't know where she went once she left our room."

"Mrs. Shepherd, please mind the halls until I return."

"Yes, Mrs. Rutley," the cook said before hurrying out the door.

"The rest of you, follow me." The headmistress headed straight to the front door. The sun was still peeking over the horizon, but long shadows were collecting over the grounds. How would they ever find her before darkness set in?

"Should we break into smaller groups, Mrs. Rutley?" Julia asked. "We have no idea in which direction she headed."

"She will likely keep to the road," Mrs. Rutley said as she hurried down the portico steps without stopping.

"There she is!" Theodosia shouted.

Indeed, just passing the large oak tree was Emma Hunter, carpetbag hanging from one hand.

"Emma!" Mrs. Rutley called. "Emma, please wait!" She lifted her skirts and began to run, and all seven girls, including Julia, did the same.

Julia's heart panged when Emma turned to face them. Her lower lip was quivering, and her face glistened from still-falling tears. The girls gathered around their friend, forming a protective circle.

Taking Emma's hand, Julia said, "Now you must tell us, what is wrong?"

"I'm sure you saw the man with my parents today," Emma said, her voice hiccupping. "That was the surprise my father had for me. He is nearly sixty, and my father has given him my hand in marriage."

Several of the girls in the circle gasped, and Julia shook her head in disbelief. "When are you to be married?" she asked.

"Once my schooling is completed in January, father will collect me, and my mother and I'll begin the preparations for... my wedding." She dropped her carpet bag and sobbed into her hands. "And I'll do it all alone, for Father has said none of you, not you, Julia, or Diana, or any of my friends, may be in attendance. That is why I wish to run away. I'm so frightened!"

Julia pulled her friend into her arms and spoke soothing words. How could any parent want to see their daughter married to an old man? She searched her friends' faces, each wearing a pained expression.

Yet, when her eyes fell on Mrs. Rutley, she was surprised to find the woman smiling.

"Emma," the headmistress said as she ran her hand down Emma's hair, "January is far away, and many things can happen between now and then. But running away is a foolish act. Not only do you have nowhere to go, but you have friends here who care for you."

"We do," Unity said.

"I do, too," Ruth said. The others voiced their agreement.

"You see?" Mrs. Rutley said. "There is no reason to fear what has not yet taken place. Even I am here for you."

Emma wiped at her eyes. "Thank you," she said. "Thank you all. It does help to know that I have such wonderful friends. But what will happen once I'm married off and have no one to go to for advice or help?"

Julia worried her bottom lip. If only she had words of comfort, but none came to mind.

Yet, as so often before, Mrs. Rutley had the solution. "Come, girls," she said, leading Emma to the ancient tree. "I want you all to form a circle around this tree. Join hands, just like that."

A cool breeze flitted several of the girls' hair and the bottom hem of their dresses as the sky turned a bright pink.

"In all my years here, I've never met a group of girls quite like you. Each of you is special in her own way, and I feel that I don't misspeak when I say you are like sisters."

"That is a perfect description," Julia said as she glanced around the circle. "The bond we share is strong."

"I have three older sisters," Louisa said, "and I feel closer to everyone here than I do to them."

Diana laughed. "I would be an only child if it were not for my sisters here."

"All of you are part of a sisterhood," Mrs. Rutley continued. "But such a bond cannot be completed without a secret to share. Emma has already revealed hers. Each of you must now share one secret without fear of reprimand, even from me. Now, who will be the next brave soul?"

"I'll go next," Ruth said. "I fear my husband, whoever he may be, will think I'm far too wild and want to tame me. I'll need someone to whom I may write when the fear becomes too overwhelming."

Diana shared next. "My father has had numerous affairs and continues to do so," she said in a quiet voice. "I hate him with all my heart and soul for how much he hurts my mother with his roguish ways."

"My father," Unity said as she dabbed her eyes with a handkerchief, "uses his fists on my mother. I fear that one day he may take her life before anyone is able to stop him."

Each girl shared a secret from her heart. Whether it be about themselves or a family member, each secret was sacred, and Julia would never repeat a single one.

Julia was the last to share, and by that time, she was much more self-assured than if the others had not included theirs beforehand. How brave her sisters who spoke before her were!

At first, she considered telling them about Matthew, but after hearing what the others were enduring, she realized that her worries were far less terrible than theirs. Therefore, she said, "I worry about marriage and what my future holds, just as so many of you do. But my greatest fear is that I will not be there for you, Emma, when you are hurting as you were today. Or for you, Ruth, to see that you behave." The others giggled at this. "But what I fear most is that when some of us leave come January, our bond will break forever."

"My concern," Mrs. Rutley began to everyone's surprise, "is that I'll never see any of you again. Each of you holds a special place in my heart." She took a deep breath. "Now I'll confess a secret to you. I was once married, and like many of you have mentioned, he never loved me. Although I had a friend to whom I could turn, many ladies do not for fear of judgment. That is what makes our bond that much greater, for I believe we will never judge one another. By sharing our most sacred secrets, we have formed what I'll deem a Sisterhood of Secrets. Our next step is to make a pledge that will bring peace today to Emma and to every one of us in the future."

"What sort of pledge?" Louisa asked.

"That whether it be tomorrow or many years from now, if any one of us is hurting, if even one of us has a need, we must only ask for help from another member of our Sisterhood, or all if need be, and we shall answer that call." She looked at each girl, a stern expression on her face. "Before you agree, consider what I'm proposing, for your commitment will be great. No pledge should be made lightly and without thought. Will you be willing, years from now, to travel a great distance to help Emma if she makes the call? What if you have children who need you and Theodosia requests your aid?"

The group fell quiet. This was a serious commitment, indeed.

Finally, Julia said, "No matter what, if any of you request my aid, I will be there. That is my pledge to you."

"I also agree," Jenny said firmly. "I care not what life may bring, I will come."

"No matter where I am," Ruth said, "I will be there for you."

One by one, the remaining girls made their vow, and by the time it returned to Mrs. Rutley, her eyes were bright with unshed tears.

"You may always call on me for help," she said. "I'll do whatever I can to make your life better. I, too, pledge this—to answer your call if you so need."

Julia smiled and glanced at Emma. Gone was the anguish, replaced now with a smile. In fact, as each girl took her vow, the weight of what they had shared before lifted, and for that, Julia was thankful. Yet it was more than that, it was as if they were no longer the young girls who had arrived at the tree only moments ago. They had become women, many of whom would soon be married.

"Mrs. Rutley," Ruth said, "this old tree... I have an idea if you are willing to agree to it."

Julia stared wide-eyed as Ruth produced a small penny knife from her skirts. Why would a young lady wish to carry a weapon on her person? Because it was Ruth, of course.

"May we carve our initials into the trunk of the tree as a reminder of our pledge?" Ruth asked. "It can be our way of signing an agreement."

What Julia had expected was a refusal, but Mrs. Rutley smiled and replied, "I think that is a wonderful idea, Ruth."

Each young lady carved her initials into the soft exposed section that had once been a limb but had been trimmed away. Julia made certain hers were right next to those of Emma. It was a magical experience, made all that more special when Mrs. Rutley added her initials amidst theirs.

"Now," the headmistress said as she turned to face the others, "let us go to bed. Tomorrow is a new day of hope." Julia did not miss the fact that Mrs. Rutley had slid the knife into her pocket, but Ruth was wise enough not to ask that it be returned to her.

Julia slipped her arm through that of Emma, and Diana picked up the carpet bag. As she looked at each girl, Julia realized that they were no longer simply friends. They were now sisters willing to come running if called.

Chapter Thirteen

Although Matthew should have had his attention on Lord Templeton, he could not help but think of Julia. Just this morning, he had sent the invitation to dinner in two days' time and was eagerly awaiting her response.

Unfortunately, the last few days had been filled with one meeting after another. It was as if discussions of business would never end. Yet, Lord Templeton was the last gentleman on his schedule for the week, so Matthew forced his mind to return to the conversation at hand.

They were seated in the parlor, and Lord Templeton sipped brandy at odd times, sometimes even mid-sentence. Also in attendance was Matthew's uncle, Ezra, who sat in the chair to Matthew's right. The meeting was meant for coming to terms about an investment between Matthew and Lord Templeton, but Matthew did little of the talking. Yet that was not all that uncommon. His uncle tended to commandeer the majority of conversations, a fact to which Matthew had become accustomed.

"It is, therefore, the reason I must ask for the majority stake in this venture," Templeton was saying. "It's I who has seen to all the arrangements, just as it shall be I who will see to working out the smaller details."

"And His Grace welcomes your offer and agrees to the terms you have set forth," Uncle Ezra said. "I believe this will be beneficial to us both."

Matthew frowned in frustration, which was an odd reaction for him. Could he not speak for himself? Was he not the duke? "I can do this myself," he mumbled.

"My apologies, Your Grace," Templeton said, "but did you say something?"

Matthew had not realized he had spoken the thought aloud.

"I believe you may have heard our butler," Uncle Ezra said with a laugh. "He is losing his hearing and tends to speak much louder than necessary." He stood. "Would you like to refill your glass?"

"One more cannot hurt," Templeton replied and went to the sideboard.

Uncle Ezra leaned in, his breath hot on Matthew's ear. "Can you not control your outbursts?" he demanded. "Do you want this man to think you have already lost your mind?" Without waiting for a response, he joined their guest.

Blood pounded in Matthew's head. He was becoming like his father more and more every day, and that frightened him. Then a thought came to him. Had Julia not said that she, too, spoke her thoughts aloud from time to time? He had seen it for himself when she had called him handsome. From what he had heard, her father did not suffer with any form of madness, nor did any other member of her family. And Julia herself was far from suffering any form of mania or other illness of the mind.

She may not be here to bring him the luck he needed at this very moment, but her image would do just as well. Had she not said he was a confident man, one who would also be a great duke? That memory gave him the assurance he needed to take the next step.

Rising from his seat, his heart pounded in his chest as he approached the two older men. "Templeton," he said, pleased to hear not a flicker of uneasiness in his voice, "your offer is fair only to you."

"Matthew!" his uncle hissed, but Matthew ignored him.

"You seek the majority share but offer the minority investment."

"His Grace may have consumed too much brandy," his uncle whispered to their guest.

Matthew closed his eyes and focused on Julia's image once more. He was the Duke of Elmhurst!

"If we are to come to an agreement, I insist that we split sixty-forty, the sixty going to me and the forty to you. It's only fair. You say you will do the majority of the work, but that is untrue. Not only shall I be investing the larger sum, but I'll also have as much responsibility to see it carried to completion as you. If I choose to dole out the responsibilities to those on my payroll rather than seeing to things myself makes little difference. No, that is untrue. If I do that, it means I'm putting in far more than sixty percent of the investment. Either way, if you don't agree to these terms, I wish you all the best with securing other funding."

Matthew ignored the glare his uncle gave him as Lord Templeton took a sip of his brandy. After several moments, he said, "My offer was not meant to offend you, Your Grace. Like your father before you, you have a sharp business mind. I agree to your terms."

Matthew slowly released a lungful of air. It was now twice in as many weeks that he had come to a business agreement, and he had Julia to thank.

It was nearly an hour before Lord Templeton left Hardwick Hall, and Matthew walked the man to the door. As Hickson helped him with his coat, Lord Templeton said, "I'll have the appropriate documents sent over to you in three weeks. Good afternoon, gentlemen."

As soon as the door closed, Uncle Ezra rounded on Matthew. "What you did was risky," he snapped. "We need that man's business to expand our fortune. I would suggest you not do such a foolish thing again!"

When his uncle turned to leave, Matthew caught him by the arm. "Why is it that when I act like the duke you say I should be, it frustrates you? Julia believes I'm already a great duke, yet someone who shares my blood does not. It makes no sense whatsoever."

A sneer formed on his uncle's lips. "So, you are now taking advice from a silly girl in training rather than from your family? What would she know about business or about being a duke? Her father is nothing more than a baron, and a newly titled baron at that! You would be better to keep away from her. Do what you must to purchase the land from Mrs. Rutley and then put both women behind you."

Matthew would not use this moment to reveal his offer of courtship. "Why do you have such hatred for those women?"

His uncle waved a dismissive hand and walked away, leaving Matthew to follow him back to the parlor.

Yet, Matthew wanted answers. "Why do you not approve of Julia? Has she said or done something to offend you?" When his uncle refused to respond, he added, "Well, she and Mrs. Rutley will be my guests for dinner Saturday evening. I do hope you show her the respect she deserves, for I value her friendship."

His uncle walked over to pour himself a measure of brandy. "Miss Wallace will one day become a fine lady. Anyone can see that she is wise, but she is not good enough for you."

"Uncle—"

"Please, allow me to finish and I'll never speak another word against her. As your father's death drew closer, he oftentimes had sudden moments of clarity. Do you remember?"

Matthew nodded. "I do. They were brief, but they brought Mother a bit of relief, even if the time was short."

"Exactly. It was during one of those rare moments that I pledged to watch over you, to see you become the duke your father dreamed of becoming. If I'm to be honest, it has become my dream, as well. Your friendship with Miss Wallace..." He paused and sighed heavily. "I have my reasons for disapproving, so I'll say no more on the matter and honor your request."

"Thank you, Uncle."

"I do make one request of my own," his uncle said as he came to stand before Matthew. "In six weeks, we'll conduct a series of meetings here that will determine the future of the dukedom. Imagine the vast amounts of land we'll purchase! The hotels, tea shops, and taverns built around them, which will also be ours! A person will not travel without seeing what we have done." Then his uncle smiled. "I have yet to speak of any trade of wool or farms we'll acquire. The desperate peasants will be throwing themselves at our mercy, begging for the chance to work for us. This will be the last chance to restore the family name to its previous glory. I ask that you make a pledge to me that from now until then, you will do everything I ask to see the Colburn name raised once more. Allow me to pass to you the knowledge your father was unable to give you, due to his circumstances."

What his uncle asked was reasonable. No, it was honorable. But Matthew had requirements of his own. "I must be informed of every decision along the way. I am not a spectator, Uncle. After all, we are discussing my estate."

"Yes. Yes, of course," his uncle said with a wave of his hand.

Feeling confident, Matthew added, "And once these contracts are completed, you will leave all the necessary decisions pertaining to the dukedom to me? Without question?"

As he was wont do to, his uncle rolled his eyes. "I do hate repeating myself, but yes."

"Then you have my word as a Colburn that until then, I'll work with you as I've done thus far and listen to your instruction."

Uncle Ezra clasped Matthew on the shoulder. "Thank you." He walked toward the door but then paused. "I wish you would have told me about our guests for Saturday. I had already extended an invitation to another, but one extra space at the table for friends will not be a bother, will it?"

"Did you invite Lord Templeton?" Matthew asked.

"No," his uncle replied. "Lady Dyer."

The idea of having the baroness at the same table as Julia was not appealing. "Perhaps we can arrange another dinner with Lady Dyer," Matthew suggested.

His uncle raised an eyebrow. "Would uninviting her not be rude? Is there something about Lady Dyer you detest?"

"No, of course not. I think well enough of her. I had simply thought..." Matthew could not think of a valid excuse that would appease his uncle.

"This does not pertain to Miss Wallace, does it? Could it be that she is intimidated to be in the presence of a woman far better than she? Or is it you feel something for the baroness and don't wish to share your table with another woman?"

With the influx of questions, most of which Matthew did not care to answer, his ire grew. He could have challenged his uncle, but instead, he paused. If he and his uncle were to go to war with words, let it be a worthy battle. Not an argument over which guests to have at dinner.

"I've considered your request," he replied. "I see no reason Lady Dyer cannot join us."

When his uncle left the room, Matthew began pacing. He and the baroness were on friendly terms, but he did not want Julia to believe they were closer than they were. Was he making too much of a simple dinner?

Yet, even as he thought this, he wondered why his uncle felt the need to invite the baroness to dinner to begin with.

As he was apt to do, Matthew walked into the ballroom to gaze upon the portrait of his father. Yet, he frowned upon seeing the place bare where the portrait typically hung.

"Hickson!" he shouted.

The butler shuffled into the room. "Your Grace?"

"Hickson, where is Father's portrait?"

"In the attic, Your Grace," Hickson replied. "Lord Ezra requested I remove it there yesterday."

Matthew clenched his fists at his side. "Is this not my home?"

The butler nodded. "Of course, Your Grace."

"Then why would you do as my uncle requests? And without conferring with me first?"

"Because for now," his uncle's voice boomed through the large room, "I'm helping you, Nephew." His uncle was not alone, however. Beside him walked Lady Dyer, the skirts of her red dress flowing around her ankles. Although Matthew did expect the baroness for dinner, he had hoped Julia would arrive first to allow him the opportunity to explain the other woman's presence.

"Your Grace," Lady Dyer said, dropping into a well-practiced curtsy. "I'm honored to once again be a guest at your table. I don't have the words to thank you enough for your kind invitation."

Matthew stifled a frown. Was she under the impression that the invitation had come from him? "You are most welcome. There is no better way than to spend an evening breaking bread with friends." His eyes shifted to the tall clock. Julia would be arriving at any moment. "Perhaps we should—"

"Come along, Hickson," his uncle said. "The baroness wishes to speak to His Grace in private, and they have no need for two old men hovering over them."

"Hickson," Matthew called, not taking his eyes off his uncle, "tomorrow you will return the painting to where it belongs."

"Yes, Your Grace," the butler said with a diffident bow.

Lady Dyer leaned in and whispered, "Your uncle is very funny. It must be a joy to have him so near, a great person from whom to receive counsel."

"He has been a great support," Matthew replied truthfully. "Did you have a request? My uncle mentioned you wished to speak to me about something."

The baroness nodded. "Last week at your party, I spoke to a gentleman..." Her words trailed off, and a blush spread across her cheeks. "Forgive me, I should say no more." Her gaze had dropped to the floor, and she appeared distressed.

"Did this man offend you in some way?" Matthew asked. She shook her head. "Then what is it you find so difficult to tell me?"

Lady Dyer sighed. "The same man I saw at your party, the one who mocked you? I saw him again in town. He was speaking to two others, and I heard your name mentioned."

A chill ran down Matthew's spine. "People will talk, my lady," he said. "We must learn to ignore what they have to say."

"That may be true, Your Grace," she said slowly, "but they said you were mad. Needless to say, I may have done something that will make you think poorly of me. I would be quite distressed if you no longer wished to be my friend."

Matthew stared in utter confusion, but before he could form a question, she continued.

"My grandfather also suffered from a form of madness," she said, "and to hear them mock you as they were, I admit I lost my temper. I gave them the sharp edge of my tongue, for no one speaks of my friends as they did." She wiped at her eye. "I was told that I embarrassed myself, and that no one would be willing to invite me to any gathering given by the *ton,* but I could not help myself. What they were saying was far worse than what I said, and I could not allow them to bring you more shame, Your Grace."

Blood pounded in Matthew's head. A widow had come to his defense, and these men believed they could ruin her name? The idea was preposterous. "Do you know who these men were?" he asked.

"I do not, Your Grace."

"Well, I'll learn their names," Matthew said. "But for what you did for me, I thank you. And I assure you, your name remains in good standing as far as I'm concerned. I'll ascertain others see it as I do."

She gave him a wide-eyed stare. "You would do this for me? A widow whose name is steeped in gossip?"

"I do it for a friend," Matthew said. What she had done was honorable and being treated so terribly for defending him was appalling.

"Oh, thank you!" she said, throwing her arms around him. "Truly I'm fortunate to call you my friend."

The embrace was awkward, but Matthew patted her back all the same. What else could he do?

When he released her, however, his heart nearly exploded when he saw Julia and Mrs. Rutley standing in the doorway, his uncle behind them. Would they see that the embrace was done in innocence?

"Miss Wallace," he said as he walked over to them. "And Mrs. Rutley. You remember my friend, Lady Frances Dyer?"

Julia held her head high, but the pain behind her eyes was unmistakable. "I do." She curtsied. "It's good to see you again, my lady."

"I've never been more pleased to have such honored guests in my home," Matthew said. "In fact, there are no others I would rather have around me."

When he caught Julia smiling, Matthew let out a sigh of relief. Their courtship was not public knowledge, so why was he explaining himself?

"Your home is lovely, Your Grace," Mrs. Rutley said. "Has the ballroom recently been redecorated?"

"My mother had it redone six years ago." He paused. How had the woman known?

"Dinner will be served shortly," his uncle said. "Come, let us take our seats."

The dining room glowed from the setting sun, but several candles lit the table settings. Matthew sat at the head of the table, his uncle beside Lady Dyer to Matthew's left, and Julia beside Mrs. Rutley to his right.

Once everyone was seated, a footman poured the wine. "Please, tell me about your week, my friends. Mine was filled with business matters, and I would hate to bore you by speaking of it." This brought about polite laughter. "Miss Wallace?"

"My week was filled with studies in poetry and philosophy, two subjects I enjoy immensely."

Matthew smiled. With her hair pulled up and set with a simple comb in the shape of a butterfly, the word beautiful did her no justice. He could have stared at her all night, but he forced himself to look away.

"Mrs. Rutley," Lady Dyer said, "I've heard wonderful things about your school. I hear it's highly esteemed."

"I appreciate you saying so," the headmistress said. "But it's the students who make it great. I'm merely there to guide them through what they already have inside them."

"May I ask how you came to purchase such a fine estate?"

Matthew wondered at the strange question, but the door opened, and a line of footmen entered, carrying trays laden with the first course.

"I'm curious as well," Uncle Ezra said as a footman set a bowl of soup in front of him. "Tell us, Mrs. Rutley, how does a woman of the gentry afford such a luxurious home?"

Mrs. Rutley smiled. "It's quite a long story. I would hate to monopolize the conversation by telling it. Would you not agree, Your Grace?"

"We can wait to hear it another time if you prefer," Matthew said.

Taking his spoon, he dipped it into the pea soup and brought it to his lips. Again, he lowered the spoon but made the mistake of glancing at Julia. She was watching him, and for reasons he did not understand, his head became light. His spoon promptly fell from his fingers and clattered into the bowl, splattering soup onto his face and the front of his coat. He grabbed a serviette and dabbed at the splatter, issuing apologies all the while.

When he glanced at Julia again, she turned away and coughed, but not before he caught her stifling a laugh.

Soon, the bowls were removed and the next course arrived. The aroma of succulent lamb in wine sauce and roasted potatoes filled the room as his uncle led the conversation.

"I have no doubt that Matthew will become the greatest duke the Colburns have ever known, but there is still much work to be done. Sadly, his father left a blemish as an heirloom, but we are seeking to restore the dukedom to the glory it once portrayed. Although Matthew has inherited many of the good traits of his forefathers, he also has taken on some of his father's habits, a curse if you will."

Matthew set his fork on his plate, his appetite now gone. "Enough!"

Julia, however, did not seem convinced by his uncle's verdict. "If that curse is one that shows a man who is noble, intelligent, and one that others look up to, then I say he should allow it to remain, for I see nothing wrong with His Grace."

Uncle Ezra snorted. "That opinion reflects your naivety, Miss Wallace. You have no idea the pain the Colburn name has been forced to suffer, nor the circumstances around that suffering."

Julia went to speak, but Matthew lifted a finger to stop her. Any argument made would only leave a bad taste in everyone's mouth, and that was the last thing he wanted. He would have full control over what was discussed at the dinner table soon enough.

"And do you agree with your uncle's suggestion, Your Grace?" Lady Dyer asked.

Matthew had not realized that the plates had already been removed without him even noticing.

"His mind is apt to wander," his uncle said with a light chuckle. "I suggested a stroll through the gardens while I show Mrs. Rutley the library. What say you?"

"I think it's a wonderful idea," Matthew replied. He glanced at Julia and added, "I think we would like that."

"Excellent!" his uncle said. "Miss Wallace, will you grant an old lord a request?"

"Of course, my lord."

"Would you be so kind as to accompany Lady Dyer and His Grace on their stroll?"

Matthew closed his eyes. His uncle could not have said anything worse. How was he to convince Julia that he and Lady Dyer were simply friends after such a request?

"Yes, of course, my lord," Julia replied in a tight voice, her eyes fixed on Matthew. "If that is what you would like."

"No, I believe the three of us can enjoy this stroll together," Matthew said. He was pleased to see a smile erupt on Julia's face. "In fact, I think it best."

Chapter Fourteen

"The first phase of redecorating will begin next spring," Lord Ezra said as Agnes walked beside him down the corridor. "Our plan is to renovate every room within the house as well as the gardens without. Hardwick Hall will be far different, more contemporary than it is today."

"The cost will be substantial," Agnes said as they stopped before the door to the library. "I imagine your coffers have filled quite well over the past few years to cover such an expenditure." How often had she told her pupils to *never* inquire into another's financial situation?

Lord Ezra smiled as he opened the door but made no response. When they entered the room, he closed the door behind them. Agnes had to force her smile to remain in place.

The library was a great room with shelves that touched both floor and ceiling, holding well over two thousand tomes. "This is an impressive collection," Agnes said. "I would guess it's among the finest outside of London. Besides those of Oxford and Cambridge, of course. Am I correct in saying so?"

The man's smirk said the pretense of niceties had come to an end. Agnes was surprised it had lasted as long as it had. "We are not here to discuss this room, now, are we?"

Agnes placed her most innocent expression on her face and asked, "What do you wish to discuss, then, my lord?"

"My lord?" Lord Ezra said with a laugh. He narrowed his eyes. "Whatever games you are playing, Agnes, they will stop this instant!"

He was no more than an arm's length away, close enough to harm her if he chose, and his breath came in short gasps, but Agnes made no move to back away from his harsh tone. She refused to allow him to bully her again. "There are no games, Ezra."

Like a snake striking, Ezra grabbed hold of her arms, pushed her against the door, and held her there. "I'm not a fool, you silly woman!" he spat. "Do you think I don't see what is happening between my nephew and that girl? Your pupil? It will stop now before it becomes too late! Do you hear me? Now!"

Doing her best to appear unruffled, Agnes looked first at one of his hands and then the other. "You will remove your hands from me, now, Ezra." He did not do as she bade. It was her turn to narrow her eyes at him. "Release me or explain why you need a doctor."

Ezra lowered his gaze to where she had the penny knife she had procured from Ruth pointed at a place just below his ribs.

"You forget the life I lived before I became a lady. Now, what choice will you make? Bleed or not bleed?"

Letting out a harsh snort, he released her. "Yes, you are right. There is no need for violence."

"It's how you have led your life," Agnes said, the knife disappearing into her pocket. "You have not changed one bit in all these years." The thought saddened her.

He shot her a scowl. "You know nothing about me," he said, walking to one of the bookshelves. "Things have changed since we last knew one another."

"Yet, many things have remained the same," she said, joining him. "You still seek to control everything around you, working endlessly to repair the world while still ignoring the flaws you have." She placed a comforting hand on his arm. This man still had good inside him, even if he could not see it. "Your anger is not with the boy, nor with Julia, but rather with yourself."

Ezra pulled back from her as if her touch singed his skin. "The anger you caused, Agnes," he said. His laugh held not a drop of mirth. "I was a happy man until I met you, and you doubled that happiness. And what do you do? You crush me beneath your slipper and make me look like an imbecile!"

Agnes recognized the rage behind his eyes, for it was just as she remembered. Reason rarely did any good when he was in this mood, but she had things she needed to say. "You never loved me, Ezra. You were merely enchanted by the idea of me. You tried to control my life, just as you are trying to control the life of your nephew now. That is what drove me away. If you are not careful, the games you play will drive away your nephew, as well."

"What do you want from me?" he demanded. "His father embarrassed us all with his outrageous behavior! The name of Colburn was held in great esteem until my brother brought it to ruin. Now I have a chance to see it restored, and I'll not have my plans ruined by my nephew becoming enamored by a pupil from your school. There are far better ladies with more prestigious titles than she who are better suited for Matthew."

As his eyes raked over her, Agnes recalled their brief romance. When it had ended, it had caused him a great deal of pain. He had blamed her for his shortcomings and had sworn that day so long ago to never love again. Apparently, he still kept that vow.

"Will you have your nephew become like you, unhappy and suffering?" Agnes asked as she walked over to one of the bookcases and touched the spine of one of the books. "He will only marry for reasons you decide. Yes, I'm aware you never married, Ezra, but that is not my point. You want nothing more than the *ton* to praise his name, for the aristocracy to gather in this home and shout, 'The duke has restored the name of Colburn!' Yet, the young man will suffer daily despite that praise." She turned to look at him. "Is that what you want?"

"If it restores the family's honor, then yes," Ezra seethed. "You act as if you have done no wrong, but I know about the man you married."

For a moment, she could not hide the worry that gripped her throat.

Ezra smiled upon seeing her reaction to his words. "Yes, I've long suspected what became of him, the very man into whose arms you ran after leaving me. The man you married soon after. The very same man who, less than a year later, died under the most unusual circumstances." He laughed, a grating sound that pebbled her skin. "And I know much about the woman with the sordid past who may have contributed to his death." He took a step forward, and Agnes pressed her back against the bookcase of her own accord. "Don't think that I'll do nothing to see you ruined, for I will if I must."

Agnes squared her shoulders and lifted her chin. "I have no doubt that you will seek to harm me," she said. "After all, if you care nothing for your own nephew, why would you care for a widow such as me? Do what you must, Ezra, but hear me now. If you do try to harm me, I shall assure you of one thing."

"And what is that? If you mean to threaten me, then say it."

The man for whom she had once cared was now cloaked in hate. "I make no threats," she said. "But I can assure you that the peace you wish will never return. Acting out in anger only makes matters worse, not better." She walked past him and to the door before turning and adding, "I'm well aware that my words mean nothing to you, but the man for whom I once cared was a kind man, and I believe he still resides within you. You would do well to search him out, Ezra, for he is the only one who can save you from the dire future you are making for yourself and your family."

Ezra barked a laugh. "That man, like your husband, is long dead, and like your former beau, he will never be seen again."

Agnes shook her head and left the room. When the door closed behind her, she sighed. Memories of the past attempted to escape from the recesses of her mind, but she pushed them back. They could be considered another day.

The sudden sound of breaking glass followed by cursing made her shake her head. No, Ezra would never change. And that was regretful.

The path that snaked through the gardens was just wide enough for two people to walk together, and doubt coursed through Julia as she followed behind Matthew and Lady Dyer. Playing the chaperone for the man for whom she cared and another woman was not what she had expected Lord Ezra to suggest.

She should have known that the evening would be less than ideal when she witnessed Matthew embracing the baroness in the ballroom. Yet, even as the doubt plagued her at that time, Matthew's smile had erased it away. If he were truly interested in Lady Dyer in a romantic way, why would his smile be so warm?

Her uneasiness returned, however, during dinner. How could Lord Ezra treat his nephew with such disregard? His words had been biting, and with each scathing comment, Matthew's face had become a deeper shade of red and his knuckles whiter as he tightened the grip on his fork. So often, he spoke of his uncle in such high regard, yet she had come to know Matthew far too well to be duped. There was something to their relationship that was off, although she could not place what that something was.

None of that compared to the irritation she felt now. Julia was no fool, but Lord Ezra implied as much with his request. He may as well have come right out and said, "You are not good enough for my nephew, girl! He is already spoken for."

Why had Matthew not set his uncle straight? And why the secrecy about their courtship? Though Julia respected his decision not to make a formal announcement, he could have at least told his uncle. Perhaps he was waiting to discuss the matter with her father. Yes, that had to be his reasoning.

With a face burning with embarrassment, she followed the couple past a large hedge, neatly trimmed. The smell of upturned soil permeated the air as a leaf floated from a bough above them to the ground.

"Your gardens are so lovely, Your Grace," Lady Dyer lamented.

"Thank you," Matthew replied. "My mother often walked here for hours enjoying the peace provided."

"She sounds like a lovely woman," Lady Dyer said. "It's a shame I'll be unable to meet such a fine lady."

Julia abhorred the feeling of being left out of the conversation. "Your mother was a very wise woman," she said.

The couple stopped and turned to face her, and she swallowed visibly. Who was she to be a rival to a lady who had already endured her debut and had learned how to handle men? Well, that simply meant Julia would have to work harder to prove she was a viable rival.

"I'm surprised that so many leaves still hold strong," Julia continued, "refusing to fall although the weather has become cooler."

Lady Dyer shivered. "Miss Wallace makes a good point. The air is chilly." She rubbed her bare arms. "Why did I not think to bring an appropriate wrap?"

Matthew, being the gentleman he was, removed his coat and placed it over the shoulders of the baroness. "That should keep away the cold."

"Thank you, Your Grace," Lady Dyer said, a blush splashing her cheeks.

Oh, why did she have to be so lovely?

"It does help." She turned and started when she saw Julia, as if she had not realized she was still standing there. "How rude of me. I should have allowed His Grace to offer you the coat first. Would you like it?" She began to pull the coat from her shoulders.

"I can go inside and retrieve a wrap for you if you would like," Matthew offered.

"There is no need," Julia said. "I'm quite warm. Shall we continue?" At least he had offered.

The sound of hurried footsteps made them all turn to find Lord Ezra joining them. "I believe your duties as chaperone have been fulfilled, Miss Wallace," he said with a wide smile. "Mrs. Rutley wishes to leave, but I can now take your place as chaperone from here. And thank you for coming to dinner. It was a pleasure to have you with us."

Julia glanced at Matthew, willing him to speak, to reveal to everyone that *they* were a couple, not he and Lady Dyer.

Mrs. Rutley joined them. "Thank you for a lovely evening, Your Grace," she said as she dropped into a curtsy. "I'm afraid the hours have slipped by, and we must return to the school."

"Allow me to see you out," Matthew said. He had yet to take his eyes off Julia. "If you would like, that is."

"I very much would," Julia replied.

"I'll join you," Lady Dyer said.

Julia's head was aching, as was her heart. She felt like a child among adults as she simply gave a nod.

To make matters worse, Lady Dyer said, "I remember when I was young, and the hour of ten was quite late." She gave a small laugh. "Oh, to be young again, with my lessons my only worries."

Julia forced a smile. "One day, like you, I'll have the luxury of attending parties and accepting invitations to dinner without thought for how late I remain. Until then, I must adhere to propriety."

The baroness's smile faltered, and Julia felt a sense of victory as they entered the foyer. Granted, her response was childish, but not any more so than the attempts made by Lady Dyer to needle her.

"I'll send word to arrange another time to call, Miss Wallace," Matthew said as he placed Julia's wrap on her shoulders.

Julia looked from Matthew to Lady Dyer and back again. "If you have time, Your Grace. But I'm the least of your concerns at the moment." She gave Mrs. Rutley a nod to indicate she was ready to leave, and they walked out to the waiting carriage Matthew had provided them.

Soon, they were seated and Julia looked out the window. Lady Dyer waved farewell.

As if she were the lady of the house, Julia thought wryly.

"If he wishes to indulge himself with her," Julia thought, "I can do nothing to stop him." Much too late, she realized she had said the words aloud. Blast her tongue!

Mrs. Rutley placed a hand on Julia's arm as the carriage lurched forward. "Your feelings for the duke have grown, have they not?"

Julia nodded.

"Do you believe you are in love?"

"I'm uncertain," Julia whispered as she twisted her skirts in her hands. "I find myself thinking of him often, and when I'm not with him, I feel... incomplete, somehow." She turned to face her headmistress. "The pledge we made at the tree, our sisterhood?"

"Yes? What of it?"

"The secrets we shared with one another… would I face reprimand if I shared another with you?"

Mrs. Rutley chuckled. "You must know that I'll never share any secrets you tell me. My role as your headmistress and your guardian is to keep you safe. If what you wish to share may harm you in some way, I urge you to tell me."

Julia swallowed hard. "Matthew… that is, His Grace asked to court me, and I accepted. I believed it was a beautiful gesture on his part, but now I see Lady Dyer in his company. Why would he make the request and not tell his uncle the truth?"

"Have you told Emma?" Mrs. Rutley asked. "Or your parents for that matter?"

"Not at all! Emma may be my closest friend, but I cannot share the news just yet. I promised not to reveal it to anyone. And as for my parents, they… they have found another man to court me and likely to marry me. It's best if I keep that secret…" Her words trailed off as the realization hit her. "Matthew has his own reasons. I understand that now."

"His Grace has a great burden to bear in pleasing his uncle."

Julia frowned. "I know it's wrong to say this, but I don't like Lord Ezra. He is a cruel man, and I don't trust his motives."

What she had expected was a stern reprimand, but instead Mrs. Rutley simply nodded.

"What do I do, concerning Lady Dyer?" Julia asked. "What if Matthew comes to realize that she is a better match for him than I?"

The carriage slowed to turn down the lane that led to the school, and Mrs. Rutley squeezed Julia's arm. "Was the task I gave you to fend off other women? Or even to get the duke to court you?"

"No, Mrs. Rutley," Julia replied despondently. "I was to bring him luck and to keep him happy, so you can sell him some of the land."

"And have you brought him the luck he sought?"

Julia nodded. "He says I have."

The carriage stopped, and the door opened. "Then I say you continue doing what you are meant to do. That should be your only concern."

Frowning, Julia replied, "Very well." As she alighted from the carriage, however, a sudden burst of rebellion coursed through her. "But Mrs. Rutley, luck does not truly exist. How am I to provide what is make believe?"

"You may not believe in luck, but he does." Mrs. Rutley placed a hand on the side of Julia's face. "He has enough belief for the two of you. Trust in that."

Chapter Fifteen

Guilt, frustration, and doubt warred inside Matthew as he sipped at his brandy in the parlor. Since Julia had left, he found he could not take his mind off her. So many questions swirled, such as, why had he not gone after her when she had made her departure? At the very least, the woman who championed his abilities deserved an explanation.

What was his uncle thinking, asking Julia to chaperone? Did he not realize it had been an outright insult?

Finally, what sort of game was Lady Dyer playing? Not once since making her acquaintance had the woman been overtly coquettish, but Matthew could not shake the feeling that her motives were suspect. Yet, what proof did he have? None.

The door opened, and the woman in question entered the room. "I've never seen a man so consumed with business as your uncle," she said as she closed the door behind her. "He can talk for hours if he wishes to do so. Luckily, he remembered a task he must complete, which allowed me to escape."

Her light laugh was like a chorus of bells, but Matthew kept a careful eye on her as she approached him. If she began showing signs of familiarity, he would put a stop to it immediately.

That was unfair. Not once had she been inappropriate in his presence. So why did he feel the need to protect himself?

"My apologies, Your Grace," she said, flushing. "I was only teasing about your uncle. I do like him."

Matthew had not realized he was frowning. "No apologies needed. He may be my uncle, but I, too, can find his choices for topics of discussion boring at times."

Lady Dyer laughed again, her hand falling to his arm, causing him to step back. She pulled her hand away with a gasp. "I'm sorry, Your Grace. I did not mean to touch you!"

Matthew pursed his lips. "Why does my uncle want you here?" he demanded. "I find it odd that you appear at the most inopportune times." His words were sharp and direct, but he had to learn the truth. There was more at play here than simple coincidence, he was sure of it.

The baroness took a step back and lifted her chin. "I may as well be truthful," she said. "My late husband's estate has yet to find a new heir. Averill was an only child, and as far as anyone knows, he has no other living male relatives. The solicitors have searched but have come up empty-handed. As you know, I made very few friends before his death, so few of the *ton* have accepted me. Yet, your uncle took pity on me and suggested it would be good for me to leave Crestview House, even for a short time." Her gaze fell, and she added in a quiet voice, "It was never my intention to be a bother, Your Grace."

"Then, you don't have some sort of romantic interest in me?" Matthew asked in surprise.

"I should say not!" the baroness said. Then she laughed. "I find our newfound friendship welcoming, Your Grace, but I would never expect anything more. You must understand..." Her voice trailed off, and she shook her head. "It does not matter. I should go. The hour is late."

Curiosity overtook him. "Lady Dyer, wait. What must I understand?"

She shook her head. "My words may upset you, Your Grace."

"Be that as it may, please, tell me."

Sighing, Lady Dyer replied, "As you wish. I have no intention of becoming romantically involved with anyone if I can. A marriage of convenience is an old tradition that should be abolished, for if two people are to spend the rest of their lives together, they should care for one another—deeply care. Though I'm pleased to be your friend, I can never offer you more than friendship. I hope my words have not angered you, but I would rather be truthful than to lead you to believe a lie."

Matthew closed his eyes and let out a small, relieved sigh. His worries had been unfounded! When he opened his eyes once more, Lady Dyer was biting at her lower lip. "I had thought... well, that does not matter, now, does it? We are friends, and I agree that it's all we are likely ever to be. To be honest, I would prefer never to marry, for I've seen how marriages can end. I could never hurt anyone as I've seen others hurt."

Including Julia, he amended silently.

The baroness smiled. "That is why you are a great duke, Your Grace. You consider others before yourself. I've had several men call on me, even asking me to marry them, but I've refused every one of them. I would rather remain alone than to hurt a man I do not love."

This was a unique woman to have the same views on marriage as Matthew. He had few people, men and women alike, that he would consider true friends, but Lady Dyer was most certainly one of them. "If we are as good of friends as we profess, I say we use our Christian names when we are alone. Julia... that is, Miss Wallace and I do the same." He clamped his mouth shut. Why had he felt the need to reveal that?

"I can see the bond you share is great... Matthew," Frances said, smiling. "It's truly a beautiful friendship. However, I would caution you with one piece of advice if I may. A woman's sensibilities can be quite fragile, so be careful that you do not hurt her."

"I will not," Matthew said. "Thank you, Frances, for your wise counsel. Would you like a glass of wine?"

"No, thank you," she replied. "I must speak to your uncle once more before I leave." Matthew frowned, and she chuckled. "With all his talking, I was unable to ask the question I had wanted to ask when I requested to speak to him."

"Ah, I understand. I'll walk you to his office, as I was planning to take some air in the gardens, anyway."

Uncle Ezra was indeed hunched over his desk, and Matthew left Frances to speak to him.

The air had cooled considerably as Matthew descended the stairs that led to the gardens. The sun was nearly gone, the horizon painted with deep pinks and oranges, and he drew in a deep breath. Tonight had not been perfect, and much of that was his fault. Yet, with his suspicion of Lady Dyer now gone, it was time he resolved other issues, mainly those between him and his uncle. He, Matthew, was the duke, and it was about time he started acting like it. Uncle Ezra meant well, but Matthew was far too old to be treated like a child.

That conversation would have to wait, however. For right now, he wished to think about Julia and how beautiful she looked in her dress. She was everything a lady should be and more. The way she spoke, the luck she carried, everything about her was wonderful.

"I do care for her," he whispered. "But is doing so dangerous?" He could not imagine burdening her with the madness that awaited him.

His heart and mind battled, striking blows that caused his emotions to swing first one way and then the other. He looked out over the horizon, toward where he knew Courtly Manor lay, wondering what Julia was doing at that very moment and wishing he knew what she was thinking.

What began as confiding her worries with Bridget and Emma that evening became a room full of young women, the same young women who had sworn their oath just days before to come when one of the others called. Granted, Julia had not called, but when they heard of Julia's distress, they came running all the same.

Julia looked at each of her friends sitting in a circle on the floor. "There is one other secret that I'll share with you." She gave them all a stern glare. "Remember our vow to keep our sisters' secrets, now. This is very important. Do you still promise to keep that vow?"

"Of course we do," Louisa said. "Now, tell us!"

Julia laughed. Louisa had to know everything about everyone, but she kept that knowledge to herself. For the most part. Yet Julia knew that once the girl promised, she kept her word. "Matthew asked to court me, and I accepted."

Squeals of congratulations erupted in the room, and it took Julia several moments to calm the others enough to continue.

"This is why the predicament with Lady Dyer is all the more frustrating. I'm sorry I did not tell you sooner, but I had a promise to keep. Or I believed I did."

"You have no reason to apologize, Miss Julia," Bridget said, smiling. "Now, I'll retire for the night and leave you girls to talk. Unless you need something else?"

"Go on, Bridget," Julia replied. "And thank you."

There was no need to ask the maid to remain because she would only refuse. No matter how many times Julia attempted to bring her into their group, Bridget would say, "I'm a servant, Miss Julia. We may be friends, but I know my place."

The others wished Bridget a good night, and she left the room. The moment the door closed, the questions began pouring in.

"Do you think she is his mistress?" Unity asked.

"Or a former lover he refused?" Theodosia exclaimed.

Jenny nodded adamantly. "He is a duke, after all." Her cheeks reddened. "Well, it's true! My sister told me that it's not uncommon for a duke to have multiple lovers at his beck and call. Some even live in their home! Have you seen him pay particular attention to any of the servant girls by chance?"

Julia stared horrified at Jenny, but then Ruth began to laugh so loudly, everyone turned to look at her. In her hand was a silver flask, not an uncommon sight when they were all together, although few accepted her offer to share in whatever she drank.

"Jenny," Ruth said, still laughing, "was it not your sister who also asked Mrs. Shepherd if one could become drunk when eating a syllabub?" She shook her head as the others burst out in riotous laughter. "Just because it's made with white wine does not mean it will give you the same results as drinking a glass of white wine. Now, if I were you, I would not listen to a single word Jenny—or her sister—says. I, however, have seen this very same situation before with one of my sisters."

"Don't believe any of her tales," Emma whispered in warning. "A lady who drinks from a flask is not to be trusted."

Ruth frowned. "Emma, you whisper louder than Unity snores."

Emma's cheeks turned crimson, as did Unity's. "I'm sorry," Emma said. "I had not meant to be hurtful, but I considered you may be drunk, and people who have consumed too much drink tend to give ill advice."

Rather than taking offense—Ruth rarely did—she waved a dismissive hand. "We are all sisters now, so we are supposed to poke fun as much as warn one another. But I assure you, it will take far more than this"—she lifted the flask—"to make me drunk. As I was saying, my sister, Isabella, caught the eye of a baron, although every other woman vied for his attention. Let me tell you, men brag of their exploits on the battlefield but that does not compare to two women fighting over the same man!"

"Surely you don't mean bouts of fisticuffs?" Julia asked with a grimace. "I have no training in boxing, or any other form of combat, nor would I want it. Ladies simply don't engage in such sport."

"Of course, I don't mean you should learn to fight," Ruth said with an air of exasperation. "I'm simply saying that you must express to the duke exactly what you feel for him. I assume you care for him, but have you yet shared that bit of knowledge with him?"

It was Julia's turn to blush. "We have admitted that we care for one another as friends. Now, granted, I do care for him a bit more than simple friendship, but I've not yet used... that word, for I'm unsure if my admiration is that strong."

"She speaks of love," Louisa said with a proud smile. "That is what she means."

Ruth rolled her eyes. "Yes, we all know what she means," she said dryly. "This is not a complicated matter, Julia. The next time you are with the duke, you must tell him that you care for him as more than a friend."

Julia frowned. "And what of Lady Dyer?"

"Once the duke hears your confession, he will fall in love with you, just as the baron did my sister, and he will forget about that red-headed hussy!"

This had most of the others falling over with laughter. Leave it to Ruth to speak so bluntly!

"However," Ruth added, "once you have told him how you feel, there is one more thing you must do."

"What?" Julia asked.

"The next time he requests to call on you, refuse him. Tell him you are not available. Let the man suffer and worry."

"I don't know," Julia said, knitting her brows. "Would it not be better to accept rather than play games?" The more she considered it, the more she did not approve. "No, I'm a lady now and shall conduct myself as one."

Ruth heaved a heavy sigh. "I don't think it wise, but I respect your decision. Now that we have sorted that out, which of you would like a sip?"

Julia, Emma, Jenny, and Diana refused, but the others partook. Unity sniffed at the flask before taking a sip and choking on the harsh liquid.

"What is this?" she asked between gasps.

"Rum!" Ruth said, grinning from ear to ear.

Unity scowled. "That is the foulest thing I've ever consumed in my life! How can pirates stand it?"

Julia closed her eyes. If Mrs. Rutley or Mrs. Shepherd were to find them there consuming alcohol, there was no telling what sort of punishment would be doled out, even to those not drinking.

As the girls broke off into smaller groups, Julia stood and walked to the window. Although she was unable to see Matthew's house from here, she could not help but wonder what he was doing at this moment. Was what Ruth said true? Should Julia ignore him the next time he called?

An arm settled around her shoulders. "Don't worry," Emma said. "You are a beautiful young lady, and His Grace smiles at you and no one else, I'm sure of it."

Julia leaned her head on Emma's shoulder. "Thank you. I do feel better after sharing with everyone. Matthew and Lady Dyer may be friends, but he cares for me, and that is what matters most."

She did not include that Matthew also had not expressed having deeper feelings for her, but she had no doubt that he cared more for her than simple friends. If only he was here to hold her, to let her know that all was well between them. Although she could not see him, she believed that he was, at this very moment, thinking the same.

Chapter Sixteen

At least three times a year, Mrs. Rutley arranged for select pupils to call at the home of a titled family, to allow the girls to learn the inner workings of a larger household. Few of the students who attended the school came from homes with more than three servants, and therefore they had little experience interacting with a housekeeper and butler who had other staff beneath them. Finding such ladies willing to lend their expertise would have been difficult if the headmistress was not acquainted with so many families of all walks of life.

Julia stood in the grand foyer of Egerton Estates, home of the Coombs family of landed gentry. Mrs. Amelia Coombs wore a welcoming smile as she paced in front of the girls, the skirts of her blue dress swishing around her ankles.

"Ladies," Mrs. Coombs said in a voice that carried around the room, "I'm so pleased to have you as my guests this morning. Mrs. Rutley informed me that you will soon be completing your training and, thus, will be off in search of a husband. It's my hope that I'll be able to further the wonderful instruction you have received at the school by introducing the practicality of running a household. Are there any questions before we begin?"

Abigail Swanson raised a hand, and Mrs. Coombs called on her. "My father has arranged for me to marry a marquess. After all, marrying any lesser man is fruitless. Surely, I don't need this instruction, for I'll have an abundance of servants to accommodate my station. Will the running of the house not fall to one of the upper servants, so I'll not have to fuss over it myself?"

Julia stared at Abigail in disbelief. The girl's vanity and her overall outlook on life always gave Julia pause. Did she not see that her words were outright rude? After all, Mrs. Coombs was not titled, yet she was willing to share her expertise with those who did not have what she had.

Mrs. Coombs did not seem annoyed in the least. "Your staff will do your bidding, for they will be in your employ as much as they are in the employ of your husband. Do you believe there will never be a time when you must instruct them on your wishes? If you prefer lamb for dinner, or you would like a fire built, despite the day being warm, how will your servants know this if you don't request it? You also must know how to approach your servants, for good help is difficult to keep. If you mistreat those in your employ, they may leave you to find work elsewhere, leaving your housekeeper or butler—or perhaps even you, if you are not careful—to not only hire but also train the person taking his or her place. The interim time can be quite inconvenient, I assure you."

Julia took an instant liking to Mrs. Coombs. She was pleasant in her speech, but her words were also direct and to the point.

Abigail pursed her lips. "I suppose so, but I find conversing with those beneath my station makes me feel... dirty." She gave a dramatic shiver. "I feel as if I've fallen in the mud."

Mrs. Rutley stepped forward. "I suggest we save our questions for after the lesson. I'm sure Mrs. Coombs has much to teach us, and we would not want to miss out on any of her wise instruction."

"Please, follow me," Mrs. Coombs said. "We will first go to the kitchen." Not once did her smile drop. If it had been Julia in her place at that moment, she was unsure how she would have responded to Abigail's rudeness.

"Don't be worrying about the porridge," an aproned woman was saying to two younger girls, likely scullery maids if Julia were to hazard a guess, "it tends to stick to the pan a bit."

Several of the pupils giggled, but a sharp glance from Mrs. Rutley quieted them.

"Mrs. Drake," Mrs. Coombs said, "these are the young ladies I mentioned to you earlier."

The cook's cheeks turned a deep crimson upon seeing she had an audience. "It's a pleasure to meet you," she said, bobbing a quick curtsy. The scullery maids followed with curtsies of their own before the cook shooed them away.

Mrs. Coombs turned to face the pupils. "Now, ladies, pay close attention to how I address Mrs. Drake. Quite often, I'll confer with my housekeeper about meals and such, but if she is out, or if I must make a change to the menu, I'll oftentimes come directly to the source." She turned to face the cook and added, "I'll have two guests joining us for dinner this evening, Mrs. Drake, but they will be arriving at seven rather than at our usual six o'clock dinner hour. I know we planned to have a simple meal tonight, but I believe we should have something a bit more appropriate. I suggest tomorrow's dinner for tonight. Will you be able to get the pork chops on such short notice?"

"Aye, Mistress, I can," the cook replied. "And what about adding a soup course, too? I've a new recipe for a wonderful tomato soup."

"A most excellent suggestion," Mrs. Coombs replied. "Please, add it." She then turned to the pupils. "Notice that I have no need to shout instructions or belittle the servants to get what I want. It's as I said before, if you treat your staff with respect, you should see great results. Is that not right, Mrs. Drake?"

Mrs. Drake gave an emphatic nod. "Most definitely so, Mistress. I've been employed by all sorts, but after working for Mrs. Coombs, I doubt I'll ever have to look for new employment. As long as I don't send up burnt food." She chuckled at this, and several of the pupils joined her, as did Mrs. Coombs.

Julia made mental notes as she observed. The exchange should have been standard behavior, but she had heard how cruel some employers could be. She did not wish to be known as one of them.

When they were finished in the kitchen, they observed as Mrs.

Coombs spoke to the butler about the wine that would be served with dinner, followed by a pair of maids instructed on readying the parlor for her guests.

"Now normally, I would speak to Mrs. Pragman, my housekeeper, and she would instruct the maids, but I intentionally sent the housekeeper into town today for the sole purpose of this demonstration."

"This is all so fascinating," Julia whispered to Ruth as they made their way to the drawing room. "We have only a maid of all work, so my mother only has to instruct her. I cannot imagine having so many staff!"

Ruth snorted. "Your dream may be to employ a house full of servants, but my life will be far different. I plan to board a ship and travel to all sorts of distant lands. Who needs servants for that style of life?"

Julia frowned. Ruth always insisted on doing the exact opposite of what society dictated. If she had her way, she would be working as a sailor on one of those ships! Mrs. Rutley would collapse in shock if she were to hear of the plans Ruth had.

The drawing room was decorated in a tasteful blue and white. One set of couches and chairs was covered in blue-and-white striped fabric and another set in white with blue flowers. Dark blue drapes flanked great windows that looked over an opulent garden.

Julia sat between Ruth and Jenny on one of the couches as Mrs. Coombs spoke with Mrs. Rutley. When they were done, Mrs. Coombs turned to address the girls. "I'm having tea brought up, so I'll give you some time to chat amongst yourselves."

Thoughts of one day running her own home played in Julia's mind, but the home she envisioned was Hardwick Hall. It would be her responsibility to make certain everything ran smoothly, all to make Matthew's days easier. At night, they would dine together, sharing what they accomplished during the day. Once dinner ended, they would go to the parlor, or the drawing room for coffee, or perhaps go for a stroll through the gardens.

The best part would be that as a married couple, they would be allowed to engage in a kiss without fear of chastisement. And although they had yet to share in such an intimate moment, she knew the day would come when they would.

"It has been nearly a week since you last saw the duke," Ruth whispered, breaking Julia from her thoughts. "Why is that?"

"He is a duke," Julia replied. "His days are filled with important appointments. Romance cannot be a priority." Ruth raised an eyebrow, and Julia added, "I did receive a letter from him yesterday, explaining that he has been very busy, but he wishes to call on Sunday."

Ruth frowned. "Sunday? But that is still four days away. What if that other woman takes the opportunity to catch his eye by going to him while you wait for him to come to you?"

"Ruth is correct," Jenny said, inserting herself into the conversation. Not an uncommon act, that. "You certainly don't want to wait too long and risk losing him to her."

Julia had managed to put thoughts of Lady Dyer out of her mind, but now they had returned. As did the former worries she had been able to keep at bay.

"As I said," Julia said, "he has written to me, expressing his sorrow for being unable to call. If he is interested in Lady Dyer, why would he take the time to write to me?"

Jenny, who was always one to quickly have a change of mind, nodded in agreement. Ruth, however, shook her head. "You cannot leave it at that," she said.

"What do you expect me to do?" Julia demanded. "Send word that Sunday is unacceptable, and I wish to see him sooner? Do you not think that is a bit forward?"

"That is what I would do," Ruth replied. "Tell the man that you must meet with him. If he comes, you will know that he only has eyes for you. If not, the other woman has him already under her spell. At least you will know the truth, which is far better than living with your head in the clouds." What was meant as sarcasm, Ruth had taken literally. It was so like her.

"I'm content with waiting for the right time," Julia said, though that was not the complete truth. She missed being in the company of Matthew, and if he were here, she would tell him as much. She touched the pocket of her dress where she kept the handkerchief she had yet to give him. "It does not matter. One simply does not demand the presence of a duke whenever she wishes."

Ruth stuck out her chin. "Then I'll do it. I'll speak to him myself and tell him that you require his immediate attendance."

The servants arrived with the tea service, and Julia sighed. "Do whatever you wish," she said. Anything to get her to drop the subject. As much as she adored Ruth, sometimes the girl could be more foolish than anyone could imagine. No matter how much Julia argued, no matter what evidence she produced, nothing she said could make Ruth change her mind once it was made. If anything, Ruth would become all the more mulish.

As the girls sipped at their tea, Mrs. Coombs gave final instructions, this time around entertaining guests.

"Now, I realize you have received extensive training on how to entertain, so I'll not spend a great deal of time on the subject, but..."

As Mrs. Coombs spoke, Julia imagined hosting a tea once she and Matthew married. Then a brilliant thought came to mind. She would invite the Sisterhood over for tea in five years from today, so each member could share how their lives had gone after leaving the school.

"I'm a duchess," she would say. *"But you are my friends, and you are always welcome in my home."*

All eyes turned to her, and she stifled a groan. Once again, her mouth had voiced her thoughts! Abigail shook her head in disgust.

Yet, as so many times before, Mrs. Rutley came to Julia's rescue. "Julia is right in saying that we must welcome all guests in our home, regardless of title, as friends. Politeness will get us far in this world."

Julia gave the headmistress a grateful smile.

As they readied themselves to leave, each girl thanked Mrs. Coombs for opening her home to them before heading outside. When it came to Julia's turn, she said, "Thank you, Mrs. Coombs, for inviting me into your home. I've learned so much from you today, and I look forward to using all you have taught me in the future."

"You are most welcome, Miss Wallace," the woman replied. Then she lowered her voice and added, "Mrs. Rutley has told me much about you. I must agree with her that you will do well as the mistress of the house one day."

Julia could not help but grin before following the others to the carriages. As she climbed into one, she sighed. One day she would be a duchess, for she wanted to marry no one but Matthew. Not so she could gain the title but rather because she could not imagine being married to anyone else.

Chapter Seventeen

"Miss Larina Oswald is young and beautiful," Henry, Lord Bannerman said to Uncle Ezra. The old earl claimed to be five and sixty, but Matthew suspected he was far older. "She will be a prize for any man who claims her hand in marriage. Her father has the sense to select her suitors carefully, but if a duke were to call, the others would be tossed out on their ear." He chuckled at this. "Only a prince could outdo a duke, after all."

Matthew offered a polite smile to the man whose hints were as obvious as the rather large nose on his face. For years, Matthew had heard the whispers of his mother's friends bragging about their daughters, all in hopes that Matthew will bend an ear. Yet, Julia was the closest he would ever come to considering marriage, though he had not said as much to his uncle and certainly not to Lord Bannerman.

As the earl and his uncle continued to discuss Matthew's future as if he were not there, Matthew allowed his thoughts to wander to Julia. It had been six long days since he had last seen her, and it seemed that Sunday was still far away, even if it were merely four days. He had considered calling this afternoon, but to arrive unannounced would only embarrass her.

"I say that for now," Uncle Ezra was saying, "we concentrate on this estate you are hoping to sell."

Indeed, Lord Bannerman wished to sell a large estate near Cambridge, for according to him, "his old bones can no longer handle traveling so far." The idea of a home in Cambridge pleased Matthew, but when he had asked why the earl's son would not inherit it, the old man had snorted. "Because he will only let it rot if I left it to him."

"Yes, I believe His Grace will agree to the terms you have set forth," Uncle Ezra said. Matthew frowned. Once again, his uncle felt the need to speak for him. Yet, before he could respond, his uncle quickly added, "And as to your granddaughter, he will be happy to call on her, but beyond that, there are no guarantees it will go any further."

"I had not expected any," Lord Bannerman said with a chuckle. "I find the terms of our agreement quite favorable."

Of course you find them favorable, Matthew thought. He got exactly what he had requested. Furthermore, Matthew had no interest whatsoever on calling on this man's daughter. Julia was the woman who brought him the luck he needed to be successful. Just thinking of her gave him the courage to speak.

"I'm so pleased," Uncle Ezra said with a wide smile. "Now—"

"Although I agree that what you are asking for your Cambridge estate is quite reasonable," Matthew said, not caring that he had interrupted his uncle, "I must believe we can come to better terms. I'll offer you one hundred pounds less and don't tell me that the property is worth more. Furthermore, I'll decline the offer to call on your granddaughter. I mean no disrespect to her, nor to you, but that is my final word on the subject."

The earl frowned. "I only request that you call on her once, Your Grace. If you show an interest in her, other suitors will follow."

"Bannerman is right," his uncle said. "There is no harm, and the young lady lives not thirty minutes away from here."

Matthew began to nod in agreement out of habit, but then Julia's voice entered his mind. *You are a great duke, one worthy of respect.*

Smiling at the thought, he stood. "I believe you are a man of integrity, and I have no doubt that you have your granddaughter's best interests at heart. However, I'll not argue or give excuses for my refusal. You may sell me the estate or not, but either way, you and I'll remain on friendly terms. In saying that, I also ask that you, in turn, respect and not take offense to any decisions I make."

The room fell silent for several moments, and then Lord Bannerman slapped his knee and barked a laugh. "You are so like your father! He was always firm in every decision he made and refused to budge no matter how hard I pushed. He was admired by everyone for that very reason."

Matthew was taken aback upon hearing such words of admiration about his father. How wonderful it was to know that he was much more respected than Matthew had realized!

Then his uncle's words tore his gladness to shreds. "Oh yes, my brother was once a stubborn man who was decisive in everything he did. Sadly, it was the later years that created the embarrassment we seek to replace."

Lord Bannerman stood, his wrinkled hands struggling with the buttons on his coat. "The previous duke, God rest his soul, was never an embarrassment in my eyes," he said. He then turned to Matthew. "I agree to your terms concerning both my Cambridge estate and my granddaughter. You are a shrewd businessman, Your Grace. I hope I did not offend you with my attempts to bargain."

"Not at all," Matthew replied. "The best businessmen make every attempt to make as much profit as they can. That is how success is measured, is it not?"

"I could not agree more," the earl said. "And I'll have the proper documents sent over within the next month." He put out his hand, and Matthew shook it. "So like your father," the earl said with a chuckle.

Matthew glanced at his uncle, whose face was stony. "Allow me to walk you out," he said. Once outside, Matthew glanced behind them to make certain they were alone. "You knew my father well, did you not?" he asked the earl.

"Very well, Your Grace," Lord Bannerman replied. "His death saddened me greatly, for though we often spent a great deal of time haggling over business, he was also a friend."

"When my father became ill, did you find it difficult to work with him? I know rumors circulated amongst the *ton*, but I'm finding myself unable to untangle myself from his legacy."

The earl rubbed the bridge of his nose and sighed. "I must be honest. At first, I thought your father was merely indulging far too much in his brandy. He did enjoy his brandy, that man. Yet, I came to realize that his issues did not stem from overindulgence but rather from a sickness of the mind. That is nothing about which to be embarrassed, for illness can inflict any of us. In fact, I advised your mother while a friend of hers sought out a proper physician to see if he could be cured of what ailed him."

"I was not aware of that," Matthew said. "Thank you. It's a relief to know that my mother found comfort from friends during those terrible times."

The old man turned away and coughed. Taking out a handkerchief, he wiped his mouth. "The *ton* will always ridicule its own. It has always been, and will likely remain thus, until the end of time. As I've advised my granddaughter, if you live your life for others, you will find yourself in misery." He clasped Matthew on the shoulder. "Let them share in their gossip, Your Grace, for they will never change. You, on the other hand, just keep making your father proud, and you will always see success."

A sense of pride washed over Matthew, and he smiled. "Thank you. Your granddaughter is a fortunate young lady to have your wise counsel."

Matthew considered the earl's kind words as he watched the man step into the carriage. Although being a duke and earning the respect of his peers was important, surely that did not mean he should have to bend to every beck and call to do so. It was a relief to hear that his father was not the embarrassment he had thought. If the earl believed this, surely others did as well. In fact, the more he considered it, the only rumors he had heard came from Uncle Ezra and a handful of his closest friends.

A seed of doubt sprouted in Matthew's mind. Why had his uncle made the rumors seem worse than they were? The man did fret over every point of contention no matter the size, so perhaps he had done the same with this.

Feeling renewed, Matthew found he wanted to tell Julia about his newfound sentiment on life. Yet, he would have to wait until Sunday, no matter how much he hoped to call on her earlier.

Movement caught his eye as a man he had never seen before walked up the lane. He was a commoner, made clear by his patched trousers and wide-eyed look as he approached Matthew.

"Y-your Grace?" he asked with a deep, unpracticed bow.

"Yes, and who are you?"

"I'm Jeffrey, Your Grace. Jeffrey Simmons, the cobbler's son. I was told to deliver you a letter."

Matthew frowned. Why would the cobbler wish to send him a letter? He had not been there for many months and had long ago paid his account in full. Taking the letter, he unfolded it and began to read.

Your Grace,

I am a friend of Miss Julia Wallace, and I am writing this letter on her behalf. Your tendency to ignore her for the baroness Lady Dyer is causing Julia a great deal of heartache. So much so, that I fear she may never recover.

Therefore, if you care anything for Julia, and value her as a friend, I request that you meet with her at the outbuilding in the back of the gardens of Courtly Manor when the clock strikes ten. The messenger before you is unaware of the contents of this letter but has been instructed to await your response of either yes or no, which he will return to me.

It was unsigned.

Matthew sighed. He wanted more than anything to meet with Julia, but trespassing on the grounds of the school was not a very noble act. What if they were caught?

Yet, if Julia was indeed in pain as the letter indicated, he was willing to take the risk. An image of him grasping Julia's hand and jumping across the brook came to mind. It had been a simple act, but it also had brought about such wonderful feelings. Was this no different?

"Tell the author of this letter that my answer is yes."

Chapter Eighteen

Dinner that evening at Mrs. Rutley's School for Young Women consisted of braised beef, bread, and a portion of potatoes with a thick gravy Julia typically would have found delightful. Despite how wonderful the food was, however, and with the weekend on the horizon, her thoughts would not deviate from Matthew. He was to arrive on Sunday, and she would finally be able to present him with the gift she had made for him, a symbol of her growing affection. It was not an extravagant item—it contained no gems or gold—but she had labored over it for several hours, all to please him.

She giggled. Perhaps she should drop it on the ground for him to collect for her! No, that was silly. Young ladies did not drop handkerchiefs to capture a man's heart; only girls played those games.

Once dinner was completed, Julia followed Louisa from the dining room. Mrs. Rutley, who had not been present at the table, stood in the foyer dressed to go out. This was strange, for the headmistress rarely left the grounds at such a late hour unless she had important business to which she had to attend.

Yet, what the headmistress wore did not speak of a business appointment. She wore a silver-threaded white gown better suited for the Royal Court, and her hair was piled upon her head in an intricate coiffure. Never had Julia seen her look so lovely! One would have thought a woman dressed so regally would also have donned a smile, yet Mrs. Rutley wore a mask of worry.

Julia and Louisa approached the headmistress. "Dinner this evening was quite lovely, Mrs. Rutley," Julia said, smiling. "It had to be the best meal Mrs. Shepherd has prepared since I first arrived." *This* was what her training had her saying? How would discussing dinner get her the answers she so wanted?

"Do make sure you tell her," Mrs. Rutley said as she pulled a glove over her hand. "I have matters I must attend to this evening, so I shall speak with you tomorrow."

Julia nodded and helped with the door. She was surprised to find an ominous black carriage waiting and stifled a shiver.

"Now, who is hiding behind those heavy curtains?" she mumbled under her breath as Mrs. Rutley stepped into the vehicle.

Mrs. Shepherd came up behind Julia, giving her a right start, and said, "Now, don't go nosing into Mrs. Rutley's business, Miss Julia. You girls have enough to worry about without tacking on what isn't your concern."

"Does Mrs. Rutley have a romantic interest, Miss Shepherd?" Louisa asked.

Julia nudged her friend. Leave it to Louisa to ask such a question.

"What?" Louisa asked with a glare. "I've heard rumors that she recently has been seen in the company of a gentleman."

Mrs. Shepherd gave the girl a stern look. "There're also rumors about a cook with such a terrible temper, girls have gone missing from the school where she works because they couldn't keep their mind on their business. Now, what were you saying?"

Louisa paled. "Nothing, Mrs. Shepherd."

"That's what I thought," the cook replied with a firm nod.

Julia could not help but grin as she took Louisa by the hand and led her to the staircase. "You cannot ask such questions about Mrs. Rutley, Louisa!" she said. "What has come over you?" She pursed her lips. What had come over her, Julia, for asking such a question of one of the nosiest people she knew?

"I'm simply curious, is all," Louisa replied. "Although, I must admit it would be lovely if Mrs. Rutley met a kind gentleman. Does she not deserve someone wonderful?"

"I agree," Julia said, "but we must remember that we are ladies, and ladies don't speculate nor ask their cook such intimate questions about the headmistress. After all, we may never be seen again!" This had them doubling over with laughter as they ascended the stairs.

Louisa entered her room, and Julia continued on to hers. As she passed the room belonging to Ruth and Diana, she heard harsh whispers coming from inside. Nothing good ever came from harsh whispers in the bedchambers of a young ladies' school.

"Ruth!" Julia gasped as she entered the room to find four girls sitting in a circle—dicing! "What are you doing? This must be one of the most unladylike activities a woman can be caught doing!"

"We are only playing for fun," Ruth said. Then she grinned at the others. "And a few coins."

"I would have thought you of all people would know better, Diana," Julia snapped. Diana lowered her head in shame. Oh, she most definitely knew better! "Theodosia and Unity at least have an excuse, for they are younger, but you, Ruth, are already seventeen and you are eighteen, Diana. You are both far too old to be making such imprudent decisions!"

The true problem was Ruth. Never had there been a girl more stubborn. If Julia ordered her to stop, Ruth would likely take the dice back out the moment Julia left the room and resume the game. Unless Julia could convince her otherwise. After all, Ruth had a good heart and cared for others, despite her propensity to get into a great deal of trouble.

"Ruth," Julia said in her most beseeching tone, "the others respect and admire you so very much that they are willing to break all the rules if you ask them. However, I know you care what happens to them. Do you wish to have the *ton* gossiping about Diana, that she was once caught dicing? And what of Unity and Theodosia? They don't need something like this threatening their future, now, do they?"

Ruth heaved a sigh. "Julia is right," she said, gathering the dice and returning them to the cloth bag she held. "The game is over. We should not be doing such things, not if we wish to become ladies." She pointed a finger at each girl. "Therefore, if I catch any of you playing games of chance, in any form, mind you, you will be forced to deal with my wrath!"

Julia smiled. Ruth was not so difficult to manage, even as stubborn as she was, as long as one appealed to her heart.

When she reached her room, Bridget was waiting. "I heard what you told Miss Ruth. You make a wonderful leader. All the young ladies listen to you."

"I don't feel like a leader," Julia said as she dropped onto the edge of her bed. "But I suppose one does not choose such a role as much as she is presented with it."

"You see?" Bridget said with a wide grin. "That's why you lead. You're brilliant! Now, would you like me to help you change for dinner or would you prefer to rest first?"

"I suppose we can begin now," Julia replied. "I wanted to discuss what I should wear when Matthew calls on Sunday."

"I would not worry about Sunday."

Julia's heart jumped into her throat, and she turned to find Ruth standing in the doorway. "And why is that?" she asked.

Ruth closed the door and grinned. "Because he will be in the garden at ten tonight."

"Whatever do you mean?" Julia demanded. "Matthew is not due to call until Sunday."

"No, he will be here when the clock strikes ten," Ruth said as she ran a finger along the coverlet of the bed. "At least, that was the time I told him to come."

Julia could only gape in horror. "You did what?" she said, choking on every word.

"Don't look so surprised. I told you I would contact him, and you even gave me permission to do so. Do you not remember?"

With a frown, Julia did remember. What had been meant to placate her friend while at the home of Mrs. Coombs had been taken seriously. Drat the girl!

"Therefore," Ruth continued, "I sent him a letter explaining that you were suffering from a terrible ache in your heart, and if he cared anything for you, he would come. If he does not, then you will know for certain that he has no intention of courting you, nor has he ever."

"Please tell me you are joking!" Julia said. "I cannot meet him at such a late hour! Mrs. Rutley will never allow it."

"But Mrs. Rutley is away for the evening and not due to return until well past midnight."

Julia frowned. "And how do you know that?"

Ruth shrugged and replied, "I make it my business to know where Mrs. Rutley is at all times. Why do you think I rarely get caught when I am... well, doing whatever it is I should not be doing?" Her grin was as mischievous as ever.

Julia's mind was whirling. Not only would she have to sneak out of the house—a feat she did only once since arriving and vowed never to do again—but what if the others learned of this transgression? She did not want to set a bad example.

Yet if she did not, Matthew would take her absence as an insult and may never speak to her again. She wanted to both strangle and hug Ruth for this.

She turned to Bridget. "I wish you had not heard, for now you are in the most uncomfortable position of being an accomplice to this outrageous misdeed."

Bridget frowned. "You know I can't allow you to do this, Miss Julia. I'd certainly lose my position, not to mention how angry your father's going to be when he hears of it. I don't think I could bear it."

Julia nodded. "I cannot ask you to take the risk. If you wish to leave now, you may. I can dress myself." She shot Ruth a glare. "Or you will help me dress. After all, this is your fault."

Ruth dropped onto the edge of the bed, rolling her eyes. "You worry too much. Mrs. Rutley will not even be here, and I shall order the others to remain in their rooms until you leave."

"And if they ask why?"

Ruth shrugged. "I shall come up with an excuse they will believe."

"And what if Mrs. Shepherd catches me?" Julia asked. "You know how she roams the corridors at night. Her ears are as keen as a fox's. If she were to catch me, everyone within ten miles will hear her shouting."

"All will be well," Ruth said with certainty. She glanced at the window. "Though, you should decide soon. The hour grows late, and you still are not dressed for the occasion."

Julia looked from Bridget to Ruth and back to Bridget again. "I cannot lie. Doing this is goes against all I've been taught, but I have so much I must tell Matthew. Plus, I need assurances from him. I worry enough that I may lose him, but if I don't meet him tonight, losing him may as well be guaranteed. That will not bode well for me." She took a steadying breath. "You are not only my lady's maid but also my chaperone. What I ask is much, but I shall do what I can to keep secret that you knew about any of this. Your opinion matters much to me, and I would feel far better if you saw your way to give me your consent."

The room fell deathly quiet, and Julia began to lose hope. She had every right to make her own choices without receiving permission from Bridget, but she also trusted the woman's opinion.

"If I agree," Bridget said after what seemed an eternity, "I expect you to follow several rules."

"Of course," Julia said.

"First, you will remain on the grounds."

Julia nodded. "I'll not leave the gardens."

"Second, you are not to go alone. Don't give me that look, Miss Julia. I'll follow you, just as I'm supposed to as your chaperone. I refuse to allow you to be alone with any man, even if he is a duke."

Julia laughed. "I see no problem with you being nearby. I don't plan to spend my time in his arms."

"You'd be surprised how many ladies end up in a gentleman's arms when they hadn't planned to," Bridget said. "Now, for the final rule. You're taking a great risk by meeting a man in the gardens after dark, so you must promise me that you'll make the most of it. Tell him exactly how you feel. Don't hide it any longer."

"I swear to you that I will."

"Then, let's get you dressed," Bridget said as she walked over to the wardrobe. "If anyone happens to find their way to the gardens, I'll tell them I'm there for fresh air. If you hear me say this, know that I'm sending you a warning."

Julia embraced her friend. "Thank you. No matter what happens, you will always be with me."

"I shall tell the others that you said they should be abed," Ruth said as she walked to the door. "Good luck!"

Moments after Ruth left, Emma entered the room. Keeping from her friend what she was doing would be impossible. Therefore, she explained her plan and received a promise that Emma would tell no one as long as Julia told her everything upon her return to the room.

Time flew, and it was not long before Bridget stepped back from Julia and said, "You look lovely." She had chosen for Julia a gown of deep blue muslin with white lace on the neckline and sleeves. A sapphire pendant hung from a blue ribbon around her neck, and matching sapphires dangled from her ears.

The door opened, and Ruth entered, a smile splitting her face in two. "It's time."

Chapter Nineteen

Ruth had promised to distract Mrs. Shepherd as Julia and Bridget hurried through the corridors of the house and out to the gardens at five minutes before ten.

"Oh, Bridget, is it not lovely?" Julia whispered, stopping to look above them. "What a magical night it will be!"

The sun had long set, and the sky glowed with a waxing crescent moon and more stars than Julia had ever seen. If not for the light given by these heavenly objects, they would have had to bring a lantern with them, leaving them vulnerable to be seen by anyone looking out a window. Now however, they could run along the shadows unseen.

"Indeed," Bridget replied as she adjusted the wrap on Julia's shoulders. "Come now, let's find your duke."

Fear clutched at Julia's heart. What if they were caught? Well, it was too late to worry about that now.

As they neared the outbuilding, however, a voice made both women freeze.

"Bridget, is that you?"

"It's Mrs. Shepherd!" Julia whispered. "How did she know you would be here? It's over before it even started! My life is ruined!"

"Hide! Quickly, now. I'll send her away somehow."

With a nod, Julia glanced around for a place to take cover. The outbuilding offered plenty of protection, but she feared what creatures crawled within it. The nearest tree would do little good, for it was far too young and thin to hide behind. Then her eyes fell on a pile of timber alongside the outbuilding. Perhaps she could climb it and hide atop the building. Mrs. Shepherd would not think to look up there, would she?

"Julia," she whispered to herself, "you are worse than Ruth!"

Praying nothing would attempt to crawl beneath her skirts, she clambered up the timber, pulled herself to the roof, and flattened herself on her stomach just as Mrs. Shepherd and Bridget came into view.

"I'm just glad it was you out here," Mrs. Shepherd said. "When Miss Ruth comes to chat me up, it's usually because one of the girls is up to some sort of mischief."

Bridget laughed. "I understand your concern. Those girls can be quite a handful." She looked around and inhaled deeply. "There's nothing like a bit of fresh air before bedtime."

Dust tickled Julia's nose. *No, please, do not sneeze!*

"Since we're out here," Mrs. Shepherd said, "I'd like your opinion on something."

"I'll do my best," Bridget said.

"There's a man in town that I quite fancy," the cook said, lowering her voice to the point that Julia had to strain to hear her, "but he's a bit of a scoundrel, seeing as he pinched my bottom the last time I saw him."

Julia had to cover her mouth to keep from bursting into giggles. Her face burned with the effort. At least her nose no longer tickled.

"We should discuss this farther away from the house," Bridget said, putting an arm through that of the cook. "My mother used to say that voices travel easily on the wind."

"That's a brilliant idea," Mrs. Shepherd said.

Soon, their voices faded away.

Julia removed her hand from her mouth, sucked in a lungful of air, and sat up. She caught movement from behind a nearby tree. Matthew was glancing from side to side, likely searching for her.

"Matthew!" she called out in a loud whisper. "Matthew, I'm here!" She waved her arms above her head to grab his attention.

"I cannot see you," he whispered back. When she laughed aloud, he glanced up and took a sudden step back. "What are you doing up there?"

She leaned over the edge and replied, "I can explain later. Should I come down?"

"No. Let me join you." He peered around the building. "How did you get up there?"

"I climbed the timber pile there," she said, pointing. "But do be careful."

It was not long before his face appeared above the roofline. "Do all pupils in this school require gentlemen callers to climb up the sides of buildings in order to speak to them?" he asked as he pulled himself up.

Julia laughed. "No, but I must admit I find watching you do so most gallant."

Matthew smiled as he joined her. He was even more handsome beneath the stars than the last time she saw him. "I must admit that the request to meet you here was unusual, but I came to assure you that Lady Dyer and I are nothing more than friends. I know you saw us embrace, but it was not as it appeared. Well, it was an embrace, certainly, no one can deny that, but—"

She placed a calming hand on his arm. "Matthew, I believe you."

A smile spread across his lips, like a young boy earning praise. "That is a relief."

"As to the letter you received concerning this meeting," she said, "Ruth, she is one of my friends here, sent it without my knowledge. I nearly did not come, but I knew I must." She giggled. "Mrs. Shepherd almost caught me, which is how I came to be on the roof."

Matthew laughed and pulled his hair behind an ear. "I'm glad I agreed to come." He leaned back on his elbows and looked up at the sky. "I've never seen so many stars."

Julia followed his gaze and sighed. "They are amazing," she said as she joined him, not caring if her elbows became dirty. "I often believe that when night falls, a thick curtain is pulled across the sky, and the stars are merely pinholes in the fabric that allow the light to trickle through."

She inched her hand toward his and was pleased when he clasped it. Such a simple act brought her comfort while at the same time caused her heart to beat to a new rhythm. They sat there in silence for several minutes, hand in hand, and although they spoke no words, it was as if they had spoken a thousand.

"Your thoughts on the stars are wonderful," he whispered. "I've often considered the stars are our dreams and a reminder of what we desire." He sighed. "It has been years since I gazed at the stars. I'm glad I came, for there is nothing more beautiful in all the world."

She turned to look at him and was surprised to find him looking at her. Her cheeks burned to the point she worried they would set fire to the outbuilding. "I have a gift for you," she said, reaching into the pocket of her dress and pulling out the handkerchief. "I hope you like it."

He pulled himself up and took the handkerchief from her. "Is this your work?" he asked. When she nodded, he said, "It's very well done, exquisite even. I'll cherish it forever." He folded it and placed it into his inside coat pocket. "This will allow me to tap into your luck when we are unable to be together. It has been a miserable week without your company."

If her face was fire before, it was lava now. "You don't—"

"No, it's true," he said. "I felt so lost, so alone. Yet every time I pictured you or brought to mind your words of encouragement, not only did my happiness return, I felt as if I were the duke I should be."

"But you are a wonderful duke in your own right," she said, replacing her hand in his. "Never doubt that."

"I don't when you are near. You have brought me back to life, and like the stars, you remind me of my dreams."

His words were like sweet music to her heart, and she remembered her promise to Bridget. Now was the time to tell Matthew her true feelings for him.

"We have become friends," she said as she stared at their intertwined hands, "brought together by the most unusual of circumstances. Yet I no longer see you as just a friend." She worried her bottom lip. How could she admit what she had sworn would never be? "I've come to care for you deeply, Matthew. So much so that my heart hurts when you are not nearby. I feel vulnerable and alone without you to protect me. I need you."

He placed a hand on the side of her face. "And I need you more than you can ever realize." Moving his hand behind her head, he pulled her toward him and pressed his lips to hers. It began as a mere touching of the lips, light and innocent, soft and tingling.

As the air around them seemed to heat, so did the kiss. A sense of urgency rose between them, as if there was a need to use every moment, every fraction of the seconds they had together. Soon, the world was spinning around them, and if he had not had such a tight hold on her, she was certain they would have flown into the sky.

When the kiss ended, she drew in a deep, calming breath, willing her heartbeat to slow. How had she forgotten to breathe?

They were quiet for a few moments as they settled back onto the roof, now lying on their backs to look up at the stars, clasping each other's hand.

Matthew placed his free hand under his head. "When we first met," he said. His voice seemed as loud as a shout. "I believed you were a thief, but that opinion has since changed."

Matthew had never considered himself a strong man, not until he lay upon the roof of that outbuilding, holding his hand in hers. Now, a protector rose inside him, as if he wanted nothing more than to shield her from every problem she would ever face, to keep her safe for all eternity.

His intentions for this night had simply been to assure her that he had no interest in Lady Dyer. Granted, he had hoped to express that he cared for her, but the possibility of doing so had been an uncertainty. He had argued with himself since responding to the invitation as to whether this night would be the right time to speak what was on his heart. What if they continued this strange courtship only to have it come to an abrupt end? That would most certainly cause her further heartbreak, and having her hurt was the last thing he wanted to do.

When Julia shared her feelings with him, however, the doubts began to crumble like the walls of the ruins that dotted the land. Yet, it had been her whispered words of needing him that collapsed the final barrier around his heart.

Passion overtook him as he pulled her close and kissed her sweet lips. Never had he experienced such yearning, such hunger, as in that moment. It was as if her lips soothed and assured him that all was fine. Ending the kiss was one of the most difficult things he had ever done in his life, but he knew in his heart that he had to temper the flames that roiled inside him before they took their passion any further.

Now he had to consider how much he should share with her. He had yet to express to her his fear of becoming mad. The signs that he was following after his father were already appearing, but he had no idea how long before they took complete control of his faculties.

He turned his head to look at the serenity on Julia's face. Never had he encountered such beauty as he did upon seeing her, with her hair splayed across that rooftop, to create a perfect frame for her lovely features as she gazed up at the sky.

No, he could not share such horrible news with her when she was so happy. He would eventually, for not telling her would be unfair. She had every right to know what sort of future lay before them, for the chances of the malady passing to his children was much too high. No woman should be forced to birth a child destined for madness like his mother had. He had seen too much suffering to allow it to continue.

Yet, he could tell her some truths. "When we first met," he whispered, "I believed you were a thief, but that opinion has since changed."

"I would certainly hope so," she said, but the corners of her mouth twitched as she said this.

Matthew chuckled. "Be that as it may, I feel the need to explain myself to you."

She turned to look at him. "There is no need—"

"But there is, Julia. Please, allow me to say what must be said."

"If you must."

"My reasons for seeking your company were selfish, for I wanted just a piece of the luck you possess, all so I could increase my land holdings. However, I must make a confession."

"Oh? Please, tell me."

"Since I was a young boy, I received training on how to conduct myself as a man of great title, but the day I was to take on the dukedom came much sooner than I had hoped. With my father gone, the only person I had was my uncle, and yet I still felt alone, felt uncertain." He shifted to his side and placed his other hand atop their clasped hands. "Then you, Miss Julia Wallace, came into my life, and all that changed. Now you have me taking risks in so many ways. I mean, look at me leaping over brooks and climbing rooftops."

The sound of her laugh was like a chorus of angels, and he would not have been able to stop the barrage of words that tumbled from his lips if he had tried.

"But what you have shown me is just a part of a bigger lesson—to believe in myself. I must admit, it has been a very long time since I've done that, and I have you to thank for my newfound confidence." He chuckled. "Would you have ever imagined a man of my station admitting aloud such shortcomings?"

"You are but a man," Julia said with a radiant smile. "All this strength of which you speak? It was inside you the whole time. The problem is that at some point you forgot, but you should be proud, for you now remember."

Matthew could not shake the feeling that if this hidden strength had been inside him as she pointed out, then why had he not remembered until she came into his life? No, it was her luck that brought this strange new sense of being. Yet, he would not point this mistake out to her, for he would do nothing to erase the smile she wore at that moment.

"Each day we are apart," he continued, "I find myself lost and searching for the happiness that I've come to realize only exists when I'm with you. Without you, my hopes and dreams disappear, closing up like a white daisy after dark."

He paused for a moment to roll onto his back again and study the stars, giving himself time to consider his next words. His mind shouted that he should not reveal his true feelings for her, that doing so would only hurt them both in the end. He could not continue to court her in secret and then later break her heart.

Yet, as he considered these thoughts, he turned to find Julia staring at him with a smile so radiant, it could have put the stars to shame. Perhaps he could trust that a future together was not destined to fail, for even if he were to go mad, he would rather be with her than alone.

He sat up on one elbow and faced her. Bringing her hand to his lips, he kissed it. "I care for you, Julia, deeply. So much so that it hurts. Does that sound foolish?"

She smiled up at him. "Not at all, for I feel that same pain when I'm not with you."

"Then I say we continue our courtship," he said. He leaned in close, kissed her forehead, and said, "One day, I shall call you my wife."

Her arms encircled his neck. "The day I may call you my husband will be a wondrous day, indeed," she said. "Then I shall be in your arms forever."

So great was his happiness that he wanted nothing more than to shout it from the rooftop, but instead he whispered, "We shall continue to share our dreams, filling the sky with so many stars, the light will blind all who gaze upon them."

"I would like that," she said as her lips brushed his.

They shared in one last kiss, one that he knew brought them even closer together if such a thing were possible. When it ended, he retook her hand in his and lay back on the roof beside her.

Julia pointed up at the sky. "Do you see that line of stars there?" she asked.

He squinted and searched where her finger indicated. "I do."

"To the right, a new star has appeared. That is my dream of marrying you, and now it shines for all to see."

"And the one above it?" he asked. "That is my dream of becoming the husband you need, one who will honor and cherish you above all else."

For how long they lay there pointing out one star after another and sharing the dream attached, Matthew was unsure, but with each dream

Julia shared, his affection for her grew. The night was perfect and one he would never forget.

After several moments of silence, Julia whispered, "If this night is a dream, I never wish to awaken."

Giving her hand a gentle squeeze, he said, "I can assure you that this night is no dream. This is our eternity."

As he studied their dreams in the sky, the sound of footsteps made his breath catch. Julia clutching his hand told him she, too, was concerned.

"Miss Julia?"

Julia released a loud breath and sat up. "It's just Bridget."

"Miss Julia, we must go. It's past midnight."

Past midnight? How had time gotten away from them? Matthew helped Julia climb from the rooftop. The urge to hold her close to him was strong, but he released her.

"Shall I see you Sunday?" Julia asked.

"You will," he replied. "I shall be here at noon as promised."

Julia smiled at him before following her companion to the house. Once they were out of sight, he sighed. The night had gone far better than he could have ever expected.

As he made his way to where he had hobbled his horse, he took a moment to look up at the stars once more. He found himself unable to stop smiling.

"They are our dreams, Julia," he whispered. "And just as the stars in the sky, they will remain forever."

That is, if he could live forever. Then, perhaps madness would be unable to claim him.

Chapter Twenty

As Julia and Bridget headed back to the house, Julia had to stop herself from skipping like a young girl. "I've never felt more alive!" she said in a harsh whisper. "This has been the loveliest, most fantastic night any lady could ever have. I don't know how I'll ever thank you."

"Just promise me you'll never ask me to do anything like this again," Bridget said. "I had to endure listening to Mrs. Shepherd's romantic interests." She shivered visibly. "You've no idea how difficult that was! And then worrying about you only made it worse. Promise me this is the last time."

"I promise," Julia said, hugging the maid. "Thank you for all you have done."

They entered the house, and Julia lit a candle that sat on a table beside the door. "I must hurry and get to bed before Mrs. Rutley returns."

"It's a little late for that concern, Julia."

Julia spun about to find the headmistress standing in the doorway leading to the corridor, her own candle in her hand.

"O-oh, Mrs. Rutley," Julia stammered. "Did you have an enjoyable evening?"

"Out for a late-night stroll, were you?" Mrs. Rutley asked, ignoring Julia's attempt to keep the focus on her.

Julia hated lying to Mrs. Rutley, but she certainly could not be truthful, either! "We—"

"Of course you were," the headmistress said, cutting off Julia. "It really is a lovely night for a stroll, but it's quite late, so perhaps we should be off to bed."

With a sigh of relief, Julia nodded. "Yes," she said with a forced yawn. "I must admit that I'm quite—"

"I do have to wonder, though," Mrs. Rutley continued, speaking over her. "Why was such a fine steed tied to one of the trees along the entrance to the property? And this was no common horse, for even I know that the animal is property of a duke."

Julia could take it no longer. "I'm so sorry, Mrs. Rutley! Ruth arranged for Matthew to meet with me in the gardens, and although I'm still unsure why I agreed to her imprudent plan, I did. Please, don't be angry with Bridget. I convinced her to go with me as my chaperone. If you must punish anyone, let it be me."

Mrs. Rutley shook her head. Her disappointment was clear. "Bridget is not one to be easily swayed, Julia. Regardless who is at fault, I cannot turn a blind eye to one of my girls sneaking out of the house to meet with a man, be he a duke or otherwise. Not this time."

Julia gave a despondent nod. What had she been thinking agreeing to such an outlandish rendezvous?

But you had such a wonderful time! she thought.

No! You could have waited to share what you felt for him in a more appropriate setting! You deserve every bit of punishment Mrs. Rutley heaps on you!

"Bridget, we shall speak tomorrow," the headmistress said. "For now, I would like to speak to Julia alone."

"Yes, Mrs. Rutley," Bridget said, bobbing a quick curtsy. She shot Julia what seemed a look of sympathy as she scurried from the room. Julia would most definitely need to offer further apologies later for putting the maid in such a precarious position.

"Come with me," Mrs. Rutley said in a firm voice that lacked its usual compassion. Never had the headmistress sounded so severe. At least not with Julia. "Put out your candle for now and sit."

Julia did as the headmistress bade, her heart pounding in her chest as she sat on the edge of the chair, her hands clasped in her lap.

Mrs. Rutley sighed. "My brightest student, the one I trust to guide the others, sneaks away into the night to meet a gentleman?" She walked over to the window, her back to Julia. "I'm at a loss for words."

"I truly am sorry for my actions," Julia said. "And for upsetting you."

The headmistress turned. "Tell me everything that transpired in my absence. Leave out not a single detail. If I suspect you of lying or withholding information, I'll see you returned home tomorrow."

Julia swallowed hard. "Yes, Mrs. Rutley," she said as she stared at her hands, though the words seemed to catch in her throat. "It began after dinner. I was in my room, preparing for bed, when Ruth entered." For some time, Julia explained all that happened. Well, perhaps not everything. Their shared kisses were a secret she could not share, for then Mrs. Rutley would have cause to send her home. If she were expelled from the school, her parents would never forgive her. And she would never forgive herself.

"Then Bridget and I returned to the house," Julia said. "And that is everything, I swear!"

It was a relief when she finished her telling. Now she was ready to accept whatever punishment set before her if it meant being allowed to remain at the school.

Her ears perked, however, when she heard what she suspected was a... sniffle?

"So, you do care deeply for him," Mrs. Rutley said in a voice so quiet Julia had to strain to hear. "Hope has once again returned to fight against the darkness that fills Hardwick Hall."

Julia frowned. "The darkness, Mrs. Rutley?"

The headmistress ignored her question. "Come with me," she said, walking to Julia and waiting for her to stand. "You must swear to me that you will never leave here at night like this again—escort or no. Do you swear?"

"I do," Julia replied with fervent agreement. "I'll swear any vow you wish, but I shall never do anything to disappoint you ever again."

To her surprise, Mrs. Rutley hugged her. "I so enjoy hearing stories of great romances such as yours," she whispered in Julia's ear. "For it gives me hope. But remember, there are many things that may stand in your way. If you care for him as I believe you do, you must fight for him. Do you understand?"

"I do," Julia replied as the embrace broke.

Mrs. Rutley smiled, although it contrasted with the sadness that rested on her features.

"May I ask a question, Mrs. Rutley?"

"Of course."

"I know little about the man you married, but have you ever been in love?"

The headmistress sighed. "I was, but it was long before I married." She gave Julia a stern look. "But that can never be repeated, especially to the other girls. They have no reason to know my business. Is that clear?"

Julia nodded. "It will be our secret," she said. "But I do have one more question to ask. Don't worry, it's not about you, not exactly."

"Go on, then."

"I've come to realize that I admire Matthew very much. But how will I know that I love him, if I ever do?"

Mrs. Rutley took Julia by the hand. "Trust me. When that day comes, you will know, for love surpasses any joy you have ever felt. Now, you should be off to bed."

Although it was not the answer Julia had hoped to hear, she did not want to test her luck further. Matthew may believe her luck could hold against any problems, but she was not so sure.

As she made her way to the door, however, she stopped and turned to face the headmistress. "And what of my punishment?"

The room fell quiet for several moments before Mrs. Rutley replied, "Too many have been punished in the pursuit of love. Your promise to never sneak away has wiped away any need for discipline. But if you break that promise..."

Julia could not help but smile as she closed the office door. She may not have understood the reason Mrs. Rutley chose not to punish her, but she was relieved not to be sent home.

So, the headmistress had once loved, had she? If she had loved before marriage, why had she not married the man she loved? Well, that was certainly none of Julia's business.

What had her mind churning as she returned to her bedchambers was Mrs. Rutley's insistence that Julia "continue to fight" for Matthew. Why would she make such a statement? After all, she and Matthew had expressed their admiration for one another, so what could ever come between them now? Nothing as far as Julia was concerned.

Or so she prayed.

Matthew awoke the following morning with a renewed sense of hope. Gone were the worries that had clung to him like moss on a rock for the greater part of his life. The return journey home after his time with Julia had him feeling as if he were walking among the clouds. A seed of doubt had shouted at him from the back of his mind, doing all it could to tell him not to allow his feelings for her to grow, to hold them back and lock them away as he always had. Yet, what a relief it was to ignore those doubts!

After seeing to his morning ablutions, his valet, George, helped him dress before he went downstairs in search of his uncle. The man had guided Matthew since his father's passing, but it was about time that Matthew took the reins of his own life so he could set out on his own. If all worked out as planned, Julia would be at his side. If Uncle Ezra disapproved, so be it.

At the bottom of the grand staircase, Hickson greeted him with a deep bow. "Good morning, Your Grace. Shall I have tea brought to your office?"

"Yes, please," Matthew said. "And have you seen my uncle? I must speak with him."

"He is in the gardens, Your Grace, and has been for the better part of an hour."

"How unusual," Matthew said, scrunching his brow. "Wait to have the tea sent up. I wish to speak to him first."

"As you wish," Hickson said, bowing again.

Matthew walked to the door that led to the gardens. Droplets of dew clung to the grass, creating a glittering effect that reminded him of the stars at night, which, in turn, reminded him of the previous night. Up ahead, he caught sight of his uncle with his hands clasped behind his back, craning his neck as if in search of someone.

"Good morning, Uncle," Matthew said as he approached. "What brings you out into the fresh air so early?"

His uncle gave him a quick nod and let out a sigh. "We have many busy days ahead, and the most important days of them all draw nigh. I cannot help but wonder if it's all in vain."

Matthew chuckled. "I can assure you that is not the case. Have I not heeded your advice and prepared for the road ahead?"

Uncle Ezra rounded on him. "Then may I ask why you lied to me? This problem has nettled me to the point that I'm unable to sleep."

"What lie have I told?" Matthew asked, taken aback. Never had he seen his uncle so out of sorts. "Please, tell me so I'm able to clear up any misunderstanding, for that is the only way to explain why you believe I would lie to you."

"And now you have lied to me twice," his uncle snapped. "Well, I suppose it does not matter. I know my place."

Matthew frowned. "Enlighten me, Uncle."

His uncle sighed. "Can I assume that your late-night jaunt was to meet with Miss Wallace?"

"How did you know? I told no one, not even Hickson."

Reaching into the inside pocket of his coat, his uncle produced a carefully folded letter. "You really should not leave your correspondences lying around if you wish to keep secrets, Nephew. They can unravel a dukedom faster than the wagging tongue of an old woman if they are found by the wrong person." He handed the letter to Matthew. "I had gone in search of you, and when you could not be found, I could not help but wonder where you had gone. When I found that letter, I realized the truth." All anger left his voice, replaced by a softness that sounded strange coming from him. "You care about that young woman, do you not?"

"I do," Matthew replied. "I know you don't approve of her, but I can assure you that she is a good and worthy woman."

Uncle Ezra looked up and sighed. "I'm sorry, Brother. I've failed you."

Matthew frowned at this, but before he could comment, his uncle continued, "You are right, I don't approve of the young lady, but I've never hidden my disapproval. Therein lies the deception. You told me that you had no romantic interest in the girl when, in fact, you do."

"But I did not lie, Uncle. At the time you asked, I had no interest in her, not in any romantic sense. Now however, my feelings for her have changed. I never set out to care for her, it just happened. You may as well know now that I've asked Julia to allow me to court her, and she has accepted. Now, I've not spoken to her father, but I plan to do that very soon."

Matthew braced himself for the rebuke he was certain would come, but instead, his uncle smiled. "Just as I thought would happen." He turned and walked away.

Staring after his uncle, Matthew said, "I'm confused. Are you not angry that I've chosen to court her?"

Uncle Ezra stopped and turned back to face Matthew. "I admit that I am... disappointed. Tell me, you once said that you did not believe in love. Have you changed your opinion on this matter?"

"Well, although I'm not yet ready to confess love—"

His uncle took a step forward, his lips pursed. "One day you will become mad like your father was, forcing Miss Wallace to suffer as your mother did. Is that love?"

Matthew found himself unable to respond. The words his uncle spoke pierced his heart but also angered him. "Proceed with care, Uncle Ezra."

Placing a hand on Matthew's shoulder, his uncle sighed. "I've had a very good reason to counsel against you and Miss Wallace developing any sort of association. Anyone can see you have cared for her, even as far back as the party. But you must come to the realization that one day you will break her heart. This is your life, Matthew. You can control whom you hurt with the decisions you make. I just make a couple of requests, the first being to consider her wellbeing above your own. That is the mark of a true gentleman, a goal I aim for at every turn, although I fail more often than I succeed."

Guilt plagued Matthew. His uncle was here to counsel him, and Matthew threw aside his wise words, without thought for all he had given up offering such counsel.

"I'll consider what you have said, Uncle. You said you had more than one request. What else do you wish?"

"Before you make this important announcement of courtship, will you wait at least one month? The *ton* will be alight with gossip, and people will wish to call to give their congratulations and hear when you will announce your engagement. You know how they are. We must focus our attention on these business affairs we have scheduled at the end of the month. Once that is completed, once we have made the agreements that will see us set up for life, you may do as you wish, and I shall support whatever decision you make. Just as I do now."

Matthew could not help but smile. His uncle's request was reasonable, and with his pledge of support, how could Matthew say no? "Don't worry, Uncle, I shall keep it secret until these affairs are complete."

"Good," his uncle said with a wide grin. "Now if you will excuse me, I must leave and will be gone all day."

Wishing his uncle a good day, Matthew considered the man's words. Although he wished to shout his courtship from the mountaintops, his uncle's counsel was wise. The *ton* had a tendency to do whatever possible to tear each other apart, and the announcement of an engagement, or even the courtship of a duke and a young lady from the school, would give them the fodder they needed.

Once the agreements were made, however, everyone from the local butcher to the King himself would know what he thought of Miss Julia Wallace. The woman for whom he cared, and somehow suspected might even love.

Chapter Twenty-One

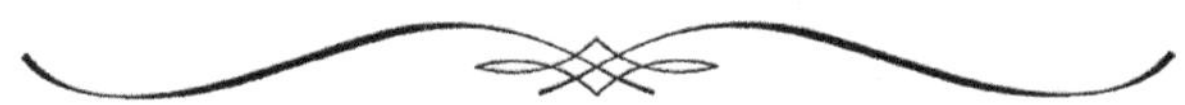

Like the loose thread on the hem of a coat, Ezra understood that everything he had planned, everything for which had he worked so hard, was unraveling. His fool of a nephew was being led astray by a girl unsuited for him. If dire steps were not taken, Ezra would lose all control over the dukedom and the wealth and luxury it offered him, sending the plans for his future crashing to the ground like a boulder dislodged from a steep cliff.

The carriage jostled, and he grasped hold of the handle above him, cursing. All had been going exactly as it should have until that chit of a girl entered their lives. The more time Matthew spent with Miss Wallace, the less Ezra was able to dominate him, and he was growing weary of watching his plans spiral out of control.

To make matters worse, his attempt to exploit Lady Dyer had been an utter failure. What he had expected was to have her use her womanly wiles to attract Matthew, but her feeble attempts at flirting were as alluring as a nun performing charity work! Her house was the first on his list to call on today. Perhaps he should call on Agnes Rutley as well.

"Women!" he cursed.

Clenching his fist, memories from years ago came to mind, memories of a time when he had called on Agnes. It had been only a brief period of time, but her beauty and mind had intrigued him. Once he professed his love for her, however, she admitted that she did not share in his admiration. Within a fortnight, she had received another suitor, and it was not long after that the two were married. She may as well have slapped him in the face!

Then Rutley had died under the most unusual circumstances. A drunken tumble down the stairs of the very house Agnes used for her school. What many did not know—and what Ezra did—was that the man rarely drank more than a polite sip during a toast. What happened that night could not have been clearer in Ezra's mind, and he anticipated the day the woman who had broken his heart would be held accountable for her crimes.

Ezra was so lost in his thoughts that he was startled when the carriage came to a stop in front of Crestview House. He alighted from the vehicle and hurried to the front door, his jaw clenched.

"My lord," the butler said when he opened the door, bending at the waist.

Ezra ignored the servant. "Where is she?" he asked as he pushed into the foyer. The butler blinked at him, as if he were speaking a foreign language. "Your mistress, where is she?"

"In the drawing room, my lord," the butler said. "Allow me to announce—"

"Get out of my way," Ezra snapped as he pushed past the butler and marched down the corridor. The door to the drawing room was open, and he entered the room, closing the door behind him with a violent *bang*.

"Lord Ezra, what a pleasant surprise," Lady Dyer said, smiling broadly. She raised the teacup she held. "I just had tea brought up. Would you like a cup?"

He glared at her as he walked over to where she sat in one of the window seats. "I don't want any tea," he snarled. "I want control over my nephew's estate, but now that may not happen. Your task was simple. You were to catch the boy's eye and keep him away from that Wallace girl, but you failed." He grabbed her wrist, and Lady Dyer gave a cry of pain as the teacup went crashing to the floor. "Perhaps you can explain to me why I'm in the position I am."

The door flew open, and Ezra released his hold on the baroness. The butler looked inside. "Is everything all right, my lady?"

"Y-yes, Pearson," Lady Dyer said, rubbing her wrist. "All is well. Leave us."

Pearson gave a doubtful look but left the room, nonetheless.

When the door clicked shut, Ezra rounded on Lady Dyer once again. "Matthew has become enamored with that girl from the school. He even wants to court her!"

Lady Dyer's eyes glistened with tears. "I tried," she said. "Every attempt I made failed. I'm unsure what more I can do. It's clear that he cares very much for her."

Ezra rubbed his temples. Why did women have to weep at every turn? "My next stop will be the bank, to notify them you are no longer able to pay your debts to me. In three months, this estate and everything within it will be mine. You will be cast out to the streets, a destitute widow with whom no man of substance will consider even having an affair. And you have no one to blame but yourself."

"Please," the baroness sobbed, "give me one more chance. I'm doing my best to win him over, but it has been far more difficult than I expected. You must realize that he sees me as a friend, not a lover."

Ezra tilted his head. "Then perhaps how he sees you must change."

Her eyes widened. "Surely you don't mean—"

"Oh, do be quiet, woman! Don't act as if you are some untarnished maiden."

Removing a handkerchief from the sleeve of her dress, she wiped the tears from her cheeks. "I don't wish to hurt him, my lord. He is a good man and does not deserve to be mistreated. Not to mention the guilt that plagues me—"

"You know exactly what will happen if you refuse," Ezra said with a sneer. "Not only will you lose your home, but I shall have such rumors spread about you that even a stable hand will refuse to marry you!"

The baroness nodded. "I know the power you possess, my lord, for you have done as much with whispers about your nephew. If you are willing to make him and everyone who knows him believe he is going mad, I don't doubt what you can convince others to believe about me, a woman who does not share your blood."

Laughing, Ezra placed a hand on her cheek. "You are much more intelligent than I thought if you guessed that. But if I hear one word, even in jest, that I'm responsible for my nephew's madness, or his belief in his madness, I shall see you sent to London to work as a prostitute. And trust me, I can do it without question, even to a widow of a baron. Do I make myself clear?"

She fell to her knees. "No, please!" she sobbed. "I'll do as you ask, just please don't send me to such a terrible fate!"

He stared at her with disgust. She was weak, but that also made her more malleable. "You are to send Matthew a letter today. In two days, you will send him another. Then, you will send him one every day after until he responds as we wish."

"And what shall I write, my lord?" she asked.

"A story," he replied. "One so sad, so tragic, that he will rethink his decision to toss you aside. Then, my dear"—he helped her stand—"when the time is right, you will do exactly as I say."

"W-what will that be?"

He took her by the arm, lightly this time, and guided her to a chair. "Sit and I shall explain the entirety of my plan to you."

Once he began, he did not stop until he had detailed every aspect of his expectations of her. If she did as he asked, Matthew would be so riddled with guilt that he would have no choice but to marry the baroness.

"Not only will you save your home," he said when he finished, "but you will also become a duchess. Whatever you desire, you will receive. You will never want for anything again, for you may be married to my nephew, but your partnership will be with me. It is I who shall have full control over the dukedom, through you. I shall express what I want, and you will relay my wishes to Matthew as if the ideas come from you. Now, do you understand what I'm asking of you? And what will happen if you fail?"

Lady Dyer nodded, her gaze lowered. "Yes, my lord. I shall begin immediately."

Chapter Twenty-Two

Julia took a deep breath as a cool breeze tousled her hair, and the sound of the trickling brook soothed her soul. Three weeks had passed since she and Matthew had confessed their feelings for one another on the roof of the outbuilding, and in that time, they had met four times.

Today, Saturday, Matthew had surprised her with a return picnic to the place they had leapt across the brook together. She closed her eyes. Was there anything more romantic than a picnic? Perhaps naming stars was its equal.

Hearing a mumbling, she looked over her shoulder to find Matthew struggling to set out the blanket as he wanted—perfect. Not giggling at his efforts was difficult, for with each tug of one corner, the opposite rose, and he would groan in protest to return to readjust that one.

Julia turned to help, but Bridget motioned for her to remain where she was. What was the woman playing at? If he needed her help, she would give it to him.

Then, after one last exasperated sigh loud enough to echo across the field, Matthew placed his hands on his thighs and studied his handiwork. "There," he said proudly. "Not as simple an endeavor as I expected, but I overcame the stubbornness of it."

Julia nodded, but that giggle fought against her pursed lips. He spoke as if he had conquered some foreign land!

"Allow me," he said, taking her by the hand and helping her sit. "Miss Bridget?"

Bridget waved him away. "I think I'll watch the water flow for a bit, if that's all right with you, Miss Julia."

"Of course," Julia replied. She would have to thank the maid for allowing her and Matthew a bit of relative privacy. How did women with strict chaperones get much-needed time alone with their beau? She was certainly lucky, indeed. Or so Matthew would say.

Julia turned her attention to Matthew. "I must admit, I was uncertain who would best whom, you or the blanket." She just could not resist a bit of teasing. "It was a lengthy battle, but the duke did prevail in the end. Well done!"

Matthew laughed, a sound Julia had come to enjoy greatly. "If such victories impress you, Miss Wallace, perhaps I should describe the skirmish I had with my coat this morning."

It was Julia's turn to laugh, but it was short-lived, for Matthew was gazing at her as if she were artwork at a museum. Not only were her feelings for this man increasing, but they were also growing tenfold each time she was with him. Even Bridget had commented, not two days earlier, how the permanent smile Julia wore was a joy to see.

Although she enjoyed Matthew looking at her, it also made her a bit uneasy. Who hoped to be stared at? She decided to change the subject. "So, what have you done since we last met? Is all well for these most important upcoming meetings?"

Matthew had explained the magnitude of what he would receive once the agreements were made. Apparently, he was to gain several hotels and a variety of farms that included both land and homes he would rent out to farmers and their families. Although the negotiations were scheduled over a week, Matthew said he hoped to come to an agreement on all terms within three days. Too often, when one spent too much time discussing the particulars of a sale, one of the parties wanted to convolute the proceedings.

"I look forward to them," he replied. "I cannot believe I need to wait only one more fortnight. Of course, I have no illusions they will be tedious and likely heated. Everyone hopes to gain somehow, of course, but I shall have you with me the whole time, so I'm not overly concerned." He removed the handkerchief she had stitched for him. "Your gift, shown in your handiwork, will bring me luck."

Julia smiled, but she wanted to pummel him! Why could he not see that it was he who created his own success, not some object or person?

Oh very well, she did not truly wish to strike him, but a well-placed slap across the cheek was always recommended for hysterical women. Why could it not be used to make a duke see reason?

"Soon, no one will be able to travel between Cambridge and London without seeing at least one property I own. Just imagine! I shall become a great duke everyone will admire." He reached into the basket and removed a bottle of wine.

"Are you not already a great duke?" Julia asked. "So many already admire you, myself included." She took the glass he offered her. "Have you not realized that greatness does not come from the acquisition of property but from within?"

"You may see it that way, and it may also be true, but you must understand that I must succeed where my father failed." She went to speak, but he raised a hand to forestall her. "This is important to me, Julia. Please, I need your support in this endeavor."

"I do wish to lend you my support," Julia said, her heart clenching at the thought that he would believe otherwise of her. "You should know I wish you to succeed."

He grinned at her "Good." He raised his glass in a quick toast and took a drink.

Wishing to change the subject, Julia said, "Mother wrote, but I'm waiting to reply. I want to tell her of our courtship. May I at least tell her now? My parents plan to come in January to collect me before we go to London to make my debut. But January is still so far away, and I thought it wise that my parents know as soon as possible."

Matthew shook his head, much to her disappointment. "I want no one to know just yet." His brow knitted. "You have not told anyone, have you?"

Julia shook her head, but guilt welled up in her for lying. Yet, she had made a pledge to her friends, that they would keep one another's secrets, and her courtship was one of them. Explaining this to Matthew would not only upset him, but it would breach the oath she had made to her sisters. And to him. Why did fealty have to be so complicated?

Plus, his relieved expression was far more suited for his handsome features than his look of worry. "Good. As I said, I would prefer to wait until after the completion of my meetings. It will do no good for the *ton* to be alight with gossip before then."

How could an announcement of courtship be considered gossip, and somehow hinder the proceedings of what he hoped to gain from these gatherings? And did he believe her mother was a gossip? The very idea was insulting. Then again, most women, rich and poor, tended to spend a great deal of time talking about others behind their hands. Come to think of it, men wagged their tongues just as much. Perhaps it was simply a trait all humans shared. Or most, anyway.

He placed a hand on hers. "I swear to you, the moment I've completed my negotiations, you and I shall both write to your father. Then I shall proclaim to everyone that we are courting. Indeed, I shall shout it from the rooftops, so both young and old will know of it."

"I cannot wait," she said honestly. She took a sip of her wine to give her time to consider her next words. "I realize you have much on your mind at the moment, but I would like to share what is on mine."

He had been reaching into the basket and stopped to raise his brows at her. "Go on, then. Tell me. But if it's a philosophical debate for which you are searching, I'm not in the mood to argue." He removed two small bundles from the basket, which turned out to be cheese and bread. "After all, I would not want to best you again."

She gave him a look of mock affront. "Is that what you think?" she demanded before laughing. "But no, I've been considering our future life together as of late. As well as our eventual wedding and the marriage thereafter." She clutched her hands together at her breast and sighed. "Oh, the adventures we shall have, and the stories we shall share! Just think, many years from now, we will be quite old—or rather you will be. I shall retain my youthfulness for eternity!" She laughed. "But when we do, we shall share stories with our grandchildren of days such as today!"

Rather than smiling, Matthew frowned.

"Matthew?" she asked. "Have I said something to upset you? If so, I did so unintentionally."

"No," he replied. "You have done nothing wrong." His expression did not match his words.

"Are you certain?"

He shook his head. "No, I was thinking of Lady Dyer, is all."

For a moment, Julia could only stare into her wine. Any attempt to drink it would have her choking. Why would her speaking of marriage conjure thoughts of another woman, especially Lady Dyer?

Although he had been named the Duke of Madness by many of the *ton*, Matthew thought the Fool of Elmhurst was a more appropriate title. Their afternoon picnic had gone so well—perfectly, in fact. So, why had he felt the need to mention the name of Lady Dyer? He had not been thinking about the widow at all but rather the future of which Julia spoke.

At first, she had made him smile with her regaling of their growing old together. Yet, when she mentioned grandchildren, his mind had ground to a halt. Rather than the lovely images her words should have conjured, his visions were discomforting and troublesome.

One in particular rose above the rest. It was far into the future, and Julia wore a worried expression for, like his father, Matthew had wandered from the estate. A small party of servants had been dispatched to search for him, and it had taken them several hours to do so. When he returned, the Julia of his vision was in tears as he shared with her his adventures of speaking to animals he had encountered in the nearby woods.

Matthew had witnessed this very horror play out between his parents. His mother's weeping had carried through the corridors throughout that night and other nights before and after. He held no delusion about a happy, normal life, for he knew what destiny had planned for him.

When Julia had asked if she had upset him, he had not wanted to take away her dreams by placing the blame on her for his sudden burst of melancholy. She had simply expressed what any young woman would have in the current situation. So, he said the first thing that came to mind that had nothing to do with him and Julia. This just so happened to be the letters Lady Dyer had been writing to him over the past few weeks, telling of her courtship with a man from the landed gentry.

"No, I was thinking of Lady Dyer, is all." As soon as the words left his lips, he knew they were wrong. What a fool he was! If this was not a sign of his impending madness, he did not know what was.

He searched his mind for any way to change the subject, but he found none. Perhaps he could alleviate the worry that had crossed her lovely features.

"I received word that she is being courted by a gentleman," he said. "I suspect that he will eventually marry her." This was not an untruth, and her current situation mattered little to him, but at least it pushed the conversation toward the reality that he and the baroness were not romantically involved.

"How lovely for her," Julia said, taking a sip of her wine.

An awkward silence fell between them, and Matthew offered her a bit of cheese.

"No, thank you."

Again, silence. He had to say something, anything! "It appears everyone wishes to be married," he said with a chuckle that sounded forced even to his ears. "The reading of the banns will take place day and night to schedule everyone in." His attempt at jesting fell flat, even he knew this.

Julia nodded, consumed the remainder of her wine in one fell swoop, and handed him the empty glass before smoothing her skirts. Women smoothing their skirts when they had no need to do so was never a good sign. "I did not mean to make you uncomfortable with my talk of marriage," she said. "Would you rather discuss something else?"

His heart ached. What he wished to discuss was his fear of the future, but if he did so now, he would hurt her all the more. "No, I have no problem talking of marriage. My mind is just consumed with my upcoming meetings. Wait, we have already discussed that." He searched his mind for another topic of discussion. "Mother wrote to say she will be visiting for a month."

Julia's eyes lit up. "How wonderful!" she said. "You must be so happy. I think it will be good for you to have family with you again."

He frowned. "I have my uncle," he said. "Do you not like him?"

"He is your uncle and blood. I would never speak ill of a relative, even if I disapproved or disliked him." Then she quickly added, "Not that I do. Disapprove or dislike him, that is."

"Please, give me your honest thought of him. I promise not to become angry with you."

She took several moments before responding. "I... I think he is overzealous in his guidance of you," she said, staring in the direction of the brook. "You are the duke, not he, and I worry that his influence has restrained you in some areas."

Her words were like silk, and he reached over to take her hand. "You are a very perceptive woman, Miss Wallace. I had not wanted to burden you with my troubles, but I've spoken to my uncle at length about this. Once the negotiations are completed, I'll push ahead on my own. Until I'm married, that is."

The blush that crept into her cheeks made her even more beautiful. "There is never a burden you must carry alone. You may share anything with me without fear of judgment."

He squeezed her hand. "For that I'm truly grateful."

"I look forward to the day I meet your mother," Julia said, smiling. "I do hope she finds me worthy of taking the title of duchess. From what you have told me about her, she is tenacious and strong, and I hope to win her approval."

"I have no doubt that you will."

"I imagine she will want to help plan the wedding," Julia said. "I would not mind, for it will be a wonderful way for us to bond, and she can also teach me about what it means to be a duchess."

Matthew simply nodded, but worry filled him. In this time of bonding, would his mother warn Julia of the dangers of marriage and what it was like to care for a madman? The more Julia spoke, the tighter the knot in Matthew's stomach became. When the pain became unbearable, he stood.

"I'm sorry, but I must leave. I did not realize how much time has passed, and I have work piling up on my desk that must be completed by this evening." The lie burned his tongue, but if he did not get away soon, he would likely say something he would regret.

He reached for her hand to help her stand.

"I understand," she said. "I imagine you have much to prepare. Do you believe you will have time for us to meet again?"

As he considered her question, he patted the place where the handkerchief was hidden away. He did need to prepare, but the thought of not seeing her before then left an unpleasant feeling within him. Yet, if every encounter they had consisted of a discussion of marriage, perhaps it would be best if they did wait.

"How about this?" he said. "Let us plan to meet again the day after the last day of negotiations, and if you would like, you may write to me."

She laughed. "I think that is a lovely idea."

Matthew repacked the basket and collected the blanket, and soon the trio was in the carriage heading toward the school. As the vehicle trundled along, he considered what they had discussed. He had to admit that the majority of their time together had been quite pleasant, just as it always was.

Once he had seen her deposited at the school, he returned to Hardwick Hall, light of heart. As soon as he stepped from the carriage, however, his uncle burst from the front door and bounded down the stairs. Never had he seen such panic on the man's face.

"I'm so glad you are here!" he said.

Then Matthew saw a folded parchment clutched in his uncle's hand. "What is wrong?"

His uncle pushed the letter toward him. "Here. Read for yourself. I'm unsure what to do."

Unfolding the paper, he recognized the flowing handwriting immediately.

Lord Ezra,

. . .

I find myself indebted to you and His Grace for the kindness you have shown me over the past months. However, I have one more request to make of you, if I may. I would like to seek your sage advice on matters far too personal to be contained in a letter. I had considered consulting His Grace, as I have done over these last weeks, but with his sparse replies, I can see that I may have become burdensome.

Matthew winced at this. The baroness had not become a burden, but he found that replying to dozens of letters in such a short period of time insurmountable.

In short, I am in desperate need of advice, for my very livelihood, my heart, and my estate hang in the balance. Please, inform me of a date and time when we may meet so I may receive the wisdom I so need.

Matthew refolded the letter and slipped it into his pocket. "What does she mean that these matters of her life 'hang in the balance'?"

Uncle Ezra sighed. "I learned recently that the estate that belonged to her husband is nearly bankrupt. I've made every attempt to help her, but apparently his coffers were already empty when she married him."

"And the matters of the heart?" Matthew asked with a frown. "She did mention in one of her letters that a man has been courting her. Perhaps it has something to do with him."

His uncle leaned against a nearby column and peered out over the estate. "I'm torn. We have the upcoming negotiations to occupy us, but if we ignore the plea of a lady widow who is in distress, I shall be consumed with guilt." He turned to look at Matthew. "I must admit, I seek your wisdom on this, Nephew. I'm at a loss as to what to do."

A sense of pride coursed through Matthew. Rarely did his uncle ask for his advice in any matter. Plus, Lady Dyer was indeed a lady widow in distress.

"During our party last month, she defended my name," Matthew said. "Therefore, the least we can do is make time to listen to her troubles and do what we can to relieve them."

His uncle knitted his brows in thought and then replied, "Indeed, you are right. That is what a friend would do. Perhaps we can have her over for dinner Saturday evening, and we can discuss whatever has upset her so terribly. Only if you believe it's best, of course."

Matthew smiled. Twice now his uncle had sought Matthew's permission rather than making commands. Julia's assessment of the relationship between him and his uncle had been one of an older man forcing his will on the younger, but now his uncle was releasing his hold and trusting that Matthew would make the right decisions.

"Yes, let us do that. I shall pen a letter this evening to extend the invitation. Yet before I do, I would like to share some ideas I have concerning some matters of business."

Uncle Ezra clasped him on the shoulder and smiled. "You are the duke—and a wise man—and I'm ready to listen. Perhaps it's time I begin to learn from you. If you are willing to teach me, that is."

"After all you have done for me," Matthew said with a laugh, "how can I refuse?"

Chapter Twenty-Three

As they had done on nearly every other Saturday, the pupils of Mrs. Rutley's School for Young Women headed into town for the day. Some were off to order new dresses while others had only a few coins to purchase a tart or some other small treat. The walk was less than two miles, and Julia enjoyed the conversations in which she and her friends shared. The forests that flanked the road kept their voices from traveling, unlike how easily one could be overheard by curious ears within the walls of the school.

"My husband," Diana was saying, "will simply have to understand that I want no more than two children. I shall be much too busy with my own affairs to raise more."

Unity frowned. "But what if they are both girls? Will your husband not want an heir? A woman in the village where I live had eight girls before she finally produced a son. You may meet the same fate." She made a valid point.

Julia's thoughts turned to Matthew and the children they would have. She could imagine her young daughters wearing fine dresses and bows in their hair. The boys would look as dashing as their father in their tailored coats.

Julia was so lost in thought that she yelped when a hand grabbed her arm and pulled her to the side of the road. A moment later, a passing carriage trundled by, the driver yelling obscenities that made her cheeks heat.

"If you keep dreaming about the duke," Ruth said in an admonishing tone worthy of the headmistress, "you are liable to be squashed." The others laughed.

"Thank you," Julia gasped as she glanced around to make sure no other vehicles were coming. "But I was not thinking of the duke."

Ruth's roll of her eyes told Julia that she did not believe her.

The streets of the Village of Chatsworth were bustling with carriages and pedestrians.

Ruth snaked an arm through that of Theodosia. "We shall be at the cobbler's," she said. "Would anyone like to join us?"

"I would like to," Jenny agreed. She turned to Diana. "And you?"

"Oh, yes," Diana replied, poking the toe of a shoe from under her skirts. "I can always do with a new pair of shoes."

"I must look for a new hat," Louisa said.

Unity grinned. "Oh, yes! There is nothing more wonderful than new hats!"

Julia leaned toward Ruth and whispered, "Now remember, they look up to you. I know you say you are going to search for new shoes, but there is no need to mention the cobbler's son."

Ruth responded with a feigned look of shock. "As if I would do such a thing!" Then she lowered her voice. "I'm well aware that most believe I'm unruly, but I have no interest in that boy, not in the way you are thinking. He has simply been able to procure various items I've needed and been unable to find without his assistance. Just because he has a nicely shaped calf has nothing to do with anything."

Julia shook her head as the girls walked away, knowing full well what items of which she spoke. One was probably the tiny penny knife she had produced when they carved their initials into the great oak tree, and another the silver flask she likely had hidden somewhere upon her person.

"What would you like to do?" Emma asked. "I spent all my allowance, so we may go anywhere you choose."

Julia looked up and down the high street. "I shall buy us a scone later, but for now, I wish to visit the jeweler."

They passed dozens of people, most racing as if they had urgent business to complete. As they approached an alleyway, Emma paused and motioned ahead of them. "Cutting through here will be quicker, and we will not have to fight our way through the crowds."

Shadows filled the narrow space as Julia considered whether they should enter. It was never wise for a lady to walk alone through areas where few tread, or so Mrs. Rutley had always counseled. Yet, she was not alone if Emma accompanied her.

"Very well," Julia said. "But if there are any strange men, we must ignore them. No banters, no attempts at bravery. Agreed?"

Emma laughed. "Agreed."

Once the cooler air hit them and the odor of rubbish assailed their noses, however, Emma clasped Julia tightly by the arm. "Do you think there are murderers hiding here?"

"Of course not," Julia replied, although she was not so sure. "Come, let us hurry."

With swift steps, they walked past the stacked crates and the doors that led to the back entrance to the various establishments. When they passed one door in particular, a strange noise caught Julia's attention.

"It's a gaming hell," Emma whispered. "I heard they never close, not even at night, and men of all sorts play games of chance or drink. Apparently, terrible fights break out in these places quite often."

Julia studied the leaning structure. It had perhaps a dozen windows, and the raucous sounds of yelling and laughter emitted from them. "All the more reason we should hurry, Emma. Come, this is no place for a lady to be caught gawking!"

It was a relief when they reached the sunshine at the opposite end of the alleyway. They made a left and paused at the window that looked into the jewelry shop.

"I did not know you could afford such luxuries," Emma said with wide eyes. "Do you plan on purchasing a necklace?"

"My parents are as poor as yours," Julia said with a snort. "I'm here to look at betrothal rings. I would like to guess which one Matthew plans to buy for me."

Emma giggled as they entered the shop.

The proprietor, Mr. Pollard, was a short, thin man with a pair of spectacles perched on the tip of his nose and a tiny magnifying glass attached to a strap around his head. He looked them over before greeting them. "Good morning, ladies. It's lovely weather we are having today, is it not?"

"Indeed, it is, sir," Julia said. "I wish to look at betrothal rings." The glasses slid down his nose in what she could only interpret as annoyance.

"You are aware that it is a man who makes such a purchase?"

"I am quite aware," she said. "I only wish to browse." Fearing the man would ask them to leave, she added, "The one who will be proposing to me mentioned you by name. That is the reason I came to your lovely shop."

The man's frown reversed. "Why, of course. You will find several examples in this case here." He walked over to one in particular and produced a wooden box displaying a variety of rings. "Allow me to show you these." He pulled a silver band from the box and handed it to her.

"It's lovely," Julia said with awe. "May I try it on?"

"Of course."

She slid the ring over her finger and put her hand out to admire it from afar. How could such a simple band mean so much? It was a sign of commitment, but Julia knew it meant much more. One day, Matthew would give her such a ring, and she hoped the day came sooner than later. To think the same man who had once accused her of theft would soon ask for her hand!

Seeing the jeweler frown, Julia asked, "Did you create this ring, sir?" Julia asked. "The craftsmanship is wonderful."

"I did," the jeweler said, his voice filled with pride. "I've been creating jewelry for nearly thirty years now, and I enjoy it today as much as I did when I first began my apprenticeship. Whenever I see my creations enjoyed by ladies such as yourself, it brings me great pleasure."

Reluctantly, she removed the ring and returned to the man, who turned to Emma. "And you, miss? Do you see any that catch your eye?"

"No, thank you," Emma replied. "I have no need."

Julia winced at the sadness in her friend's voice. Emma was destined to marry a man for whom she cared nothing. Yet perhaps she could help lift the girl's spirits.

"Pretend that Lord St. John is choosing one for you." Granted, the man was a rogue and likely the worse person Julia could have suggested, but Emma's face lit up just the same. Julia glanced at the proprietor, but the name did not seem to faze him in the least. Thank heavens.

Choosing a different gimmal ring, this one a pair rather than a trio, Emma slipped it onto her finger, a dreamy look in her eyes. "My name will be Emma St. John when I marry."

Oh no, what have I done? Julia asked herself. "Come, Emma, let us go to the tea house. Thank you for your time, Mr. Pollard."

They returned to the alleyway. It truly did cut a good bit of time rather than going to the next street. "After we purchase our scones, I say we join the others at the millinery." Emma nodded, and Julia slipped her arm through that of her friend once more. "You have a lovestruck look. Surely you would not truly entertain the idea of marrying that man."

"If he were to propose, I would not be so rude as not to at least consider it. He is quite handsome, after all, and a lady should not be so quick to dismiss him."

This made them both laugh, but as they drew closer to the gaming hall, the shouts that had been inside earlier were much louder. Standing in the doorway were two men arguing.

"Baron or not," the one inside was saying as he pointed a finger, "we'll not extend you a farthing more credit until you pay what's already owed! Now, the next time I see you, you'd best have enough money to cover your bill or don't bother coming back at all!"

"But my coat is inside," the baron said. "What am I supposed to do, run around town in nothing but my waistcoat?"

"Until you pay off your debt, we'll say your coat's a form of collateral. But don't worry, I'll take real good care of it for you." The burly man burst out in laughter that became muted when the door slammed shut.

As soon as the baron turned, Julia recognized him immediately. As did Emma.

"That's Lord St. John," Emma whispered. "Julia, you must agree that there is no man more handsome or more noble than him in the entire world."

Indeed, Lord St. John was a handsome man with his short, dark wavy hair and chiseled, although unshaven, jawline. Yet she could not in good conscience say he appeared noble, not when he stumbled down the single step, cursing and reeking of stale ale. His clothing was so disheveled, it appeared he had slept in it for several days. Or had not slept at all.

He stopped and eyed Julia and Emma. "Ladies," he said, lifting an imaginary hat as he swayed before them.

"Forgive us, my lord," Julia said. "We wish only to pass." She took a step forward, meaning to walk past him, but he held up a hand to forestall them.

Emma wore a ridiculous grin. What did she see in such a disgusting man?

"You may pass," he said, his voice slurring, "but I have a question I would like answered." He looked at Emma. "What is your name, for I believe I've seen you before and thought you beautiful."

Julia pursed her lips. If he believed he could get Emma to give such information, he was quite mistaken. How many times had Mrs. Rutley instructed them never to give their name to a man before being properly introduced?

"Miss Emma Hunter," Emma replied readily. "And I already know your name, my lord. You are Lord St. John. You once winked at me, and I've never forgotten. In truth, I've thought of that day often."

Julia gaped at her friend. Had she forgotten all her training?

The baron grinned. "Indeed, that was I who did that, Miss Hunter, and I assure you it was the first and only time I gave such attention to any young lady."

Emma giggled, but Julia considered pulling her friend toward the exit. By the hair if need be!

"Now, Miss Hunter, allow me to say that you may pass, but I shall require a toll."

"A toll, my lord?" Emma asked. She was enjoying herself far too much.

"Indeed. And I'll offer you a bargain of one kiss for two to pass, as long as that kiss comes from you, Miss Hunter."

Julia had heard enough. Baron or not, Lord St. John was no gentleman. "I believe I speak for both Miss Hunter and myself when I say that we are ladies and don't engage in such nefarious activities. Now, please allow us to pass so we may return to running errands."

She turned to Emma to tell her they were leaving, only to find the girl with her eyes closed, her lips puckered, and her head tilted upwards! To Julia's horror, the baron placed his hands on either side of Emma's face... and kissed her on the lips!

"Don't forget that you have now been kissed by a baron," he said. Then he gave a shaky bow and walked past them. "Good day to you, ladies!" he shouted without turning. "Especially to you, Miss Hunter."

"Oh, Emma, what have you done?"

Emma opened her eyes and sighed. "I'm uncertain, but it was more wonderful than I ever imagined! I feel as if I could float above the footpath rather than walk upon it. Do you believe it's love I'm feeling?"

Julia had to get Emma back to civilized society as quickly as possible, so she pulled Emma by the arm and forced her to walk. "Of course it's not," she snapped. "I suspect you have become drunk by the spirits on his breath, they were so strong. Now come, before you decide to kiss someone else!"

What frightened Julia the most was that her friend had fallen in love with that man long before she even knew him!

Chapter Twenty-Four

Saturday arrived sooner than Matthew had expected. He had spent the week preparing for the business meetings, which would not only increase his wealth but also would help him gain a great deal of recognition from his peers. Yet throughout all the preparations, he could not help but feel a twinge of guilt about Julia. She had waited with the patience of an angel for him to announce their courtship. Initially, he had hoped her parents would visit so he could handle their courtship properly, but even he had to admit that January was much too long to wait. Granted, he could have taken the time to go to them, but with his current commitments, he simply did not have the time.

Matthew glanced at his reflection. Taking his uncle's advice to wait had been a good choice, for he was in no state to make the perfect impression on Julia's father. His eyes were red and his face thin after too many days of working far too late into the night and rising before the sun, all so he would be as ready as he could possibly be for the coming week. He had assessed the cost of land and the building of the various hotels, including how many rooms each would offer and how much they would charge. Soon, numbers blurred into one another, tea shops became farms, and wool became shillings. Everything had muddled together by the time he had gone off to bed, but he was proud of the work he had completed.

When Lady Dyer arrived at Hardwick Hall for dinner, Matthew stood beside his uncle as Hickson invited her into the foyer. She wore a blood-red gown that went nicely with her auburn curls. Despite her stately appearance, sadness and dismay crowded her features.

Matthew bowed to the baroness. "Lady Dyer, I'm so pleased you were able to come."

"Thank you," she whispered. Then she sighed. "Once again I've come to burden the Colburn family with my troubles. How do you ever put up with me?"

"Now, there will be no such talk," Uncle Ezra said. "Not in the company of friends. You are not a burden, I assure you. We are here to listen to your woes and to share any crumbs of wisdom we may be able to conjure. Something my nephew has taught me as of late."

Pride straightened Matthew's back. His uncle had made great changes over the past few weeks. Gone was the overbearing man, and in his place was one filled with compassion. Lady Dyer's presence this evening was testimony to that.

"Please, come in," Matthew said with a smile as he offered his arm. "Let us eat and enjoy one another's company, and after, we shall discuss what is troubling you. Upsetting oneself while eating is bad for the digestion, after all."

And that they did. The food was delicious and the discussion pleasant, but a cloud hung over them, or so Matthew felt, as they waited for the inevitable conversation to come.

"And how has your week gone?" Lady Dyer asked of Matthew.

Matthew gave a weak smile. "Preparing for an important gathering of several business associates has been somewhat overwhelming, but I admit the challenge is invigorating. I find myself anxious to see the results of our hard work."

"How wonderful for you," the baroness replied. "My week has also been far more of a challenge than that to which I'm accustomed. I have few friends, and with Gregory gone... no, we shall discuss that later."

Matthew was curious about this Mr. Gregory Thompson. Lady

Dyer had often mentioned the man and their growing admiration for one another in her letters. So, he had jilted her, then.

The remainder of the meal went smoothly, and when the last course had been removed, Uncle Ezra stood. "I say we move to the drawing room. I shall have coffee brought up unless you would prefer something a bit… stronger?"

"Is it wrong that I would prefer sherry?" Lady Dyer asked, her cheeks turning pink.

Uncle Ezra laughed. "Certainly not, and I'm sure Matthew would prefer brandy, as would I." He tilted his head toward the baroness to indicate to Matthew he should help her stand.

"Allow me," Matthew said as he pulled out her chair. He offered her his arm, which she readily accepted, and they walked together to the drawing room.

Once they were seated and the drinks had been poured, Matthew smiled at the baroness. "In your last letter, you stated that you fear losing your home. So many are suffering in these trying times."

She blushed as she looked down at the glass in her hand. "I find admitting as much embarrassing, but the estate is in near ruins. I've sold all the artwork, the many adornments Averill had purchased over his lifetime, and any other items of value. My bed may be the next item I sell, and I'll be left to sleep on the floor. If I'm able to keep the very floor, that is."

The idea of this woman suffering any more than she already had since losing her husband rankled Matthew. He could not simply give her money outright—that would be inappropriate and likely refused—but perhaps he could offer her a loan or contact her financial adviser about investing in one of her husband's businesses.

"If you don't mind my saying," Uncle Ezra said, "you would be better off marrying a man who will be able to pay off the debts Averill accumulated, thus saving you and your home."

Lady Dyer frowned. "But if I were to marry, would I not live in another home? The home of my new husband?"

Uncle Ezra smiled. "Consider it a wedding gift to your heir."

Although Lady Dyer nodded her agreement, Matthew could see that her worry did not decrease. She was clearly hiding something.

"This man, Mr. Thompson, can you and he not marry and thus put everything to rights?"

The baroness let out a choked cry and covered her face with her hands. "That is just it," she said. "Gregory is gone."

"Gone?" Matthew asked. "Gone how?"

His uncle shot him a stern glare. "It's quite clear what she means, Matthew. The man jilted her." He stood. "I believe this topic would be much easier if I left the two of you alone. Matthew has some experience with matters of the heart, but I have none. I fear my presence will only serve as eavesdropper rather than contributor, and this matter is far too private for eavesdropping. I shall leave you in Matthew's capable hands."

"If you believe it appropriate," Lady Dyer said. "And I thank you for considering my privacy."

Once his uncle was gone, Matthew leaned forward in his chair. "Now, tell me what happened. Did this man hurt you in some way?" When she did not respond, he added, "Frances, we are friends, and although I wish to help, I cannot unless you tell me what occurred."

The baroness heaved a sigh. "You are right, but may I request that you sit beside me? I fear someone may overhear, and that would just add more shame to an already terrible situation."

Rather than arguing that she had nothing to fear—their servants did not spend their time listening at keyholes or peering through windows—Matthew walked over to sit beside her on the sofa. "Now, tell me what has happened."

"Oh, Matthew," she lamented, "I'm a horrible woman! I must confess what I've done, but I'm so frightened what you will think of me."

"There is no need to fear me," Matthew said. "I'll not judge you."

A smile crossed her lips, and her eyes lit up as she placed a hand on top of his. "No, you would not, for you are a wonderful friend. You have always been honest with me, so I shall be honest with you. Gregory proposed to me, and I refused. When he pleaded with me to explain why, I told him the truth." A tear rolled down her cheek, and she quickly wiped it away. "That truth crushed him, and now I'm conflicted as to whether or not what I revealed was the right thing to do."

"What did you tell him that was so terrible?"

She glanced at her now empty glass. "May I have one more? For courage."

Nodding, he collected their glasses and went to refill them. He had consumed far too much wine at dinner, and now on his second glass of brandy, his head was beginning to spin. He needed to be careful, or he would become drunk. What good would he be to the baroness in that state?

"Yes, she is quite beautiful," Frances said.

"Sorry?"

"Julia, Miss Wallace, she is beautiful."

Matthew frowned. "Why are you speaking about her?"

"You just said you thought she is beautiful, and I was agreeing," Frances said with a knitted brow. "Or did you not mean to speak your thoughts aloud?"

His breath caught. How many times had he voiced his thoughts without realizing? Yet, he had not been thinking of Julia but rather his concern of becoming drunk. With a pounding heart, he returned to the sofa and handed her the sherry.

"You were speaking of what you revealed to Mr. Thompson," he said. "Go on."

"Yes well, when Gregory proposed, he professed his love for me. And therein lies the crux of my trouble. I don't love him, nor could I ever." She dropped her gaze. "And I told him as much. You may find it odd, but I wish to marry a man who is in need of an heir but otherwise wants only companionship. I've seen what love can do when it's lost, and I don't wish to travel that same road again."

If she had broached this subject before he began calling on Julia, he would have readily agreed with her outlook. Now however, he was not so sure.

She looked at him, her eyes glistening. "Was I cruel for speaking the truth? Or should I've lied to save him from the hurt I inflicted upon him?"

Her question was like a knight's lance piercing his heart with guilt.

He had not been truthful with Julia about his fears, and now he had created a fissure between them. How could he lie to Frances and say she had not done what was right?

"No, you were not wrong," he said. "I've withheld things from Julia, and now I'm finding I regret doing so."

"You speak of the fear that you have inherited your father's madness." It was a statement, not a question. She knew! But how? "Your uncle is concerned about you, as am I." Her eyes widened. "Oh, I did not mean to say that your uncle has been gossiping about you with me. He has simply worried about you and felt he could speak to me about his concerns." She placed her hand atop his once more. "My apologies. I should not have said anything."

Matthew chose to neither confirm nor deny his fears. The fears were his, and his alone. "What did you tell my uncle when he revealed this to you?"

"Do you want the truth?" she asked. Matthew nodded. She leaned forward to set her glass on the table. "I told him that Miss Wallace is a beautiful young lady with a lovely nature. I wish I had her disposition." She shook her head. "Yet despite her wonderful intentions, I'm unsure her spirit can endure the problems she will be forced to face once your health worsens. I suspect that it will cause her so much pain that she likely will never recover."

Bile rose in Matthew's throat, and he washed it down with the last of his brandy. Not because he was angry with Frances but rather for the fact that she had confirmed his worst fears.

"Your uncle will support you, as shall I, with any decision you make. As a woman, however, I must consider the heart of another woman. Please, don't break hers."

Matthew gave a numb nod. "Thank you for your honesty and for your wise counsel. I fear my mind is not as sharp as I once thought."

The baroness pulled her hand away in fright.

"What did I say?" he asked.

"Nothing," she whispered, although she backed away farther. "It's nothing."

"Don't lie to me now," he said, his frustration rising. "What is it I said that caused you to withdraw from me?" She looked as if he had raised a hand to her, so he forced calm to his tone. "Please, Frances, I would never hurt you."

She gave a small nod, but the fear remained in her eyes. "Wh-when you spoke aloud and did not recall, it was not the first time you have done so. You have done so on several occasions, but I've said nothing because I did not wish to upset you. When I mentioned it to your uncle, he agreed that I did the right thing."

"Are you saying that my uncle has witnessed it, as well?" Matthew asked with alarm. "Why has he never mentioned it to me?" The world began to spin around him, and he slammed a fist on his thigh to bring it to a halt. "Why is everyone keeping things from me?"

"Because we care, Nephew," Uncle Ezra said as he entered the room. "We care and are concerned for you."

The baroness rose. "I owe you an apology, my lord. I betrayed your trust in sharing what you confided in me, but the truth is, I could no longer hide it. I just hope you can forgive me."

His uncle walked around the back of the sofa and placed a hand on Matthew's shoulder. "No, Lady Dyer, it was you who had the decency to be honest. As we all should have been."

There was that word again—honest. Matthew had so many truths he had not told Julia. What kind of monster was he?

The kind that becomes mad!

"I'm sorry, Nephew," his uncle said as he squeezed Matthew's shoulder. "I feared revealing the truth would be detrimental to you, but I see now that I only made matters worse by making you believe that everything was all right."

"It's because you care, my lord," Frances said, retaking her seat. "We both care for him and don't wish to see him suffer." She set her hand atop his once more. "I swear to you that whatever you need, I shall be there no matter what happens to you."

"As shall I," his uncle said.

"These utterings," Matthew said, turning to look up at his uncle, "were they the first indication of Father's madness?"

"I'm afraid so."

"And he was gone four years later," Matthew mused. "If that is true, and I'm already experiencing them..." Soon, he would be singing down the corridors and wandering the grounds at night.

"Julia," he whispered.

Lady Dyer gave him a sympathetic look. "If you care for her, which I believe you do, then you must let her go, just as I did Gregory. It will hurt now, but in the end, it will save her. The choice is yours, of course, but I believe your uncle agrees with me when I say you must consider her future as much as you do yours."

His uncle nodded. "As I said before, it's why I've tried from the start to keep the two of you apart. I know you resented me for it, but I did not wish to see either of you hurt. You are more my nephew than you are the duke, at least in my eyes, but whatever decision you make, I'll support it."

Lady Dyer's eyes were brimming with tears as she gripped his hand tight. He was indeed fortunate to have her as a friend and to have an overbearing uncle with his best interests at heart.

"You should find the guest cottage suitable but please don't hesitate to ask if you need anything," he said. "Go and rest while I think over matters." Once she was gone, his thoughts returned to Julia, the woman for whom he cared so deeply that he wished to be in her presence forever. Yet, eternity was short-lived when his mind was destined to be lost. No, he cared for her far too much to allow her to endure such suffering.

"I shall speak to Julia," he said, forcing the words from his lips. "And although I know I risk crushing her heart, my denying her now will save her in the end."

The question was, would he survive letting her go?

Chapter Twenty-Five

Julia swatted away a fly as she waited for the last of the girls to flick out their blankets beneath the great oak tree, the same around which they had taken their oaths of sisterhood. They were here to make another.

"I'll be sad when some of you leave in January," Diana said with a sigh. "It will not be the same with you gone." She took Julia's hand and gave it a squeeze when she said the latter.

"I would not worry too much," Julia said. "We will write one another. Plus, it will give you the opportunity to become a wonderful leader to the new girls who arrive once I'm no longer here." Diana's smile told Julia that she was ready to take on that responsibility, and Unity voiced her agreement.

Sighing, Julia looked over the other girls. Regardless of her leaving, she and her friends would always be connected. Just as she and Matthew now were. Each of her friends was dear to her heart, and knowing she would soon announce the courtship with Matthew sent a jolt of excitement through her body. They would be announcing their subsequent wedding soon after, she was certain.

One week from tomorrow, Matthew would begin his deliberations, which were to last the week. These past few days had been difficult not seeing him, but she understood the magnitude of the path set before him. He needed time to prepare properly if he was to be successful in his negotiations. When he was done, they would celebrate his inevitable victory as well as announce their courtship.

Soon, she would become a duchess, a title she would carry with honor. That would be followed by children, as many as he wanted. That thought brought an even broader smile to her lips.

Yet, when she had spoken of their future, Matthew had become distant. And to think that he was thinking about Lady Dyer at that time did not sit well with her.

"Come now, Julia, he is busy with his meetings," she assured herself. "Don't think that he avoids you because he does not care for you."

A chorus of giggles told her that she had once again voiced her thoughts, but rather than denying it this time, she added, "Yes, I said that for all to hear, and I'm glad I did." She joined them in their laughter. In front of whom else could she make a fool of herself than her sisters?

The sound of hoofbeats made her look up to see a chestnut mare galloping up the drive, leaving a trail of dust behind. The rider dismounted and hurried to the door, and Mrs. Rutley greeted him.

"It appears our dear headmistress receives word from her lover," Ruth said, her eyes gleaming with mischief. "Though from which lover remains to be seen."

Jaws hung open and gasps erupted around them as Julia said, "Ruth! How could you say such a terrible thing? Mrs. Rutley is a lady and conducts herself as such. You should be ashamed of yourself, spreading wild tales about her in such a heinous manner!"

Ruth, who was leaning with her back against the tree, twirled a blade of grass in her fingers. "Remember when that black carriage collected her?"

Julia nodded. How could she not? She and Matthew had professed their feelings for one another on the rooftop of the outbuilding that night.

"Well, that carriage belongs to Lord St. John."

"What?" Emma asked as if the world had just been upended. "That cannot be possible. Tell me you are jesting!"

"I cannot, for it's true. And why would the Baron of Rake Street meet with our respectable headmistress? Do you think she is giving him lessons in philosophy?" Even Julia found herself shaking her head at this. "You see, it can only be a secret romance. I admit that I admire her for her tenacity. After all, he is at least twenty years her younger."

Emma appeared as if she were ready to burst into tears. Julia motioned to Jenny, and Jenny wrapped a comforting arm around Emma.

"We have no idea why Mrs. Rutley met with the baron," Julia said, looking at each young woman around her. "And speculation is unwise. Surely none of you wish others to make idle speculations about you." She gave Ruth a pointed look as she used her eyes to motion toward Emma. "Even you can see the sense in what I'm saying, can you not?"

Ruth's eyes went wide before she nodded and said to Emma, "What Julia says is true. I was only teasing. I'm sorry, Emma. I'll not jest like that again. I did not do it to hurt you."

With peace once again restored, Julia settled back to wait for Mrs. Rutley to join them. Hopefully, whatever message the headmistress received would not force her to postpone the Sisterhood's time together.

A shadow fell over her, and Julia looked up to see Mrs. Rutley staring down at her. "Julia, come with me, please." The woman wore such a stern expression, Julia found swallowing difficult. In the headmistress's hand she held two letters, one of which she handed to Julia.

"Who is it from?" Julia asked as she walked toward the house at Mrs. Rutley's side. What a silly question. All she had to do was open and read it to see the sender.

"Your parents," Mrs. Rutley replied. "And apparently it must be read immediately."

They stopped halfway between the tree and the portico. A sense of dread washed over Julia as she slid a fingernail beneath the plain seal. Immediately, she recognized the flowery handwriting as that of her mother.

Dear Julia,

. . .

There have been great changes since we last spoke, and I write to you with wonderful news. Lord Howe has spoken at great length with your father concerning your courtship and eventual marriage. He has indicated that he no longer wishes to wait for you to complete your training. Therefore, on Monday the 16th, your father and I will collect you from the school. I expect you to be packed and ready to leave, for you know how your father hates waiting. We have already informed Mrs. Rutley that we will no longer be needing her services.

With love,
Hortensia Wallace

The words began to blur together. "But that is this coming Monday! It's far too late for me to reply and tell them that Matthew and I are courting."

Mrs. Rutley placed a hand on Julia's arm. "Besides you and the duke, has anyone else been informed of your courtship?"

Julia shook her head. Then an idea occurred to her. "But it does not matter. Matthew will simply speak to Father about our situation. How can he refuse? After all, a duke is far better than a baron." Then her thoughts returned to her father's tirade concerning Matthew and his possible madness. "No, he will not refuse us. Matthew will convince Father we should be together. I know he will."

"You must prepare yourself for the worst. If that happens, you will return home with your parents and begin preparing for your marriage to Lord Howe."

"That will not happen," Julia said firmly. "Or rather Matthew will not allow that to happen. He pledged to protect me, and he cares for me. I shall make certain he is here when my parents arrive so he can speak to Father." She paused, her eyes widening with fear. "Oh, Mrs. Rutley, Matthew's meetings begin that Monday! He will not be able to call, for he will be far too busy. We agreed not to see one another until after his business is completed to give him time to prepare, but I must speak to him and explain what has happened. If I do not, he will come here and find me gone!"

Mrs. Rutley tapped her lips with a finger. "This is a conundrum," she murmured. "Here is what I suggest. Send word to His Grace to meet with you tomorrow. I shall excuse you from your lessons for the day, but you must make up the work that night. You may be leaving soon, but you are still a student here. Understood?"

Julia nodded, and when Mrs. Rutley stared up at the sky, she looked up to see a bank of dark clouds threatening a storm.

"Then hurry," Mrs. Rutley said, "for I don't like what I see coming."

Julia frowned as Mrs. Rutley hurried back inside. When she glanced back at the sky, she knew she had little time before the storm hit.

"Ladies," she said as she joined her sisters, "we must speak, for I've received the most unsettling news." She told them of the letter and her concerns of her father's refusal of Matthew. "My worry is that because Father thinks him mad, he will refuse his request, especially on such short notice. My father has never been one to back out on his word and if he has already made an agreement with Lord Rowe, I may be destined to a life I don't want. What do you think?"

Unity said, "He will see how much you care for the duke, which will make it impossible for him to refuse." Her certainty was like a salve.

"I think your father will realize the wealth the duke has, and his greed will change his mind." This came from Jenny.

Ruth, however, stood, and the look she wore made Julia uneasy. "I say it does not matter what your father wants. If he says no, you will simply run away and marry the duke, anyway. He cannot stop you once you are already married. I heard that if a couple goes to Scotland, they don't require banns to be read or for parents to give their permission."

The very idea of doing such a bold act did not sit well with Julia. No matter how much she adored Matthew, no matter how much she wanted to be with him, she could never bring her family that much shame—or herself and Matthew, for that matter.

She turned to Ruth. "May I ask one last favor of you? I must meet with Matthew tomorrow. Will you send him a message? Tell him to meet at the brook. He will know."

Ruth scrunched her brow. "You write the letter, and I shall see it gets to him. I believe the gardener owes me a favor."

"Thank you," Julia said just as the first spits of rain began to fall. "Mrs. Rutley is worried, but I believe all will end well. Do you agree?"

Rather than affirmation, the others shrieked when a great clang of thunder shook the ground beneath them, and rain burst forth from the clouds. They gathered their skirts and ran toward the house, some using the blankets to cover themselves from the deluge. Once inside, Julia went straight to her room and wrote her letter. But would Matthew heed her call?

Rain pelted the windows of Hardwick Hall, and thunder caused those very same panes to rattle. Matthew watched as the gardeners collected their tools and rushed to find shelter.

Although he had made the decision the night before concerning Julia, he had yet to inform her. Doing so by letter was a cowardly act, and he was no coward. No, he would have to wait until next week to inform her of his decision. These negotiations, unlike all the others, were ones he did not look forward to attending. The last thing he wished to do was hurt Julia, but in the end, she would thank him for his consideration for her future. She deserved to be with a man who could take care of her the way she deserved, not one she would be forced to care for instead.

After he had retired the night before, he spent many hours trying to work out any scenario in which Julia would not be hurt, yet all ended with her brokenhearted. His, too, was broken, but that mattered far less. Therefore, if he truly cared for her, he had no other choice than to tell her he could not be with her.

"Matthew?" He turned to find Frances at the door. "Am I disturbing you?"

He forced a smile. "No, please, come in. Did you find your accommodations comfortable?"

"Quite," she replied. "Although, I must admit, I had trouble sleeping. I was worried about you." She touched his arm with the tips of her fingers. "I cannot help but worry. You carry such a burden, and I have no way to help you."

He sighed. "You have done more than a dozen friends could wish for," he said. "It is I who wonders how I can help you."

She smiled. "Just allow me to always be your friend, that is all I ask."

How could he refuse? So many saw a man in his position as nothing more than a means to meet their selfish needs, but not Lady Dyer. She truly was his friend.

"You will always be my friend, Frances. And it's an honor to know a lady who possesses such dignity, such honor."

Her wince made him frown. Perhaps she was one who did not take compliments well. The discomforted look was gone so quickly, he wondered if he had imagined it.

"Allow me to refill your drink," she said, taking his glass from his hand before he could respond. She returned, a drink for herself in her other hand as she handed him back his.

He nodded his thanks, and as he took a sip of his brandy, his thoughts returned to the conversation they had shared the previous night. Four years. That was his guess as to how long he had left on this earth. Perhaps he would still have the luck Julia had given him and live another year longer, but he found it unlikely. Not only would his life end, but so would the prospect of an heir. Perhaps that was for the best, anyway. This madness had to end somewhere, so why not with him?

"Your eyes reveal more than you know," Lady Dyer said. "You should not be ashamed of your illness. I shall be here to help you through it."

"How can I not be ashamed?" he said in a voice harsher than he had intended. "Next week, I shall inform Julia that I must end our courtship so I can prepare for a madness that will claim my life. I shall never have a son upon whom I can bequeath the dukedom. Uncle Ezra and I are the last male descendants of the Colburn name, and as my uncle never married, he, too, will have no sons. It's a travesty."

Frances let out a sob and before he knew it, she had her cheek pressed against his chest. "You would be a wonderful father, Matthew," she murmured into his coat. "Your son would be a most noble gentleman. This does not need to be a story of sadness but one of hope!"

Matthew snorted. "There is no hope, Frances. I'll not marry Julia only to see her hurt. You know this. And if I don't marry her, I shall have no son."

"Then allow me the honor," she said, looking up at him.

Matthew's heartbeat increased in alarm, and he pushed her away. "What are you saying? Do you think I'll bed you for the sake of an heir?"

A tear rolled down her cheek. "I would hope you think better of me, my friend."

Guilt tickled the back of his mind. "My apologies. I'm confused and lost and therefore cannot think straight. What exactly are you suggesting?"

Setting her glass on the windowsill, she took his and placed it next to hers. "I believe we were meant to be friends, for we are very much alike, you and I. I could never marry Gregory, and you cannot marry Julia because neither of us want to hurt the ones we care for the most. Yet with another, you can still have a son."

"No, Frances, you must—"

"Allow me to interrupt just once more," she said. "I believe you should hear what I propose." She drew in a deep breath and continued. "We are friends, yet we have no romantic feelings for one another, and I'm confident that none will develop. Would you agree?"

"I would."

"Then I say that in the act of helping one another, we marry, as friends, of course. I shall give you a son, a boy who can carry your name with pride, one who will succeed where you did not. You will also have a wife who, though sad, will not be heartbroken when you are gone."

Now who is mad? he wondered. Yet, her suggestion was not unreasonable. "Are you saying that you wish to have my son and heir, who you would raise with the help of my uncle?" The baroness nodded. "A son who may be the first to break this curse that has plagued my family for generations. You would do this for me?"

"When I was ostracized and left alone, you invited me to your party, despite how much it would taint your name. You made me feel important for the first time in a very long time. I would be honored to give you an heir, my friend, for it's the least I can do." She dropped her gaze. "I would make one request if I'm to do this."

Matthew frowned. What could she possibly want? Money? Jewelry? She would have all that and more as a duchess, regardless.

"If you agree to this, you must promise me it's done in friendship and nothing more. If I do sense that something more is developing, I'll warn you, for my motive is not to have us fall in love. And although you are in control of the estate and your family, if you refuse my warning, I have every right to reside in another home."

The realization that she truly did not wish to control him brought him a sense of relief. "Without Julia, I have no intention of loving another." Then his stomach clenched. He had not yet informed Julia, and he was already considering marriage to another woman? One he did not love, to be sure, but still another. "May I have time to consider this?" he asked. "I may need several days, if not weeks, to think on it before I decide. Regardless of my answer, know that you have given me hope on this dark day."

With a kind smile, she took her wine glass just as Hickson entered the room.

"Your Grace, a letter was just delivered for you."

Waving over the butler, Matthew took the parchment from the silver tray. Hickson bowed and left the room.

My Dearest Matthew,

I realize you are very busy making preparations for your meetings next week, but I must beg of you to meet with me, for I have something of the utmost importance to share with you. Please meet me at the brook, or as you refer to it, the River Thames, at one tomorrow afternoon. I shall be waiting.

. . .

Yours,
Julia

His heart ached as he thought of the brook and the day they had jumped over it together. They had conquered one of his fears there with her by his side. He wished this encounter could be just as wonderful, just as beautiful, but alas, he knew it could not be.

"The distress on your face tells me who the sender of that letter is," Frances said.

Matthew nodded. "Julia wishes to meet tomorrow. I shall answer her call but knowing full well it will be for the last time."

Frances laid a hand on his chest. "You are an honorable man, Matthew, but you must hurt her now or see her suffer far worse later."

The baroness could not have been more correct. It would hurt them terribly, but in the end, it was for the best.

The only question was, could he reveal this terrible news and risk never seeing her again? Of that, he was unsure.

Chapter Twenty-Six

The sun had returned, and the grass beneath Julia's feet was dry as she and Bridget walked through the field that led to the brook. She could barely contain her excitement, for she had no doubt Matthew would see the gravity of the situation and rush to her aid. Once he explained the situation to her father, they could announce their courtship without fear of repercussions.

"Your dress matches the flowers," Bridget quipped.

Julia laughed. Indeed, white daisies and purple-red champions dotted her skirts, and the yellow of the fabric matched the ribbon on her hat. "You have a wonderful eye, Bridget. The way you can always select the perfect ensemble always amazes me. I don't know what I would do without you. If I were left to choose my own clothes, I would only embarrass myself."

"Oh, I doubt that, Miss Julia. You've a better eye than you give yourself credit for. Every night before I go to sleep, I offer up a prayer of thanks for my good health and for being able to serve a fine lady such as yourself. And I give thanks that He's given you beauty but not the sense to select a dress, for that would mean you don't need me anymore."

Julia gave a feigned gasp of indignation and then laughed. "Well,

I'm thankful for you. Just think, not only are we friends, but you will be there when all the important events happen. When I marry, when my first child is born... oh, for so many events! Unless you don't wish to be there."

"There's no one else I'd rather work for, Miss Julia," Bridget said, smiling. "Who else would pay me to be their friend?"

They continued to laugh and talk, and as the brook came into view, Julia's heart quickened upon seeing Matthew waiting on the opposite bank. Yet as they drew closer, her smile faded. His clothes were disheveled, his hair looked as if he had not combed it in days, and his expression beneath the stubble on his face was far less welcoming than she would have expected. Even the lines of worry around his eyes were deeper than usual.

Then a realization hit her. His work schedule had been so full, he had not taken care of himself.

"I'm so happy to see you, Matthew," Julia said as she walked to her side of the brook. "I'm glad you came because I have much I must share with you."

"As do I," he said. "It's important that you listen, for what I must say is very difficult, yet it must be said."

Julia could not help but smile. Although she adored him, she was wise enough to understand that men struggled to admit their feelings, which was why women were left with the difficult task of being the first to say how they feel. That in itself was a complication, for were men not supposed to be the first to express their admiration for a woman? With such societal rules in place, it was no wonder so many marriages were arranged!

He went to say more, but she lifted a hand to forestall him. "What I must say is also important. It concerns my father, so I shall begin if I may." He nodded. "Mother wrote to me, informing me that she and Father will be coming to collect me the morning of the sixteenth. Lord Howe has asked my father for permission to court me. Of course, he is unaware that we are already courting."

"Julia—"

"I was fearful, for I know my father can be stubborn. He has heard about your... malady, but we—you and I—we know the truth." When he looked away from her, her heart constricted. She had to address this first. "The truth is that we care for one another. Deeply, in fact. I've given it careful consideration and have come to realize just how deeply those feelings go." She paused as a gentle breeze blew back several strands of his hair to reveal eyes heavy with exhaustion. Perhaps now was not the best time to express what was on her heart, but having already begun, she could not stop the words from coming.

"What began as a means for you to find your missing pocket watch turned into something beautiful. We are more than simple friends now. We share a bond so strong that I was unsure how to describe it. Yet Mrs. Rutley explained that a day would come when I would have no choice but to express what was on my heart, and that day has come. Matthew, it's love we share, a love so strong it hurts when we are apart. A love that has brought us together and can never keep us apart. It's that love between us that my father will see and will have him readily agree when you tell him that we are courting."

She wiped tears from her cheeks. "I know you have much to do, but you must find a way to come to the school early Monday morning. Unless you would rather see me marry Lord Howe..." She gave a tiny chuckle at the absurdity of that statement. "I fell in love with you, Matthew. I don't know the exact moment it first happened, but it feels as if it has been an eternity."

Matthew turned away. Was that pain on his face? No, he loved her as much as she loved him, she had no doubt.

You must be patient and remain quiet, she thought. He needed time to consider this onslaught of information she had placed before him.

When he did turn to her, she nearly took a step back in shock.

"Julia, I... I'm sorry, but I cannot allow myself to love you."

All the air from her lungs disappeared, and the world began to spin around her, threatening to cast her to the side. And this time, she was unsure if Matthew would be there to catch her.

Matthew swore his heart ripped in two as Julia expressed her joy, for he knew what she hoped could not be. What choice did he have? He either hurt her a little today or allowed their love to grow and ultimately hurt her far worse later. The choice was not all that difficult to make.

"I fell in love with you, Matthew. I don't know the exact moment it first happened, but it feels as if it has been an eternity."

It was as if he had been kicked in the chest by a stallion. He turned away to hide his pain because she had voiced what he had come to believe for himself. If only he could tell her that he felt the same, but to do so was far too cruel. "I'm sorry," he finally said, tearing the words from his throat, "but I cannot allow myself to love you."

She took a step back, and he could feel her hurt even from this distance. He wanted nothing more than to leap across the brook and comfort her, but he knew he should not. Instead he said, "You should obey your father's wishes and marry this Lord Howe. I'm sure he will take good care of you." The words were like spoiled cabbage on his tongue, making him want to retch for speaking such a lie.

"But I don't want to marry Lord Howe," she said. "I want to marry you, the man I love. Why can you not love me in return? Have I embarrassed you somehow? Done something of which you don't approve?"

He shook his head.

"Is it Lady Dyer?"

"No."

"Then, I pray you tell me what is wrong, for our last discussion was about our future together, and now it seems you wish to cast me aside as if I'm riddled with the plague."

Straightening his back lest he fall down in shame, Matthew replied, "What we had was wonderful, but my luck has reached its end. There is nothing more for us to discuss. You will return home with your parents and begin preparations for your new life. I believe you will be happy."

"That is a lie!" she said with such vehemence that he had to take a step back. "Tell me truthfully that you want nothing more than for me to lie with another man, and I shall leave and never see you again!"

Matthew looked away, for he was unable to say the words.

"You speak of luck?" she demanded. "I tell you now that it does not exist!"

"That is where you are wrong," he cried. "My father believed in it, and so do I. You possess so much of it that your father needed you at his side. Luck is what caused me to complete my business transactions as of late. But I tell you now that the luck will run out, for it can never save me from my fate!" His breath was ragged by the time he finished.

"It was all lies, Matthew," Julia said in a quiet voice as she wiped tears from her eyes. Tears he had caused. "I never carried any luck. The story about my father was a fabrication. He does not believe in playing games of chance and certainly never in my presence."

"You lied to me? Why would you do such a thing?"

"I regretted doing so, but Mrs. Rutley asked me to. But do you think that matters now? Do you not see? It has been you all along, Matthew. You have brought on your success. You completed those business dealings and gained the admiration of those around you, not I. Nor was it your pocket watch or a handkerchief. It was you!"

What she said might be true, but that did not put an end to the inevitable. All he could do was let her go, so she did not suffer with him.

"I've confessed the lies you were told," she said. "I truly am sorry not only for agreeing to them, but for encouraging them as well. But now I want to know why you refuse to love me. Come now, tell me."

Fear clutched at Matthew's heart and froze his insides. Then he caught a blur of yellow as Julia leaped over the brook and came to stand before him.

"We have shared our feelings and our dreams," she said as she looked up at him. "Nothing can be kept secret but the truth. Now tell me, what is the truth?"

Anger coursed through his veins as he grabbed her by the arms. "I'm afraid!" he shouted, ignoring her gasp of pain. "There! That is the truth you wanted to hear. I'm frightened."

"Do you believe that I'm not afraid of what the future may hold?" she asked. "I'm being forced to marry a man I don't love, scared of living the life my mother has been forced to live, a woman afraid of her own shadow. A woman who still breathes but has long since died. Yet, you can save me from that fate, Matthew."

He barked a laugh. "But how can I do that when I cannot save myself? My fate is to end up as my father, and that will happen far sooner than I had expected. You have no idea how many nights I heard my mother weeping as she watched my father's sanity deteriorate. It destroyed her, Julia, crushed her to the point that she never was the same. I cannot—I will not—have that happen to you! Therefore, it's time we say goodbye."

She placed a hand in his, but he refused to grasp it. If he did, all would be lost.

"Next week," she said in a quiet voice, "you will conduct your meetings. Once they are completed, you will have earned the admiration of not only those closest to you but also those of the *ton*. But know this. When their voices die off, you will be forced to face your fears."

Julia turned toward the brook. "You are right. You may end up like your father. People may laugh and mock your name behind your back, for that is what cowards do." Her lip trembled as she turned back to him. "They may attempt to strip you of your dignity and say that Matthew Colburn was never a great duke, but that would be a lie. I believe you already are a great duke and will only become greater over time. Yet what I believe makes little difference, Matthew, for you must be the one to believe it. Luck and curses don't exist, and no one can know what the future holds, but if my words go unheard, you must know one thing. This fear you carry inside, release it, for it will only weigh on you until it ultimately destroys you. Look what it's doing to you now. You are creating your own fate, but you refuse to see it."

Julia dropped her hand and leaped back across. "We did this before together," she said from the opposite bank. "But now you must do it on your own." Tears streamed down her cheeks as she reached a hand out to him. "I'll always be here, Matthew. Now, come and join me and cast away your fears."

Matthew stared at her proffered hand. As she had done many times before, Julia had spoken words that had forced him to think rationally, proving to him there was hope. Yet unlike before, he could not accept her invitation, for she could never understand the pain she would one day face when his madness overtook him.

"I'm sorry, Julia. I cannot do this."

And with that, he turned and walked away, ignoring the cries that followed behind him, although they crushed his heart to ash.

Chapter Twenty-Seven

Five days had passed since Matthew said goodbye to Julia, and he felt none the better for it. If anything, he never felt more alone than he did now. His heart ached as his fingers rubbed the handkerchief in his pocket. If he were not careful, he would rub a hole right through the fabric. What he had first considered as a charm for good luck, he now understood was a token of love, a strong, yearning love Julia had confessed to him. Why had he been so afraid to return the sentiment?

No, he was showing her how much he cared for her by allowing her the life she deserved.

Now sitting in his office, he stared at the empty chairs that would soon be filled with gentlemen with whom he would do business. If all went well, his wealth would increase to such a magnitude that the King himself would be riddled with envy.

"What if, once it's done, those in the streets no longer speak my name? Then what?"

The opportunity to even consider the response to that question was cut short when his mother entered the room. She had arrived two days earlier, and although silver streaks battled to take control of her otherwise blonde hair, her youthful appearance remained.

"Did you sleep well, Mother?" he asked, standing and walking over to embrace her and kiss her cheek.

"I slept without waking for the first time in many years," she said. "And you, my son? Did you sleep well?"

"Yes, of course," he said in a rushed lie. "My bed is comfortable. So much so that I find it difficult to rise most mornings."

Her smile reminded him of the time he had broken a vase in the upstairs corridor and blamed the wind coming through a nearby open window.

"Then why do you look so tired?" Matthew searched his mind for any excuse that made sense, but before he could utter one, she added, "You may tell me anything. You should know this."

"I do know," he said with a sigh. "But my troubles are my own, and I'll not burden you with them."

His mother laughed. "You are so like your father, you know," she said, brushing back the hair from his cheek. She never approved of his long hair. "I lost count of the number of times he chose not to burden me. Come, let us take a stroll around the gardens, like we once did when you were young."

He offered her his arm, and together they walked through the house and outside. Although it was late autumn, the cold had not yet settled over the country.

"Do you miss Father?" he asked.

She glanced at him. "Do you doubt my love for him?"

"No, it's not that. I just know that as his mind worsened, you were more hurt by his actions. Or dare I say you were embarrassed? I don't blame you for running away to Scotland to hide. The *ton* can be cruel with their whispers and innuendos."

His mother came to a halt. "Is that what you believe?"

"Of course," he replied. "But I don't blame you for your choice to leave. Your name is important and—"

"My name means nothing without your father beside me," she snapped. Then she sighed. "Matthew, I care nothing for what the *ton* has to say, nor anyone, for that matter. I loved your father—I still do—and nothing can change that. But one thing is certain, I was never embarrassed by him."

"I don't understand," Matthew said, frowning. "The man wandered away at odd hours, the outbursts at parties, his talking to trees, all these things! How can it not fill you with shame?"

His mother sighed again, and they resumed their walk. "It broke my heart, knowing that his mind was failing, and there was nothing I could do about it. That is when a woman weeps the most, my son. When she knows she has done all she can, and there is nothing more she can do."

A bird flitted past them, and a hare raced across the cobbled path. Otherwise, they walked in silence for several moments.

"May I give you a bit of advice?" his mother asked.

"Yes, of course."

"Your father and I had so many we thought were friends in the *ton*, but they were not true friends. You have no idea how many praised us with their lips only to spread rumors once they were out of our presence, and most of those rumors concerned your father's ailment. Soon, none would call, nor would they offer aid. Instead, it was a headmistress of all people, a friend of your father, who helped arrange for the finest doctors."

"Mrs. Rutley?" he asked, astounded. His mother nodded. "But how would she know which doctors to approach? And why would Father give her an audience?" He was well aware of his arrogant tone, but he had to know why his father would put his trust in a woman who ran a school for young ladies.

"Agnes and I have known one another for years," his mother replied. "But that is a story for another time. The point is that those of the *ton*, those who should have been by our side, were not."

Matthew knitted his brows. "But did my uncle not search out doctors?" he asked as they came to the end of the path. "He says he did."

His mother snorted. "Your uncle thought whiskey would cure your father's mind. Ezra did what he always did. Nothing. He hid in the shadow of your father, waiting to catch whatever scraps he could, so he would not have to fend for himself. Just as he had done all his life."

Why had his uncle lied about finding his father a doctor? And was his reason for being at Matthew's side the same?

"Now, as to why I left," his mother continued, "I believe you may be either misinformed or simply have misunderstood. I went to Scotland because I was hurting. Your father was gone, and I wished to grieve on my own and in my own way. It took me far too long to realize that going was a mistake, for I should not have abandoned you when you needed me most."

He brought her hand to his lips and kissed her knuckles. "You did what you needed to do," he said, smiling. Any anger he may have had over her leaving had long abated. "Is there anything I can do to make your stay here more comfortable?"

She became quiet for a moment before saying, "I know something is bothering you, and I understand that you would prefer not to share what that something is. But don't worry, I take no offense. Whatever this problem is, you must face it or it will have you retreat as I did, attempting to find solace elsewhere."

"Did you not find solace in Scotland?"

"No," she replied. "Nor will I discover it here. Or any of the estates you now own. Matthew, solace comes from within us, not from without. That is why I've returned to Hardwick Hall, to find my own solace in the place where I came to first love your father." She placed a hand on his chest. "The answer you seek is within you. It always has been. Now you must simply find it."

"Thank you, Mother," he said as he kissed her cheek. "You have given me much to consider."

For several minutes, they spoke of less consequential topics before she excused herself, leaving Matthew alone with his thoughts. Everything he believed to be true concerning the death of his father was slowly unraveling, and a different picture was painted beneath. Yet, his mother's words rang in his mind. The answer was inside himself, advice akin to what Julia had given him.

Thinking her name conjured an image of her in his mind. What was she doing at this very moment? Her parents were to arrive on Monday, and she would begin a new life. With a new man. And that thought did not sit well with him. Not in the least.

Torment. That was what Julia felt on Sunday morning. Emma had already risen and gone to breakfast, leaving Julia to burrow into her covers. If she hid herself beneath her blankets long enough, would she be forgotten and thus left alone?

The door opened, and Bridget entered the room with the answer to that question. "Miss Julia, you must get up. It's already past noon."

"Leave me be," Julia said, her voice muffled by the covers. "My heart is heavy, and I wish this blanket of sadness to consume me."

The edge of the bed sank as Bridget sat. "What you're feeling isn't unusual, you know. Most women experience some sort of anguish of this sort at least once in their life."

"I doubt that is true," Julia said, her head still covered. "I doubt you have ever been forced to endure such heartache."

Bridget sighed. "That's where you're wrong, Miss Julia."

Julia pulled down the blankets in shock. "You? You have been heartbroken before?"

"I have. It was before I took this position. And though I hurt just as you do now, I knew that if I allowed my sorrow to drag me under, I'd drown from it. I know it's not easy, but you're a young lady now. If you don't pull yourself back up, the sadness will suffocate you in the end. Mark my words on that."

Julia waved a dismissive hand. "I doubt I shall die by lying here for just a little while longer."

She went to pull the covers back over her head, but Bridget stopped her. "That's just not true, Miss. I knew a woman who refused to get out of bed when she'd been jilted by her betrothed, the day before they were to be married. She spent *weeks* there beneath her covers, refusing to eat or drink because her heart was breaking."

"What happened to her?" Julia asked, her eyes wide.

"Why, she died, of course."

Julia sat straight up in the bed. "Died? From a broken heart?"

Bridget snorted. "More likely because she hadn't eaten or drunk anything for so long, but the outcome was the same. All I'm saying is that you can't lie here hiding in bed all day. You've too much life to live to let this one complication ruin it. It might feel as if your life is finished, but it's not, I promise you that."

Forcing a smile, Julia nodded. "Thank you, my friend. I shall heed your advice."

The blanket felt as if it were made of stone as she pushed it aside, and her legs were as heavy as iron, but soon, she was out of bed, dressed, and sitting in front of the vanity table. As Bridget brushed her hair, Julia's mind wandered. Her heart had been shattered, and like the woman in the story Bridget had told her, her appetite was gone. The future that awaited her caused such torment that she did not sleep. Or when she did sleep, her mind was filled with nightmares.

Her mind replayed that final day at the brook. She had leaped across the water and offered her hand only to have him refuse it and walk away. That had been bad enough, but when he ignored her cries, she had fallen to her knees to weep harder than she had ever wept in her life. Bridget had come and held her, assuring her everything would be all right. Sadly, the maid had been wrong, for Matthew did not return, leaving her soul in a thousand pieces. And it remained so, still lying on the bank of the brook.

She looked at Bridget's reflection. "Tomorrow we leave and begin a new journey. One I wish I did not have to take."

Bridget's lips thinned, but she said nothing.

"And although I know my fate is sealed, I cannot help but think that Matthew will return to me." Her eyes misted. "Am I a fool for believing that?"

"You're no fool, Miss Julia. You're a young lady who's in love. It's just that the man you love is blinded by his fears."

Julia sighed. "When I first arrived here, Mrs. Rutley read a passage of poetry in one of our lessons. I had thought the piece beautiful, that it depicted what love should be. Great writers say that love is this powerful force that nothing can stop, yet now I see that they are wrong. Love is for stories and poems, but it has nothing to do with real life."

Bridget set the brush on the table and placed her hands on Julia's shoulders. "I've only been on this earth a short time—granted, longer than you, but still a short time overall—and I've come to learn that love is indeed a powerful force. Your heart may be broken now, but I believe there's always hope."

Julia smiled and placed a hand atop that of Bridget. "You are the best friend a girl could ever have."

Bridget gave a mock sniff. "As I said earlier, you're not a girl anymore. After all you've been through, after all the things you've learned, you're very much a woman."

Standing, Julia embraced her friend. She was just drying her eyes when Ruth sauntered into the room. Without knocking. So like Ruth.

"It's a beautiful day today," Ruth said. "Come and join us for some fresh air."

Julia offered her a small smile. "Thank you for inviting me, but I believe I need time alone to consider some matters. Perhaps I can join you later."

Ruth gave a great snort as she marched over and took hold of Julia's arm. "It was not a suggestion, Miss Wallace. Do you think that we will allow you to spend your last day with us feeling sorry for yourself? We are hurting, too, you know."

Julia came to a stop at the top of the stairs. "Even you—?"

"Will miss you?" Ruth asked. "Of course I will." She leaned in closer and lowered her voice. "But you must not tell the others, lest they think I've become proper." She added a wink, which made Julia laugh.

When they reached the front door, Ruth grabbed a wrap and threw it haphazardly over Julia's shoulders and placed a hat upon her head with even less ceremony.

When they walked out onto the portico, Julia smiled upon seeing her friends sitting beneath the great oak tree.

"I'm so glad you are joining us," Diana said. "There is something you must know."

Julia frowned as she found a place upon one of the blankets, but before she could speak, Unity said, "We will miss you terribly, for you have been our leader for so long."

"It's true," Theodosia said. "So many times, I came very close to making unladylike decisions, but I chose not to because I knew you would not approve."

Emma nodded. "You have taught us all what true friendship means.

Not once have you refused any of us your ear, nor your heart. I, for one, am very grateful."

"If it were not for you," Louisa said, "I would have listened at every keyhole and likely gotten caught."

Jenny snorted. "You still listen at every keyhole!"

"Yes, but I don't get caught," Louisa said with a wide grin. "I'm much more careful when and where I do it."

"Well, I know I'll miss you," Jenny said. "If it were not for you, I would never have gotten through my studies." She pulled on her braid to make her point, which made everyone laugh.

"What we all are trying to say," Ruth added, "is that you have been a very important part of our education. And for that we, every one of us, are grateful."

Julia blinked back tears as she looked from one of her sisters to the next. She had so much she wished to say, yet finding the right words was difficult. How does one tell such great friends how important they are to her?

A breeze lifted the corner of the blanket, and she knew it would not be as difficult as she believed. "We are more than friends. We are sisters brought together not only by a pledge but by the love we have for one another. We may not know what the future holds for us, but it's made less frightening when we know that we will always be there for one another. You have no idea how much I'll miss each and every one of you."

The tears came and soon Julia was in Emma's embrace. "I shall miss you, my friend," Emma whispered in her ear. When Emma moved away, Diana's arms were around Julia, followed by each of her sisters in turn.

As she looked at each of her dear friends, Bridget's words came to mind, and she realized that they were true for all of them. They had arrived at Mrs. Rutley's School for Young Women as girls but would leave as ladies. It was the pride that came from that knowledge that Julia held as she and the others gathered their blankets and the Sisterhood returned to the house just as rain began to fall.

Chapter Twenty-Eight

Thunder rumbled as Matthew sat listening to one of the three men who had arrived at Hardwick Hall the previous day. Today was the important first day of negotiations, and they had come together in the office. The pelting rain on the window was so loud that it threatened to drown out all their voices.

"What you say is true," Lord Mills was saying as he drummed his fingers on the arm of his chair. "The farther away from London a village lies, the greater the risk, but the reward, gentlemen, far outweighs the risks, for there is so much potential."

Lord Campbell, a man in his early fifties with flakes of gray in his otherwise dark hair, nodded in agreement. "It's not the reward I fear, my friend. It's the risk. Most of this deal I like as farmland will always guarantee a steady income. Hotels are a safe investment in larger areas, but in these villages? Some of the wealthiest men in some of these hamlets own no more than two pairs of trousers! No, I fear that investing in these less significant villages will expose our coffers and bleed them dry."

He waved a hand at Mr. Harold Seston when the man went to argue for the fifth time this morning. "I'm not saying we should do nothing. I say we begin with perhaps half a dozen and see whether they are worth the stakes. If I am proven wrong and we see a profit, we can add more, but if we learn I'm right, our losses will not bankrupt us."

"But if we don't act on them all while the price is low and we are successful on those few," Mr. Seston argued, "others will take notice and move in on those we ignored. Gentlemen, as Lord Mills mentioned, the possible rewards are too great to pass up."

Matthew glanced at the mantel clock as the men continued to argue. Ten past eleven. They had been at it for over two hours, and still they had not initiated anything close to an agreement concerning where to first start purchasing land. The others had argued they should begin just outside of London, while Matthew thought Cambridge would be a better place to start because available properties there did not last long.

He had done his due diligence, but his uncle overrode nearly every suggestion he made. Oh, it was done with a most diffident tone and with wise arguments, but Matthew could not help but feel manipulated like a puppet controlled by a puppeteer. Did his mother not say that his uncle lurked in the shadows awaiting whatever scraps fell his way? Did some dogs not eventually attack in order to get the biggest morsel? Which in this instance was control of the dukedom?

Soon Matthew stood and walked over to the window. No one seemed to notice. Small pools of water had collected in the garden, and his mind turned to Julia, who would be leaving this morning. If she had not already.

The thought that she would be gone, and he likely would never see her again, caused his heart to ache. To know that another man would claim her as his bride only intensified the pain. It was an unjust punishment for Julia, for she had done no wrong, but the guilt alone nearly suffocated him. His motive for releasing her had been pure, but had it been the right decision?

"Gentlemen, please!" Lord Campbell shouted, breaking Matthew from his thoughts. He had not noticed how loudly they had been arguing. "You leap on me as hungry wolves after a sheep! Let us ask His Grace for his wisdom in this matter."

Matthew turned to find all eyes focused on him, including those of his uncle.

"His Grace is clearly deep in thought," Uncle Ezra said. "Why do we not continue our conversation and allow him a bit of extra time to consider his response?"

"I'm not in need of extra time," Matthew said. "Repeat the question."

His uncle frowned, but Lord Campbell said, "I was merely pointing out, again, that we are taking too great a risk with our wealth when considering these villages. Unless everyone here can guarantee the results?" He laughed at his own joke, but something tugged at the edges of Matthew's mind. "Should we proceed into an unknown future rife with risk as these men have proposed, or do we use a small sample group and proceed with others once we see the results are favorable?"

An image of Julia standing across the brook came to mind.

Luck and curses do not exist, and no one can know what the future holds.

"Well, Nephew? They are waiting," his uncle whispered in Matthew's ear. He had not even noticed that his uncle had come to stand beside him. "Don't allow them to believe you are a mad duke, or this entire deal shall unravel."

Matthew clenched a fist as Julia's voice came to mind again.

They may attempt to strip you of your dignity and say that Matthew Colburn was never a great duke, but that would be a lie. I believe you already are a great duke and will only become greater over time.

"I'm considering," Matthew said sternly. "I'll not be pressured into making a decision for worry of anyone's time but my own."

His uncle took a surprised step back, but the others nodded in agreement.

Matthew looked at the older man. "You mentioned fear, did you not Campbell?"

"I did," Lord Campbell replied. "I fear the risk is too great."

"I, too, know fear," Matthew said. A chain pulled at his heart. "For many years, I've allowed fear to guide my decisions." He reached into his coat pocket and pulled out the handkerchief Julia had given him. "A wise woman once told me that luck does not exist, and now, more than ever, I believe her."

His uncle gave a small laugh. "My apologies, gentlemen. His Grace was involved with a young lady, but—"

"Silence, Uncle," Matthew snapped. His uncle's face reddened. "For far too long, I've allowed you to speak for me, but I'm quite capable of speaking for myself. Now, back to our discussion." He turned his back to Ezra and focused his attention on Lord Campbell. "I would like to ask, has listening to your fears in the past truly helped you? Did doing so guarantee the outcome of whatever that fear guarded?"

The older man rubbed his chin in thought and then shook his head. "No, I suppose it did not." He frowned. "Now that I think on it, very little of what I feared came to pass."

Matthew nodded. "As I thought. Now, about these villages... you may be correct, we may fail, but we just as well may succeed. Have I not done my due diligence on the villages chosen for this scheme?"

"You have," Mr. Seston replied.

The memory of the time spent with Julia upon the roof of the outbuilding came to mind, and he smiled. "Then, I say we set aside our fears, for if we don't do so now, there is no telling what other opportunities we may miss."

The room fell quiet, the only noise the rain pelting on the windowpanes behind him.

Lord Campbell heaved a sigh. "What you say makes sense, Your Grace. I shall heed your advice and no longer allow fear to guide my decisions in this matter." He turned to the others. "The outcome of this plan is uncertain, but as His Grace said, none of us know what the future holds. We have only one way to know if this deal is successful, and that is to give it a try." He chuckled. "At least if it does not go well, I'll not be alone. We can all wallow in our cups together."

Matthew raised a single eyebrow. "Or we can be optimistic and experience success." It was as if a great weight had been lifted off his chest, and he knew he had to make another investment, one far more important than the monetary one he was making at this moment.

I'll always be here, Matthew. Now, come and join me and cast away your fears.

"Julia," Matthew groaned. "What have I done?"

No sooner than he had uttered the words when a woman's cry echoed outside the room. His heat quickened. Was that his mother?

At once everyone stood, and Lord Campbell asked, "Your Grace? May we be of assistance?"

"Gentlemen, please remain seated while I go investigate."

Pushing past his uncle at the doorway, Matthew hurried toward his mother, who was comforting Lady Dyer at the bottom of the staircase. "Mother? Frances? What's happened?"

"The baroness and I have been in deep discussion for the past hour," his mother replied. "There is something you must know."

Lady Dyer looked up, her lower lip trembling. "I'm not the good friend you believe me to be, Your Grace. I've betrayed you, just as your uncle has. I cannot express how sorry I am for the part I played."

"Betrayed?"

"The woman lies!" Uncle Ezra shouted as he entered the foyer. "Matthew, cast her out of our home this instant! It's clear she is only after our wealth."

Rage boiled in Matthew. "Why is it every time you mention wealth or this estate, you describe it as 'ours'? This is *my* home, Uncle, and the wealth is *mine*. It would do you well to remember that." To Lady Dyer, he softened his tone and said, "Now, explain what you mean by this 'betrayal'."

"The madness you fear? The words you speak aloud but don't recollect having thought them? It was all a lie. Lord Ezra threatened me, and I had no choice but to lie, to hurt you. But I can no longer endure the guilt created by what I've been forced to do. Do you not see, Your Grace? You are not mad!"

A flash of images played through Matthew's mind as everything became clear. From the moment his uncle had offered his aid, to the very bargain they hoped to strike this week, it had been for his uncle's gain, not Matthew's. He had been played for a fool, betrayed by his own blood while he had allowed fear to cloud his vision. But that time had passed, and a new man had risen, one whose fist shook in rage.

"Lies!" Uncle Ezra shouted again. "She is just trying to hide the truth!" He grabbed hold of Lady Dyer's skirt, causing her to pitch forward. If Matthew's mother had not had her arm around the woman's shoulders, the baroness would have tumbled down the last two steps.

Matthew grasped hold of the lapels of his uncle's coat and shoved him against the wall. "No," he growled, his nose mere inches from that of his uncle, "I see everything clearly now. You have slithered your way into my home and spun your web of deceit. Do take notice of the man who speaks to you now. I am no longer your dog to command."

"You will be mad like your father! That is a truth you cannot escape no matter what you say."

Matthew eased his grip. He knew now, more than ever, what he wanted—no, what he needed—in his life. "That may be true. One day, I may be like him, but it is a chance I must take. Just know that, like my father, I'll have a woman who cares for me by my side."

Uncle Ezra narrowed his eyes. "You made a pledge to me! Do you not remember?"

"Oh, I remember my pledges quite well," Matthew said. "But the one I made to Julia, that I would always protect her, is far more important than any I've made to you." He pushed his uncle away. "You have one hour to gather your things and leave Hardwick Hall, never to return again."

The man's jaw fell open. "You... you cannot—"

"I can and I will! Hickson?"

"Your Grace?"

"Have my horse readied. And see to it that my uncle takes only what belongs to him. If he seeks to harm my mother or Lady Dyer in any way, you and the other staff may intervene with whatever force is deemed appropriate, without fear of repercussion."

"Gladly, Your Grace," the butler said with a deep bow. He grasped Uncle Ezra by his coat and shoved him toward the staircase. Then he motioned to an awaiting footman. "You heard His Grace. Keep a watchful eye on him as he collects his things."

Once his uncle's curses and shouts could no longer be heard, Matthew turned to the baroness. "Mother will escort you to the parlor. Wait for me there, for I have many questions. But I have another matter I must see to first."

Lady Dyer dropped into a deep curtsy, her cheeks still wet with tears. "Yes, Your Grace."

With long strides, Matthew entered the office and walked around his desk. "Some matters of great importance have arisen."

"Can we be of help, Your Grace?" Lord Campbell asked.

"Indeed, you can." Matthew removed a ledger from a bookcase, opened it, and dropped it on the table where his colleagues sat. "I have here the complete expenditure for this project, from the purchase of the lands and buildings needed for the hotels, beginning with Cambridge. Not a single expense has been omitted. When I return, we'll discuss the benefits of starting there."

How great it felt to speak as the duke. No! As the very man he was! "If you gentlemen are hungry, breakfast will be served in the dining room in ten minutes. Please do not wait for me."

Without pausing for a response, he returned to the foyer and opened the door to the lashing rain just as the butler returned.

"Your Grace!" Hickson cried. "You cannot leave in this. You will be drenched, and your coat will be ruined. This is madness!"

Matthew roared with laughter as he removed his coat and tossed it to the butler. "Yes, Hickson, it is madness. And it's a wonderful thing!" With that, he bounded down the stairs and out into the driving rain that stung his face just as a stable hand arrived with his horse.

Time was of the essence, and he prayed that Julia had not yet left with her parents.

"He ain't too happy 'bout bein' out in this storm, Your Grace," the stable hand shouted to be heard above the pounding rain. "Be careful he don't throw you."

Indeed, the stallion snorted and shuffled as Matthew took the reins. He rubbed the horse's nose. "All right now," he whispered in his ear, "show me you are as mad as I am and take me to Julia without fear of this storm."

He placed a foot in the stirrup, bounded into the saddle, and flicked the reins just as a clap of thunder boomed above. The horse trumpeted a great whinny and reared, lifting its front legs into the air and threatening to pitch Matthew backwards from the saddle. Yet, he held tight to the pummel and rubbed the animal's neck.

"No need to fear," he said into the horse's ear. "We are in this together."

The horse righted itself and sprinted forward. With each passing breath, Matthew said a silent prayer that Julia was still at the school. He had so much he wished to tell her, to let her know that she had been right all along. The rain battered his arms and back, and his shirt clung to his body. He leaned forward and urged the horse to go faster.

When the school came into view, a thousand images flashed through his mind. Yet, one stood out above the rest. And as the rain pelted his face, he shouted but one word.

"Julia!"

Fear. That was what Julia suffered as she stood in the drawing room with her parents. They had arrived an hour earlier, having stayed at an inn in Chatsworth the night before rather than traveling on to the school. The storm outside raged, rattling the window frames as thunder rumbled and rain danced on the glass.

Her father stood, staring at the fire that burned in the fireplace, mumbling under his breath. His anger was as great as the storm that delayed their departure, for he had planned to leave just after sunrise, and her father despised when his plans did not go according to his wishes.

Her closest friends sat around the room, awaiting Julia's departure. Mrs. Rutley gave Julia a nod of encouragement before returning her attention once more to Julia's mother, who sat beside her on the couch.

"Mother, please," Julia whispered, making one last attempt to make the woman see reason. "I came to realize that I love him, and I know he loves me. He just cannot yet see it. So, I beg of you, allow me to remain here to complete my education and wait for him to return. I know he will."

The evening before, Julia had gone to Mrs. Rutley for advice, and the headmistress agreed to speak to her mother concerning Matthew.

Now, as she waited for the timid woman to speak, Julia held on to this one last thread of hope before she fell prey to her sadness once again.

"I admit that your story is beautiful," her mother whispered. "Every lady seeks love in life, but few find it." She took Julia's hand. "You have admitted that this man refused your offer of love. What makes you believe he will ever wish to speak to you again? I'm sorry, but your father will never allow it. Lord Howe has already asked for your hand, and you know very well your father will never be swayed by such notions of love."

Julia glanced at her father. "Then, I shall speak to him myself," she said. "Tell him the truth. Surely, this one time, I can have a say in my life?"

Her mother shook her head. "You know very well that cannot be. When it comes to marriage, he will never allow it."

The door opened, and her parents' driver peeked through the doorway. Mrs. Rutley rose to speak to him and then slipped what appeared to be a coin into the man's hand. He gave her a nod and then walked into the room, his cap clutched in his hands, and his head bowed.

"Sorry, my lord, but I'm afraid the carriage wheel's in need of repair. I'll need at least another hour. It's awful hard to change the wheel in the rain, but I'll do my best."

"An hour?" her father bellowed. "Surely it will not take you that long. I want no further delays!"

Mrs. Rutley smiled and stepped forward. "Lord Wallace is right. There is no reason to delay this journey. Is the wheel broken?"

"Well, no missus, but—"

"There you are," Mrs. Rutley said. "The first village you will encounter on your journey home is only a mere twenty miles away. If the carriage happens to capsize, I'm sure help will come. Eventually."

Julia's father mumbled and waved a hand at the driver. "Then do it quickly, man. I'm ready to return home."

Another hour. Surely, that was enough time for Julia to convince her mother that she should remain.

"Mother," she whispered, "do you see Emma over there? She is already betrothed to a man far too old for her, and it pains her terribly.

I don't wish to have the pain she is forced to endure. Please, speak to Father. Convince him to let me remain here."

Her mother bit at her bottom lip. "I cannot. He will become irate, and you know how terrible he can be when he is angry."

Julia sighed. Her mother did not refuse out of malice but rather out of fear of her husband.

"Julia!"

All heads turned toward the front of the house. Then her name was called once again, and Ruth ran to a window.

"It's the duke!" she said, her voice brimming with awe.

Whispers rose among the girls as they crowded around the window. "It is he!" Louisa said. She, of course, had been the second to see who was calling Julia's name.

Julia pushed through her friends and gasped at the sight before her. A dark stallion pranced in great circles in front of the house, Matthew doing all he could to keep it under control as the storm raged around him.

Then, the horse reared, and Julia screamed. If he were thrown to the ground and trampled by the beast, she would never forgive herself. To her relief, Matthew brought the animal under control with ease. He leaped off the horse just as a clap of thunder rattled the panes once more, sending the horse running at full speed back down the drive.

Matthew did not even look in the direction the animal ran. "Julia!"

"Matthew!" she said in a harsh whisper as she pushed past her friends and ran toward the parlor door.

"Where are you going?" her father demanded. "Can you not see how mad he is? What man in his right mind would stand outside during a storm? He is as mad as his father was! I forbid you to speak to him, do you hear? *I forbid it!*" He pointed toward the window. "You see, Mrs. Rutley I told you of my concerns, and now he has made my point for me!"

"But Father, please, you must understand. I love him!"

Her father took a step back as if she had struck him. Never had she raised her voice to him before. "How dare you speak so foolishly, Julia. You are embarrassing me."

"But it's true! I wish to marry him, not Lord Howe."

Her father's face had turned purple with rage. "Madam," he seethed at Mrs. Rutley, "is this what you teach your pupils? If so, then I shall see your doors closed for good! Now you, daughter, will sit yourself right back down beside your mother and wait for this storm to pass."

"Henry," came a timid voice, "since the day we first courted, you have made every decision, controlled every aspect of my life, and you have done the same for our daughter."

Julia turned in surprise toward her mother, who now stood with her chin raised for the first time Julia could remember. Her father could have been bowled over by a feather by his look of shock.

And then her mother spoke again. "Is it not time to allow her to make a decision on her own?"

Julia could not have admired her more.

"Has my entire family lost their mind? Not only does my daughter embarrass me, so does her mother!" Julia's father sputtered, spittle flying from his lips. "These girls must learn—"

"That their husbands should be like you?" Her mother's voice sounded stronger, and her back was straighter. "Allowing their husband's anger to make them tremble at his every word? That they should believe that their every thought, every feeling is wrong? Is that what they must learn?"

The room became eerily quiet, and Mrs. Rutley took Julia by the hand. Every eye was on Julia's father, staring at him as if daring him to say it was so.

Rather than responding, however, her father muttered something about at least his daughter would be a duchess and then nodded toward Julia.

Had her father agreed? She was not going to wait to find out as she hurried down the corridor and out the front door onto the covered portico.

"Oh, Julia," Matthew said, pulling his dripping hair from his face. "You were right! I see it now! You were right all along!"

Julia blinked back tears. "Tell me!" she shouted to be heard above the storm. "What do you see now that you did not see before?"

"The fear that ruled my life, every decision that I made was not made with my heart nor my mind but rather in fear. My uncle," he shook his head and laughed. "I learned he used my fear against me to twist what I thought of myself."

Julia smiled. "I'm glad you now see it."

"But there is more!" he said with such glee that Julia's smile widened. "When we leaped over the brook together, I learned that taking a chance is a good thing. And that night under the stars, do you remember our dreams?"

"Of course I remember," she said. "We named so many, but I recall them all."

"Well, I made a pledge to you that night to protect you," he said. "But my fear made me recant that pledge." Rain dripped from every possible part of his body from his nose, his chin, to the ends of his hair and at the bottom of his sleeves, but not once did he wipe away the wetness. "I don't know what the future holds, and I no longer believe in luck. What we carry inside is what we should allow to lead us, not a pocket watch or even a handkerchief." He patted his chest and looked down. "Which I appear to have left at home," he said with a laugh. He spread his arms wide. "You see? I even came here without it! But that thing inside us, do you know its name?"

"I do," she said as tears of joy filled her eyes. Oh, how her heart ached to say it! "I know its name."

"It's what I've been wanting to tell you for the past week but was too afraid to do so. Yet I shall say it now, right here at this very moment as rain pours from the sky. Julia, I love you! And I'll shout it from the mountaintops right this instant if I must. For I need it... No, I need *you*, for without your love, I'm nothing."

"And I'm nothing without you," she whispered. Without a thought for the pounding rain, she lifted her skirts, bounded down the steps, and ran to him. "Oh, Matthew, I do love you so!"

He wrapped his arms around her, lifted her from the ground, and turned her around in a circle. "I love you more than life itself," he said as he held her close.

Julia's tears mixed with the rain as he lowered his face and kissed her. His lips tasted of the rain that fell upon them, soaking their clothes. Her hair was plastered to her head as much as his was, and he drew her even closer, the protection he had once promised her now realized. Yet, it was more than the protection from a marriage she did not want, or even from a person who wished to bring her harm. It was the guarding of her heart, to claim it as his own, and never to let anything hurt her again. That was what she had wanted all along.

When the kiss ended, they stared into one another's eyes as rain drenched them further. Then Julia looked up to see her friends standing in front of the parlor windows, their hands clasped, and she laughed.

Unity and Jenny waved, and even Ruth wiped away a tear. Yet it was the far window, where Mrs. Rutley stood alone wearing a wonderful smile, that Julia remembered most.

Chapter Twenty-Nine

Cambridge, England, 1807

The same day Matthew had come to claim Julia, she returned home with her parents to begin preparations for her wedding, although it was not to Lord Howe. Instead, she married the Duke of Elmhurst six weeks after his business transactions were completed. He had received everything he requested, and not once had he relied upon a charm to give him luck.

Matthew had also shown great compassion to Lady Dyer. The woman's estate was now under his watchful eye, saved from bankruptcy when he invested in the trades her husband had left behind.

Uncle Ezra admitted to his wrongdoings but when he refused to show even the slightest bit of remorse, he left Hardwick Hall to reside in an estate he owned in Yorkshire.

Matthew's mother and Julia had taken an instant liking to one another, a far cry from the uncle who had once made a play to reign over the estate. It had taken some convincing, but the dowager duchess remained at Hardwick Hall, allowing Matthew and Julia to begin a future in a new home. It had been nearly two years since Julia left Mrs. Rutley's School for Young Women, and she had been far too busy to return. Yet, she remembered her life there as she read a letter from Mrs. Rutley. All the sisters had corresponded with one other, but besides Emma, her headmistress wrote the most.

"She is a wonderful woman," Julia said, refolding the letter. "I do wish I could go see her, but I believe such a journey would be unwise at the moment."

"I would say so," Bridget said as she looked at the roundness of Julia's stomach. "Soon, perhaps, but not until after the babe comes."

Matthew walked toward them, and Bridget winked and hurried away.

"Has Emma written to you again?" he asked with an amused grin. "Or is it Ruth this time? I'm always curious what sort of mischief she is into these days."

Julia laughed. "No, it's from Mrs. Rutley. She was inquiring about the land you wished to purchase from her. Are you still interested?"

This made them laugh, for Matthew no longer desired to buy the land, instead settling to work toward his own dreams rather than those of his father. That was also the reason they had chosen to live at the estate in Cambridge rather than at Hardwick Hall—to have a new beginning.

"I sense that you miss her," Matthew said.

"You do know me so well, husband," Julia replied. "I do miss her. I miss all my friends, but there are more pressing matters at hand, such as the child I carry inside me. And of course, you."

As Matthew pulled back his hair, which he still kept long, Julia's cheeks heated and her heartbeat quickened. "I find you more handsome each day I'm with you, Your Grace. And my love increases all the more."

"I did not think it was possible for my love for you to continue to grow, and yet it does. Each day blooms into something different, and yet it only gets better." He pulled her into his arms and moved a strand of hair behind her ear. "You fell in love with the Duke of Madness."

"That may have been your name at one time," she said, "but it's now the Duke of Dreams, for your dreams are what you pursue."

"You are wrong, my beautiful wife," he said, caressing her cheek with the back of his hand. "For they are *our* dreams, not just mine."

As it had many times before, her heart soared as his lips pressed against hers. Many emotions coursed through her, but above all was the protection she felt because of the pledge he had made to her.

When the kiss ended, he took her hand in his, and they strolled down the garden path as they often did. They spoke of the days and weeks ahead, and even far into the future, a subject they both enjoyed.

For the fear that had once taken hold of Matthew's life had been destroyed, replaced with not only a belief in himself but also in the love they shared. It was in that love that they walked, continuing to allow it to guide their steps, no matter what tomorrow may bring.

Epilogue

Chatsworth, England, 1825

Julia held Mrs. Rutley's hand as she wiped tears from her eyes. How long her story had taken in its telling, she was uncertain, but the headmistress's cheeks were as wet as Julia's.

"And that is the story of how Miss Julia Wallace came to meet and fall in love with a man once known as the Duke of Madness, who is now better known as the Duke of Dreams—at least to his wife. The story is filled with fear, luck, and most of all love, but no other romance novel could be as wonderful, for it's my own."

Mrs. Rutley smiled. "And what a wonderful story it is," she said. "And though I already knew it, I was glad to hear it again after all these years."

Julia removed her hand to dab tears from her eyes. "I must admit that there have been times I considered that maybe Matthew had been right about luck," she said with a light laugh. "If he had not lost his pocket watch and accused me of theft, we may never have been brought together."

"Julia, my dear," Mrs. Rutley rasped, "it was not luck that brought you together, for the truth is, the watch never went missing." The older woman opened the hand Julia had believed she was clasping because of the pain she was enduring. In it was a gold pocket watch. "You see, I had it all along."

"You... that is... I'm confused!" She took the watch and turned it over in her hand, recognizing instantly the Colburn family crest. "Mrs. Rutley, you found it and never said anything?"

Mrs. Rutley chuckled. "No, Julia, I did not find it. I stole it."

Julia's mind returned to the day Matthew had first arrived at the school. Indeed, although Julia had first collided with him, Mrs. Rutley had patted his coat, offering words of apology on Julia's behalf.

"I knew His Grace walked in fear of becoming like his father," Mrs. Rutley said. "And I also knew how much he relied on luck. The only one who could save him from an uncertain future was you."

Tears flowed freely now as Julia laughed. She leaned over and kissed Mrs. Rutley on the cheek. "Thank you."

"Thank you for allowing me to witness your growth," Mrs. Rutley said. "To see the love you have for your husband still today." She sighed. "But yours is not the only story I wish to hear."

No sooner had she said this than the door opened and a woman appeared.

"Emma!" Julia said, hurrying over to embrace her friend. She pushed Emma away and studied her. "Look how beautiful you still are!"

"As are you," Emma said. Then she lowered her voice. "And Mrs. Rutley? How is she faring?"

Julia smiled as she took her friend's hand. "I believe she would like you to tell her a story, and if you don't mind, I would like to listen as well."

THE END

Thank you for reading *Duke of Madness*!

Join Emma and Andrew as they navigate gaming hells and abandoned castles in the next book in the series, **Baron of Rake Street**. Coming February 2022!

In the meantime, check out other books by Jennifer Monroe or dive into one of the latest releases by WOLF Publishing: *Once Upon a Devastatingly Sweet Kiss* by *USA Today* Bestselling Author Bree Wolf.

Also by Jennifer Monroe

Sisterhood of Secrets

#1 Duke of Madness

#2 Baron of Rake Street

#3 Marquess of Magic

Secrets of Scarlett Hall

Victoria Parker Regency Mysteries

Regency Hearts

Defiant Brides

About Jennifer Monroe

Jennifer Monroe writes clean Regency romances you can't resist. Her stories are filled with first loves and second chances, dashing dukes, and strong heroines. Each turn of the page promises an adventure in love and many late nights of reading.

With over twenty books published, her nine-part series, The Secrets of Scarlett Hall, which tells the stories of the Lambert Children, remain a favorite with her readers.

Connect with Jennifer:

www.jennifermonroeromance.com

facebook.com/JenniferMonroeAuthor

instagram.com/authorjennifermonroe

bookbub.com/authors/jennifer-monroe

amazon.com/Jennifer-Monroe/e/B07F1MRXDN

Made in the USA
Las Vegas, NV
01 December 2021

35750176R00163